THE
MURDER
BALLAD
OF
ORCHARD BEND

a novel by
Patrick Lemieux

Published by
Across The Board Books™
Toronto, Ontario, Canada

ISBN: 978-1-926462-07-3

First Trade Paperback Edition: April, 2018

Cover Art & Illustrations:
© Patrick Lemieux, 2017

To Terry & Dennis Burns
For everything

Acknowledgments

In one way or another you all made this book possible:
Michael Wiley – Once again, your editing talents made my book better. If any errors are still to be found in these pages, they are mine alone.
Heidi Loney – For talks over lunch and drinks.
Andre Gagne – I wonder what Jeff is up to these days.
Ashley Sirianni – For being a light on dark days.
Kiran Friesen – For summer afternoons on the patio.
Tim, Mel, Emmet, Jill, Dave, Jack, Josephine, Mark and Liv – Family is everything.
Mom and Dad – Obviously.

1

April 20, 1886
Orchard Bend

Death walked the streets of our small town.

Men attacked and took Sheriff Anderson by gunpoint. Emery,
her soul ever brave, joined the effort to find him. As scared as I
was for her safety, I encouraged her to go. In the face of this
new danger, Deputy Wilson needed her. The town needed her.
No less than an hour after Emery departed my cottage with a
pair of guns on her hips and two knives beneath her duster, I
heard the whip-cracks of pistols firing in the streets. I prayed
in the dark that neither she anyone special to me would be
hurt or killed, that the doers of evil would meet God's wrath.
Soon after the gunshots, I heard the commotion outside. People
crept from their homes, still afraid after being told by Deputy
Wilson to stay indoors when the trouble began. From the
window I saw Wayne and Herman Statler passing by atop their
horses, armed with rifles. I unbolted the door and ran out to
meet them.
"Miss Adelaide," Wayne Statler said upon seeing me, "it may
not be safe yet. You and everyone else should go back inside."
They did not know exactly what the commotion was about. I
asked whether they had heard the gunfire and they said they
had not. I followed them to Church Street, where everything
became confused around us. The brothers Statler and I were
parted. They rode ahead to the cluster of townsfolk. Dread
gripped my heart and I knew tragedy befell our town.
Death had come to Orchard Bend once more.

I heard urgent voices up ahead, but could not hear their exact words until I got closer. My fears of what Death had wrought were true.

Sheriff Anderson was dead, as were two of his assailants. I pushed through the small crowd. The Statlers and several other men kept everyone at a respectable distance, but the horror was there for all to see. The sheriff was dead on the ground in the middle of the street, his body disfigured by his wounds, his injuries so ghastly I do not wish to describe them. Not far from the sheriff was another lifeless body said to belong to one of his attackers. I came upon Mick Wiley, father to one of my students, and he told me they found another body in the alley past the millinery, another of the outlaws. I cast about for Emery, but did not see her. Word came that Mr Jackson, the photographer, was found dead in his studio, not far from where we stood. Mr Jackson was a good man and amiable to everyone. My mind reeled at the senselessness of it all.

Mr Trask came from his hotel with sheets to wrap the bodies, fighting against the blustering wind. I felt no need to remain at the site of all this carnage, so turned away. A hand touched my arm. It was Mr McManus, the blacksmith.

"Miss Adelaide," he said. "Would you be kind enough to open the church? I'm sure Reverend Thomas won't mind. There are those of us who would pray for Sheriff Anderson tonight."

"Yes, of course" I replied.

Even as Emery's whereabouts eluded me —a point of deep concern— taking action in that moment brought a small amount of relief. I told Mr McManus to meet me at the church. I returned to my cottage, hoping Emery would be waiting for me, but she was not there. It seemed reasonable that she would return when she could, after the confusion of the evening had been sorted through. I wrote a note for Emery, telling her I was safe and where to find me. I left it on the table where she would see it and then picked up the lantern and matches. It was nearly dark and I arrived to find Mr McManus and a half dozen others were waiting for me. Further down the street, I glimpsed the form of Sheriff Anderson still on the ground and had to look away. I unlocked the church and left one door ajar, suspecting more people might join us. As the others sat among the pews, I set my lantern on the altar and made the sign of the cross. I considered leading a prayer, but thought better of it. What Mr McManus and the others –and myself, I confess— needed in that moment was simply to be <u>there</u>, in a quiet place. With my matches, I lit some of the candles on the wall, listening to the soft-spoken prayers. I sat at my desk and whispered the Lord's Prayer, then one for Sheriff Anderson and Mr Jackson, then one for Emery.

I gave some thought to home for the first time in a good long while. I thought about my father and our last words. I thought about my mother and her hopes for me. I thought about how the candlelight on the wall in the little church in Orchard Bend looked very much like the play of light on the bedroom wall Diana and I shared as children. I miss her most of all. Nothing can replace the love of a sister, but having Emery in my life salves some of that ache. Seven years ago, she saved my life (and saved Sammy O'Toole's life, as well) the day the murderous Underwood Gang stopped us on the road. We have since become the closest of friends.

So adrift in my musings was I that I failed to noticed more than an hour had passed. Mr McManus was still there, but others had quietly slipped out, replaced by newcomers seated in the candlelight. That made me smile. I stood up to stretch and went to the door. In spite of the cool air, I sat on the steps. Down the street, I picked out the dark forms of the Statlers by their sloping gaits, but the bodies of the fallen men were gone, taken by Mr Allman to begin his undertaking.

After a time, one by one, the church emptied. Mr McManus was the last to leave. We bid each other a warm goodbye. I closed up the church, leaving it as I found it, knowing in a few days it would be quite full for the sheriff's funeral. Reverend Thomas was in Blue Creek for a wedding, but word would travel there soon that he was needed in Orchard Bend.

I returned the cottage and found my note to Emery as I left it. She had not returned. Dread slipped into my soul, replacing the quiet peace I had found at the church. I could not shake the feeling that something greater was keeping her away. The thought of sitting in my cottage in anticipation of her return was more than I could bear, so I ventured out into the brisk, blowing eve. I would visit the jailhouse or Sully's tavern, the two places I guessed Emery likely to be. I entertained the thought that she had single-handedly apprehended one of the outlaws and was at the jailhouse now, getting to the bottom of their foul business in our town. Why would anyone kidnap and murder Sheriff Anderson? The curse of being a schoolteacher and an avid reader is that my imagination can spiral with believable, vivid scenarios.

I came to Reed's General Store and found Mrs Reed and Mr Ramsay deep in conversation. Young Wendell Ramsay sat next his father on their wagon. I crossed the street as the Ramsays pulled away. Mrs Reed turned to go inside her shop and I called her name. She pivoted with a start.

"Oh, Miss Adelaide," she exclaimed, glancing next door at Dr Shaw's office. "Isn't it most dreadful? A gunfight in the middle of town!"

"Yes, I can hardly believe Sheriff Anderson is dead," I sighed. "Did they find the other assailants?"

Mrs Reed gave me a curious look and I knew there was more to the story than just the death of the sheriff.

"Has no one told you?" Mrs Reed asked. "I mean, in all the commotion at the Town Hall, I suppose no one thought. Of course Emery Dale is your friend—"

"Please tell me what happened," I said. In fact, I _demanded_. My stomach was suddenly sick with nerves.

"Your friend was shot," Mrs Reed said.

There was such a rush in my ears as the world seemed to fall out of focus, almost as if I was outside myself. Mrs Reed took my hand and my arm, likely afraid I would swoon and fall. I am not ashamed to say I might have, but I tried to ask, "Is she dead?" I do not think I spoke very coherently, but Mrs Reed understood.

"She's alive, Miss Adelaide," Mrs Reed said. "She's alive and you best come with me."

I let her guide me inside her store. We settled in her parlour in the back, where she set about making tea. Her boys, Quinton and Gregory appeared on the stairs, but were shooed away by their mother.

"What happened?" I asked when I regained my composure.

She told me what she had heard, fragmented from different sources. There had been a gunfight on Church Street. The sheriff and two of his attackers were killed. This much I had deduced, but I did not interrupt. Emery was in the thick of the violence and there had been a third man. He fled when his associates fell and brave Emery went after him. They fought in the skeleton frame of the yet-unfinished Town Hall. Face to face with Emery, he had his chance to kill her. As she bled, he levelled his gun at her, all while bleeding to death himself with her knife in his back. Emery was helpless, wounded from two gun shots, one to her arm and one to her leg. The Lord intervened, however, and placed Sam O'Toole there to shoot the outlaw before he could fire.

This man, it was discovered afterwards, was Daniel Underwood, the son of Ernest Underwood --the man who shot me seven years ago, the man Emery killed to save me. Either by coincidence he found himself in Orchard Bend --the place where the Underwood Gang met their end-- or he came here seeking to avenge his father. Regardless, he was killed by Sam O'Toole's hand and Emery was rushed unconscious to Dr Shaw.

Even before Mrs Reed finished making tea, I wanted to be with Emery. I knew Dr Shaw was tending to her, but the need was so great I could hardly restrain myself from getting up and going next door to his office.

Mrs Reed must have sensed my anxiety, for a bottle of brandy accompanied the tea as she set the serving tray before me. "Drink up and I'll see to Miss Dale."

I poured some tea and indulged by adding some of the brandy. It did indeed steady my nerves as it warmed me up. I rose from the sofa and paced, looking at the lovely décor of the Reeds' home. A photo of Mr Reed sat on the fireplace mantle. Poor Mr Reed, I thought, dead now several months. How time slips away. He was a kind man and I do miss his smile when I visit the Reeds' store.

Mrs Reed returned and said Dr Shaw would allow me to visit Emery, but only for a moment, for she was still not conscious.

We went together and I saw Dr Shaw had dressed Emery's wounds; one on her left leg, a graze just above the knee, and one on her right arm more serious, a deeper wound in the flesh of her bicep. Dr Shaw said she was lucky neither hit bone. I took Emery's hand, hoping she would awaken at my touch, but she did not. She only slept. I saw her gunbelts wrapped neatly on a table near her. The harness with which she carried her knives hung on the wall with her duster and hat. Dr Shaw had been forced to cut Emery's trousers to get to the leg wound and they lay shredded in bloody pile on the floor near her boots. It hurt to see her in this state.

Dr Shaw said he would stay with her that night and that I was welcome to return in the morning. I thanked them both and walked back to my cottage. Exhaustion overwhelmed me not long after I lay down to sleep, but I found myself awake again four hours later with little rest. I began writing here to clear my addled brain —and it has brought me some amount of calm-- but now hours have passed and the sun crests the horizon, casting the morning sky crimson.

2

April 19, 1886
Orchard Bend

By the near dark of twilight, in the half-built Town Hall of Orchard Bend, Daniel Underwood recognized his father's guns in the hands of this woman he meant to kill. Through the pain of the knife wound in his back, through the shock and adrenaline, somehow, *impossibly* he spotted the notch on the cylinder, the subtle dent made years ago when his father Ernest once dropped the weapon in a drunken stumble.

Back at their cramped two-room shack, young Daniel, then too old to be a boy, but not yet a man, watched his father teeter about, nursing a bottle of whiskey. His father raved about the injustice of it all, that the rich were getting richer and the poor poorer.

"...And Christ Almighty I mean to take what's owed to me!" *Ernest said, waving the gun to emphasize his point. He reared back to take a long pull from the bottle, coughed, and that's when the gun slipped from his hand. The barrel was pointed at Daniel when the gun struck the stone of the hearth. In that split second the boy thought,* It's gonna to go off. It's gonna kill me.

The gun didn't go off. It clattered on the floor and Ernest barely noticed, but it left the small but recognizable dent in the cylinder.

As this woman Emery Dale now pointed the same gun at his heart, Daniel had a similar thought, *She's gonna to shoot. She's gonna kill me.*

Click.

Blood-soaked and fuelled by rage, Daniel raised his weapon as Dale pulled the trigger again. There was only another *click* and Daniel grinned.

This is what real vengeance feels like, Daniel thought. He was dying, that was clear. The bullet holes in his body, the knife in his back and the one in his gut would all make certain he'd be dead before long, but he was going to take down the bitch that killed his father and stole his guns. He had her in his sights now. Everything was moving slowly. He squeezed the trigger, but it took an eternity. The pounding of blood in his ears sounded like a slow roll of thunder.

Daniel didn't so much feel the pain of the shotgun blast, as felt the great concussive force of the shot as his chest exploded. Daniel was beyond pain even before Sam O'Toole pulled the trigger, but he was aware he'd lost his chance at revenge as the shotgun blast sent him staggering to the floor. The fall took a long time, too. He watched his gun fly from his hand even as he tried to finish squeezing the trigger. When he hit the floor, he landed on his back. There he found himself looking up at a man with gaping holes for eyes and a grotesque mouth-like maw.

The Angel of Death, Daniel thought. *You've come for me.*

No, came the voice of the shadowy man, *but your father thought the same thing. I was there at his death, too.*

Where did you come from? Daniel thought as a blackness like smoke swirled about him. The shadow-man became more distinct and Daniel no longer wanted to look at him. The hideousness was enough to drive a man insane.

I've been here a long time, the shadow said. *Like I told your father, I'm a prisoner here.*

Will I see him? Daniel asked.

There was no answer. The Prisoner looked away, beyond him. Then the Dale woman came into view. She looked at him. A hand pulled her away and there were voices, but nothing Daniel could make out. They sounded very far away and muffled, like trying to hear underwater. Dale's gaze found the Prisoner and she looked at him. As the whiteness of death took Daniel, the last thing he heard was Dale telling the Prisoner, "I know you."

The Prisoner replied, "Major, it's me!"

* * *

April 20, 1886
Orchard Bend

Dr Alfred Shaw dreamt about blood and fire and chaos. Around him, men died. Greybacks charged the camp, lighting tents aflame and impaling Shaw's comrades on bayonets. The screams of pain, the barking of orders and the hail of gunfire became a wall of noise around him. Red mixed with blue uniforms at his feet. Shaw tried to find cover, fleeing, panicked. He spotted a woman on the ground, her blonde hair matted with dirt and crimson-brown blood. Her eyes were open when Shaw approached and she grabbed his hand and squeezed.

"Doctor," she said, her voice quiet, but cutting through the cacophony around them. "What happened?"

"You were shot," Shaw said. He could see the wounds, one on her arm and the other on her leg.

She squeezed his hand, hard this time, and Shaw jerked awake.

Emery Dale lay on the exam table looking at him. She clutched his hand as he shook the nightmare away and his thoughts cleared. He realized he'd fallen asleep in the chair next to her, after telling himself he was only going to rest his eyes a moment. Still holding her hand, he stood up. Her skin was ashen and damp with sweat.

"Miss Dale," Dr Shaw said. "You've had quite an evening. How do you feel?"

"My head hurts," Dale said, letting go of the doctor's hand to massage her forehead. "And my arm and my leg. I was shot. Twice."

"Do you remember what happened?" Shaw asked.

"I was chasing three men," Dale said, "They killed Sheriff Anderson. I killed one of them in the street and Anderson must have killed the other. I found the body. The third hid in the Town Hall. We fought. I got him with both of my knives, high

9

in the back and in his stomach, but it wasn't enough. We both kept firing. He shot my arm and my other gun was out of bullets. He had me dead to rights. Then someone shot him. A shotgun blast, I think."

"Sam O'Toole shot him," Shaw said. Emery nodded, her eyes closed.

"How bad are my wounds?" she asked.

"The leg was a graze," Shaw said. "The shot to your arm was deeper. How does it feel?"

"It tingles, like it fell asleep," Emery said.

"I don't think there's nerve damage, but the muscle is torn," Shaw said. "It will heal, with time."

He looked at his pocket watch. 4:27 in the morning.

"You should get some rest, Miss Dale," Shaw said, rubbing his eyes.

"Doctor, do you remember when we first met?" Dale asked.

Shaw looked at her, at her clear eyes, sharp and perceptive, like few people he'd known.

"Yes, Miss Dale, I remember it well," he replied.

"Do you remember when I asked you about confidentiality?" Dale asked.

"I suppose I do," Shaw said. And he did, to a point. While the details of that day had faded over the last seven years, he remembered how curious it was that she'd ask that question.

"Then I expect confidentiality between us for what I'm about to tell you," Dale said.

* * *

Kneeling over Daniel Underwood's body, Emery Dale stared into the face of the shadowy figure before her. Even with the gaping holes of its eyes and mouth, she recognized it. As the world around her seemed to descend into a swirling darkness, the figure became clearer. She'd glimpsed this thing, this *person*, once before, as little more than a dark shape in a dark room, but then as now there was familiarity.

"I know you," Dale said to the shadow.

Major, it's me, the shadow responded, its voice flooding her mind.

As her body went into shock, at last giving into the traumas it had suffered that day, Dale collapsed into unconsciousness.

When she awoke, she was in a dark room, with a solitary lantern set low; Dr Shaw's office. He sat snoring in his chair next to her. Pain throbbed in her arm and leg beneath their dressings. She stared up at the ceiling, replaying the events of the late afternoon: the shootout in the street, the death of Sheriff Anderson and the confrontation in the Town Hall.

Underwood, Dale thought. *That's what the Sheriff told me with his dying breath. And he was right, the man in the Town Hall was an Underwood. The resemblance to Ernest Underwood was unmistakable. Anderson must have spotted them and they realized they were made. They grabbed him, but he eventually overpowered one of them, killed him and made a break for it. He was gunned down in the street for his trouble, trying to get away.*

Dale took in a deep breath and let out a long sigh, her nerves cold now.

They were here for me, she thought. *There's no other explanation. They came to Orchard Bend to exact revenge and Anderson got in the way. And Jackson, the photographer, killed in his studio as I tracked them.*

Dale closed her eyes, breathing deep again as a familiar and unwelcome sensation arose in her chest.

Breathe, she told herself, taking long, steady breaths. Her mind raced. She saw Anderson dying in the street again, Jackson's body on the floor of his studio, Underwood's blood-soaked face grinning beyond the barrel of the gun pointed right at her.

And then there came the shadowy man with the empty eye sockets and the terrible hole of a mouth. And there came recognition. She *knew* this hideous thing.

Major, it's me, the shadow man had told her.

Dale sat up, her skin chilled by sweat. Adrenalin coursed through her veins, dulling the pain of her wounds, but the blood rush to her head overwhelmed her and she lay back down. Deep breaths turned to gasps for air. The walls around her loomed and she clenched her eyes shut.

"I was a major once," Dale whispered. She had the proof back at her cabin, a piece of an old life she could hardly remember. "I will not give in to panic. *I will not!*"

Shaw grunted next her and Dale took his hand as he slept. Her pounding heart began to slow to a calmer rhythm. Her gasps stopped as her chest muscles first seized then relaxed, allowing her breathing to settle. Around her, the walls no longer seemed so crushing.

Dale lay there for a long time. With no clock in the room, she did not know how many minutes had passed. She held the doctor's hand, even as he started to stir in his sleep. When he began to mutter, Dale squeezed his hand.

"Doctor," she said. "Wake up."

* * *

"Can't this wait until morning, Miss Dale?" Shaw asked.

Dale paused, turning it over in her mind. The eye-less face wouldn't go away and she feared if she didn't say something right now, it wouldn't let her rest. Not tonight, possibly not ever.

Shaw's gaze felt like another weight on her.

"You served in the war," Dale said.

Shaw nodded, his expression unmoved.

"I did," he replied.

"Does it still haunt you?" Dale asked.

"Why are you asking me about this, Miss Dale?" Shaw turned away, found the urn of water on the table near him and started to pour.

"It will take some explaining and it's a strange story, but you'll have to trust that I'm telling you the truth," Dale said.

Shaw put the urn down and picked up both glasses of water. He handed one to Dale. Shaw sat next to her in his chair, looking at the floor. He sipped his water as he listened to her.

"I've been in Orchard Bend seven years now," Dale said. "The day I arrived, before we met, I woke up in the ravine west of town and I had no memory of who I was. I didn't even know my own name. I found... well, I found documentation with my name on it and a few details about my identity, but after all this time I can only remember fragments."

"Amnesia," Shaw said, not moving except to sip his water. Dale took a sip of hers and continued.

"This is the point where I ask you to trust me, Doctor. I've not spoken of this to anyone. Rose and I are—" Dale hesitated, "—*close*, but if I tell her what I know, fear will come between us."

Dale took another sip of her water.

"I served in the military, like you," Dale said.

Now Shaw did turn, his eyes fixed on her. He said nothing.

"And I have fought in war," Dale said. "I have flashes of it. There's shooting... and blood. Soldiers under my command... and the sight of innocents dying."

She waited for a reaction, but all Shaw said was, "Go on."

"Tonight, after Underwood was killed, I saw a face in the darkness staring at me, a ghost," Dale said. "I don't know if it was a memory or madness, but it was the face of one of my soldiers. For as much as I can't remember, *I know that much*."

Dale looked back up at the ceiling, feeling the pain pulsing in her arm and leg.

"Do you believe in ghosts, Doctor?" Dale asked. "Shadows that walk among us, follow us? That can be in the same room as us?"

"Miss Dale," Shaw said, standing up. "I believe that *you* believe everything you've told me, even the part about commanding soldiers. The look on your face now tells me you think I'm patronizing you. Let me tell you, I am most certainly not."

Shaw swallowed the last of his water and sighed.

"Maybe you did terrible things. Maybe you saw terrible things and it was too much," Shaw said. "You can shoot, you can handle a knife. Hell, you can even use a *sword*. So while common sense tells me you're like as not mistaken on some counts, like as not you may be right."

It was Dale's turn to sit in silence now and sip her water.

"I believe in ghosts, Miss Dale," Shaw said. "I believe they may be drawn to death the way flies find a corpse. Maybe it reminds them of what they once were, *who* they once were. Maybe they forget over time, so they walk around looking for pieces of their old life. They're attracted to death because it's how they themselves came to be."

Shaw took the empty glass from Dale and looked at it for a long time, turning it back and forth in his hand.

"Would you like more water, Miss Dale?" Shaw said at last.

"No, I'm fine," Dale said.

"Get some sleep, then," Shaw said. "I'm going to get some shut-eye in my front office."

Shaw slipped through the curtains and Dale was alone. Between the pain and her thoughts, it was a while before she fell asleep.

3

Before I resume from where I last left my narrative, I will commit to greater brevity. I wrote a good deal more than I anticipated, though re-reading the preceding passages in my journal about what happened to Emery, I find there is little I would omit otherwise.

We shall see how succinct I can be as I continue.

The morning after the gunfight, I found Emery awake when I arrived at Dr Shaw's office. She sat upon the bed, talking to him. I went to her, my heart lightened to see her better. When she saw me, Emery got up, but her wounded leg wouldn't support her right away. She caught herself on the examination bed and Dr Shaw took her arm. I was at her side in an instant, but she shrugged us off through gritted teeth.

"No," she said, not with anger, but with determination. "No, I can do it."

And though it pained her greatly, Emery forced her leg to take the weight, standing straight with only the bed to balance her.

"It will take time for that wound to heal, Ms Dale," Dr Shaw said. "I'll give you a crutch to help with your mobility, but I suspect you'll resist using it. Keep this in mind, though: you can't rush these things, the body will do what it's supposed to do and it will take as long as it takes."

"I understand, doctor," Emery said. She looked at me and took a shaky step forward. We embraced, holding each other for a long time. The darkness of the night before faded away.

Dr Shaw coughed and said, "I can prescribe something to help with the pain, if you'd like?"

"No," Emery said. "The pain is bad, but I can manage. I <u>will</u> take the crutch, as you suggested. And I'll heed your wisdom and will try not to overdo it."

Emery's face was grim. She turned to me and said, "Let's go home, Rose."

Reluctantly using her crutch, Emery shuffled out of Doctor Shaw's office, her face tight with composure against the pain of her wounds. She struggled to stand upright, mustering as much dignity as she could. To that end, she wore her duster and hat, while I carried her heavy gun belts and harness. She again waved off help as she climbed onto my buggy. My heart went out to her, seeing her wince in pain with each movement.

Seated, she let out a long sigh, <u>then</u> saw me wringing my hands. She smiled.

"Rose," Emery said, "when I bought you those gloves, I didn't expect you to wear them out fretting over me."

I had to laugh. Emery always had a talent for disarming my worry with humour.

"Merely keeping my hands warm, Miss Emery Dale," I replied, feigning offence. "You have an awfully high opinion of yourself, I warrant. That simply will not do."

"I was important enough to be shot at, Miss Rose Adelaide," Emery replied as I climbed onto the buggy and took the reigns.

"I have it on good authority that you're not the first person in this buggy to suffer such an indignity," I said. "You recall I was shot in the shoulder."

"I see. Well, now that we're even, perhaps we can leave our sad stories behind us," Emery said, looking about the street. I sensed she wanted to make haste to my cottage. It was still early in the morning, but a few passers-by paused to look at us, to look at her, and though she did not return their gaze, she knew they were watching. I drove the buggy home as quickly as I could, respecting the silence that fell between us. We passed Church Street and there Emery looked in the direction of the gunfight, deep in quiet thought.

Emery kept her thoughts to herself for the whole of the ride to my cottage. When we at last arrive, she paused after climbing down from the buggy, I expect taking a moment for the waves of pain to subside.

I had already decided to cancel school that day to stay home to take care of her, much to her protestations. I left her only long enough that morning to go to the church to post a note on the door. I returned to the cottage and found Emery in somewhat brighter spirits. I tended to her --she referred to me as her servant more than once, to my amusement-- and Dr. Shaw visited shortly after lunch to examine and re-dress her wounds.

I insisted she go right to bed following dinner and she did so with some reluctance.

The following day, we attended the wake and funeral for Sheriff Anderson and Mr. Jackson. Both men were unwed and the service began at Sully's tavern, an arrangement --I was informed-- made by the council of aldermen in the absence of immediate family. Maxwell McCabe spoke with his usual eloquence of the sheriff's many years of loyal service to the town. He announced that in the coming days, our Main Street would be renamed Anderson Street, as a lasting legacy to our fallen Sheriff. Deputy Wilson accepted the promotion offered to him and is now Sheriff Wilson.

Emery ate little and spoke even less. At her request, we seated ourselves at a table distant from the other mourners. I stayed with her for a time, but even her dry humour could not mask her desire to simply watch the goings on around her in sullen quiet. She did take a moment to speak with Gertrude McCabe. I was not privy to their talk, as I was in pleasant conversation with Eloise Picton --who is engaged to be married to David Langford this summer-- but it reassured me to see Emery and Gertrude smiling like the old friends they are. Emery told me on the ride home that Gertrude had left a standing invitation to tea at the McCabes' home. Later, the town buried Sheriff Anderson and Mr Jackson next to the church. When services concluded and the mourners began filling out of the cemetery, Emery touched my arm.

"Let us stay a moment," she said.

And so we tarried and were the final mourners there. I spoke briefly to Reverend Thomas, but Emery remained at a distance. When the good Reverend at last left, I went to her, expecting we would then take our own leave.

Emery handed me her crutch, which until then had been supporting her. She adjusted her gunbelts under her duster, squared her hat and began to limp unassisted toward the graves. It was both an inspiring and difficult thing to watch, but she bore the discomfort and her knee did not fail her. From the harness she wore, she drew one of her knives --with the fine cherrywood grips-- and traced a shape into the earth between the fresh plots. When she stood up, replacing her knife in its sheath, she looked around and found me watching her with intense interest. She winked and beckoned me to join her. I looked upon what she had carved on the ground. It was the shape of the symbol tattooed onto her arm, that of the "P" with an "L" growing out of the left side.

"Why?" I asked. "What does it mean?"

"A sign of respect," Emery said. "The Sheriff died protecting the town. Jackson was innocent."

I handed Emery her crutch and we returned home to my cottage.

Emery was insistent I resume teaching come morning. She had by now managed well with her crutch and told me greater sensation and feeling was returning to her arm --apart from the pain of the wound, which had never left. She was correct that I should return to my teaching duties, of course, but I would have preferred to stay with her at the cottage another day.

She was not far from my thoughts to-day as I schooled the children at the church, and I hurried back to her as soon I could. Imagine my surprise when I found Gertrude McCabe at my modest cottage, visiting with and tending to Emery.

We had pleasant company until Gertrude's son Henry came to fetch her. She invited us again to come to her home when Emery had recovered more.

After Gertrude had left, Emery seemed to slip into long bouts of quiet, sitting before the wood stove, her mind many miles away. At one point, she looked at her tattoo, the curious "P" and "L" shape. I gently prod her into conversation periodically throughout the evening as I write in my journal, but after a time it became clear she had much to occupy her thoughts.

I do worry for her so.

* * *

April 21, 1886
Orchard Bend

The newly appointed Sheriff Wilson sat at the bar of Sully's tavern and tried to ignore the eyes in the room watching him. He cast about for Sully, or Sully's wife, or Sully's daughter, Irene, *anybody* to pour him a damn drink.

Following the funeral, Wilson had returned to the jailhouse. Even with the cells empty and no real business requiring his attention, it seemed the place to be, where Sheriff Anderson would've gone. So Wilson went there and sat at the desk. He'd occupied the chair before, but there had been no mistaking that the chair really belonged to Anderson. As deputy, Wilson had always just been keeping it warm while guarding a prisoner or while Anderson was out on his rounds. Now, however, Anderson was not coming back. Thinking about all that had brought a lump to Wilson's throat and he found himself unable to bear another moment in the jailhouse that evening. He needed a drink and Sully's seemed the best place to be.

He looked around the bar again for someone to serve him. Irene came out of the back room with a crate of bottles, saw him and smiled.

"Deputy, I mean *Sheriff* Wilson," Irene said. "You look like a man with an awful thirst."

"Oh, Irene Sullivan, such an understatement has rarely been uttered," Wilson said.

"A day such as this requires some lubrication, I warrant," Irene said, pouring Wilson a shot of whiskey. She slid it to him across the bar and he downed it with no hesitation. It burned his throat, like swallowing fire. It felt good, a cleansing kind of fire.

"Another, Irene," Wilson said, his voice a touch hoarse. She poured another and Wilson downed it just as fast, letting out a satisfied gasp as he did so.

"Two shots to start," Wilson said. "Fitting, wouldn't you agree, Irene? One for Sheriff Anderson and one for poor Mr Jackson."

"God rest their souls," Irene said.

"We nearly didn't find Mr Jackson, did you know that?" Wilson said. "We were backtracking from the Town Hall in the wake of Dale and Underwood's confrontation. O'Toole and his son had already taken her to Doc Shaw. They were across the street, see, searching for Anderson and his kidnappers when they heard the ruckus. Sammy saved Ms Dale with a well-aimed blast of his shotgun. By the by, after all that madness, I was trying to piece together what happened, following the path of bodies back from the Town Hall. I thought it started on Church St with the Sheriff, but then Mr Trask tells me Dale had chased one of the men from the alley behind Jackson's studio. It was dark by then and I almost didn't go to investigate, but I had an inkling I should. Maybe there'd be something in that alley to help me make sense of what happened."

Wilson took another shot, winced as it went down, and shook his head.

"Lord help me, was I ever wrong," Wilson said. "Far from making a lick of sense, things got plenty worse. The rear door to Jackson's studio was open and Clarke Brewer and I went inside. When we found Jackson, I sent Brewer to tell Mr Allman he had another body to tend to, then sat down on one of Jackson's fancy chairs, the ones he uses for taking portraits, and I ain't too proud to say I felt sick at the whole thing."

Wilson looked around, making sure no one else heard that last part. Irene gave his hand a gentle pat and Wilson smiled. He looked at the bottle she was holding, but she turned away and put it behind the bar before returning to him.

"Would you like me to fix you up some dinner, Sheriff?" Irene asked. "I know you're mighty fond of our pork and potatoes."

"I am indeed partial," Wilson said. "And your mother makes the best gravy in the county."

Irene grinned and disappeared into the back kitchen. Wilson was tempted to reach across the bar, grab the bottle of whiskey and pour himself another shot (hell, he'd even take his shot straight from the bottle), but resisted. He was the sheriff now and people were around. He could almost hear Anderson growl, "Don't you dare, boy!"

Wilson snickered at the thought as Irene returned.

"What's so funny?" Irene asked.

"Pondering Sheriff Anderson's opinion of me taking his place," Wilson said. "I warrant he'd take exception."

"Nonsense, Clem Wilson!" Irene said. "Sheriff Anderson would be proud of you. You'll be a fine sheriff, a most worthy successor."

"Thank you, Irene," Wilson said. Irene touched his hand again and gave him a warm smile. He smiled back and felt some of the weight of the last few days ease from his soul. Irene left to tend other patrons and Wilson looked at his reflection in the mirror behind the bar. He was almost thirty, but somehow seemed older now. Maybe it was the badge, bigger than his old deputy's badge, heavier. Wilson took it off and turned it over in his hand.

"I'm gonna do the job right, Sheriff Anderson," he said. "I'm gonna make you proud."

He pinned the badge back onto his jacket as Irene returned. He watched her pour beer for the men playing poker, then looked away as she glanced over at him.

Gosh, Wilson thought, *when did Irene Sullivan stop being a girl? Why am I only noticing now?*

Irene went to serve the men their beer and came back to the bar. She smiled again at the new sheriff as she polished glasses. Wilson felt hot embarrassment and tried to look casual as he examined the photos on the wall. There was a picture of Main Street, with Sully's tavern in the foreground. Next to it was a family portrait of the Sullivans, Irene and her parents all gussied up in their finest. Both bore the words *Jackson Picture Studio* in the bottom right corner and Wilson's good humour slipped away. It was only for a moment, however, as he then remembered something.

"That reminds me," he said to Irene. "I have Jackson's camera sitting in the jailhouse. I don't know much about photography, but I reckon he might have taken a photograph before he died."

"What on earth would make you think that, Sheriff?" Irene asked. Wilson hesitated. Somehow her calling him 'Sheriff' had a pleasant way about it. When he found himself again, he went on.

"The lens cap was off and a plate was in the camera," Wilson said. "Remember when I said I had to sit down after we found Jackson? Well, I was sitting there and I looked into the studio proper, where he took his actual pictures. I could see the camera there in the dark with no lens cap. I looked back at Mr Jackson on the floor and I see a little round shape lying next to him. The lens cap, plain as day. Lying right there next to his hand, it was. When that sick feeling passed, I picked up the cap and put it on the camera. That's when I noticed it was loaded with a plate. I've seen Mr Jackson around town taking his photographs. We all have. I saw him load it on more than a few occasions, so that got me thinking maybe he took a picture with it before he died."

"Aren't you clever?" Irene beamed. "So why did you take the entire camera?"

"Well, I didn't know how to take the plate out of the contraption without exposing the image to the elements. I reckon that would ruin it, so I up and took the whole thing," Wilson said. "I have a mind to see if I can get that photograph developed. I just have to find a man with the know-how."

* * *

Major, it's me.

The half-moon light was just enough for Emery Dale to see by as she awoke from her dream. The face of the shadow-person lingered, leaving her cold inside, almost to the point of shivering; and this despite the warmth of the bed under the covers next to Rose. Rose lay on her side, her back to Dale, breathing deep and steady in her slumber.

Dale slipped out of bed, the black sockets of the shadow's face swimming through her thoughts. The gunshot wound above her knee itched and throbbed under the dressing, but her leg could support her well enough to make her way to her clothes. Her nightshirt was clammy with sweat in the cool air and she pulled it off in the darkness. Her right arm tingled and stabbed her with jolts of pain as she got dressed. She still had to favour her left hand as her grip was still weak in the right. Dale half shuffled, half limped to where her gun belts were slung over the bedpost. She took one of the Colt .45s out of the holster and made her way from the bedroom to the front door. She set the gun on the small table by the door and took a small package wrapped in paper from the table's drawer. She put it next to the gun. With some effort, Dale pulled on her boots. She put on her duster, put the gun in the left pocket and stepped outside.

The light spring breeze fluttered her duster about her legs as Dale set out from the cottage. Moonlight lined the clouds silver and the familiar stretch of the Milky Way seemed endless beyond.

She made slow progress on her injured leg. She passed Main Street (now Anderson Street, she reminded herself) and turned onto Church Street, pausing a moment at the site of the shoot-out days before, and then staggered on down the road. The complaining wound in her leg settled into a manageable cluster of sharp jolts as Dale made her way through the streets in the direction of the McCabe Mill. Dale could hear the lapping of water from the river. When she reached the water's edge, she walked along the shore to a landing of stone and mortar, little more than a ledge where fathers and sons liked to sit while fishing. Dale looked down at the river, guessing it wouldn't be long now, another month perhaps, before the fish came back in plentiful schools. Stone steps led down to the landing and Dale took it easy as she started her decent.

"Emery!" came a voice behind her. It startled Dale and she almost lost her balance. She turned and saw a figure on the road behind her, rushing forward.

It was Rose.

"What in heavens are you doing?!" the schoolteacher called out, her voice near panic.

"Rose, calm yourself!" Emery replied, holding up her hand.

"Emery Dale, do *not* tell me to calm myself!" Rose said as she reached the top of the bank. "You leave in the middle of the night to come all the way out *here*? I followed you, you're in no shape to be roaming the streets, let alone at *this* hour. Now I see you heading down to the water's edge. Dear Lord, you could slip and fall in!"

"Rose, it's alright," Emery said, climbing as fast as she could back up the steps. The effort sent searing pain through her leg and she came close to losing her footing as she reached the top. Rose was there and caught her.

"You see?!" Rose said. "You can barely stand."

"It's not as bad as that," Emery said, stretching the truth a little. It hurt, a lot, but after the initial wave subsided, Emery felt she could manage.

"Nonsense," Rose said. "Now, tell me what brought you out here."

"I have to do something," Emery said.

"Could it not wait until morning?" Rose asked.

"No," Emery said. "As a matter of fact it could not. It has to be done at night and I wanted to do it in private. Since you're here, though, you can share this with me."

"What are you going on about, Emery?" Rose said. The panic had left her voice, replaced now with curiosity and confusion.

"I'll show you, but first we have to go down to the landing," Emery said, leading Rose to the steps. The teacher was in her nightdress, robe, wool frock coat and boots. Hand in hand, the two descended the steps, Emery leading, but using Rose to balance. The pain in her leg was such now that she wanted to get this finished soon.

The tide was in and the water came up almost to the lip of the stone landing. Dale reached into the pocket of her duster and took out the package.

"What's this?" Rose asked.

Emery said nothing, but unwrapped it and revealed two short candles, a box of matches and two pieces of wax paper. Rose watched as Emery folded a piece of the paraffin-coated paper into the shape of a cup.

"Hold these," Emery said, setting first one candle in its cup, then the second. Emery took the box of matches and struck one. The tiny flame flashed bright and Emery looked up at Rose, who was looking back at her. The schoolteacher's eyes glistened, reflecting the tiny point of light. A sad smile came to Rose's face. Emery wanted to kiss her right there on the landing, but dared not to. Besides, she was out here for a reason. Rose never took her eyes off her.

Emery lit the candles and took one herself. It was warm, even at the base. The paraffin would melt soon.

"Now we set them upon the water," Emery said. Kneeling hurt something fierce, but she forced herself to drop to her knee long enough to place the cupped candle on the water. Beside her, Rose did the same.

In their little wax paper boats, the candles floated down the stream at once, two pin-points of light on the water. Rose took Emery's hand as they watched them ease away down the river.

Emery wondered if Rose expected her to say something, to explain, like she had at the cemetery. Rose squeezed her hand and that was all. Nothing need be said as the white dots glistening on the water drifted further and further away.

When the candles disappeared, whether from sinking under the surface or rounding a bend, the two climbed back up the steps and walked the streets of Orchard Bend back to Rose's cottage.

* * *

Rose opened the door, but Emery sat on the bench outside, sighing as she took the weight off her leg. She leaned back against the wall of the cottage and took in the spring air. Rose stopped in the doorway, watching her.

Emery smiled, shifted over and said, "Join me."

Rose wrapped her coat tight around her and sat next to Emery.

"A half moon tonight," Rose said, nodding to the west horizon before them.

"Above it is the constellation Leo," Emery said, pointing to the shape in stars. She gave Rose a wry smile. "Your sign, if I am correct that your birthday is July 30th."

Rose frowned and said, "Astrology. Spiritualism. Such ideas dally too close to *witchcraft*. Don't let Reverend Thomas hear you speak of such things. You will get an earful on the subject of fire and brimstone."

"The constellations are invaluable to navigation," Emery said.

"Absolutely. That's the function of *astronomy*," Rose said, affecting the tone she often used with her students. It was automatic and Emery had realized long before that the schoolteacher wasn't aware she was even doing it. Emery Dale found it delightful. "Astrology is altogether different. The stars do *not* govern our lives and choices. It's hogwash. The refuge of the weak-willed, those who desire to be absolved of responsibility for their actions in this life."

"I do not argue with that," Emery said. "I don't hold much stock in celestial machinations. The answers I seek are not found there."

Rose said nothing, her bright expression faltering as she looked away. Emery took her hand and squeezed it. It was warm in the cool night air.

"My dear Rose," Emery said. "Such a burden your soul carries, empathetic to so many."

"My mother once said it was a failing, forming deep attachments," Rose said. "That it left me open to sorrow, with so much of life beyond my control. But I have my faith and I have my work. And I have you."

"Thank you, Rose," Emery said. "You can't know just how much that means to me."

Emery stood up, still holding Rose's hand, and added, "But let me try to show you."

Rose took in a sharp breath at the invitation, smiled, and Emery led her inside the cottage.

4

May 14, 1953
Blue Creek

Everything was dark and wet.

Mara Dale awoke to find herself lying face down in the rain on gravelled dirt. Her left foot was cold. She opened her eyes just as lightning cut the sky. She lay half in and half out of a ditch full of water that soaked her boot right through.

Mara pulled herself up and looked around. From the side of the road, she saw streetlights marching away in either direction.

"This was not what I expected," she said aloud.

A metal box about the size of her hand lay next to her. She picked it up.

A control computer, said a voice in her head. It sounded like the voice of her captain, her commanding officer, but that wasn't entirely accurate. There was something else in that voice, but she couldn't place it. Mara set that aside as she examined the small computer more closely.

The screen had a crack in it. A small keypad slid out of the bottom. She started to press the power button, but the voice in her head said, *No! Not in the rain.*

"Of course," Mara replied. "Wet electronics make for dead electronics if you turn them on. Thanks for the heads-up."

The voice didn't reply.

She found a pocket almost large enough inside her leather jacket and wrestled the computer inside. She looked around again and that's when she saw the tiny flashing light halfway down the ditch, almost at the water's edge. Mara scooped up the piece of plastic and metal.

A watch.

The flashing display read:

DETONATION
COMPLETE

Mara stood motionless in the rain, chilled to her core and not because of the storm.

The facility, she remembered, it had been blown up. Soldiers had come. They fired on Mara and her team.

"No," she said, her quiet words almost lost as the wind picked up around her. She didn't even notice. "They fired at my team, but not at me. And the scientists were being spared, too. The soldiers needed them to work the equipment, more than likely to keep the experiments going. I was standing next to one, the lead scientist. Then the captain decided to detonate the facility..."

The watch in her hand belonged to the captain.

"She dropped it when..." Mara whispered, "...when we were pulled into the Breach."

The Breach.

The Breach was the reason for the experiments. The facility contained the Portal to the Breach, a tear in reality of some sort being studied by the scientists. Mara's team guarded the facility, but with little warning, everything went to hell. The facility went into lockdown following the President's assassination and the coup that followed.

"The captain had to destroy everything," Mara said. "She had no choice. When they started shooting my team, that was it. They couldn't be allowed to have access to the Breach. It was too dangerous."

Mara stopped speaking and realized she'd started walking along the side of the road. She looked back the way she came, unsure how far she'd travelled. In the rain and darkness, broken only by pools of white light from the streetlamps, everything looked the same. Trees lined the road with shadowed fields beyond. She couldn't even see a farmhouse.

Mara tucked the watch into her pocket and kept walking, one direction being just as good as the other when you didn't know where the hell you were.

This is the right way, said the voice of the captain. *Follow your gut.*

"If you insist," she said and let out a giggle.

When the captain detonated the facility, something unexpected had happened as explosive charges had gone off around them. From the Portal, the Breach seemed to reach out. She couldn't *see* it exactly, but she could feel it, like a great fist punching her in the stomach, punching *through* her abdomen and taking a grip on her insides. Then it pulled. The Breach consumed the lead scientist standing next to her. It pulled all of them in, even the soldiers who had just executed her team.

It had pulled her in, too.

The world had then turned a swirling grey and everything became transparent, like old, smoked glass. It had gotten darker and darker around her. At some point she had lost consciousness.

And woke up here, wherever here was.

"Maybe I'm dead," Mara thought aloud. "Maybe this is the afterlife. A lone road in a storm. I'm doomed to walk it for eternity."

The thought amused her, but she didn't know exactly why. She grinned, her face soaked from the rain. She wiped her blonde hair from her eyes and wished her jacket had a hood.

The rain lessened as she walked and after a time it stopped altogether. She looked up and saw the clouds breaking up. Stars glittered. Gusts of wind buffeted her as she looked at her wrist, only to find her own watch missing.

"Just great," Mara said. At least she had the captain's watch. She took it from her pocket and turned it on. The display cast a reassuring glow in the heavy night that surrounded her. She cleared the screen of the detonation message and found the clock app. Tapping it, the app informed her thus:

Geo-sync update
required.

Unable to acquire
signal.
<u>Manual?</u> <u>Cancel?</u>

"Shit," Mara said. "Maybe this *is* hell, after all."

She giggled again, unsure what was so funny, but the giggling turned to outright laughter before tapering off to a snicker.

"Better to laugh than cry, I suppose," Mara added. That led to another snicker as she put the watch back in her pocket and continued walking.

With the rain stopped, the view of her surroundings improved a little. Squinting through the dark, she could make out a few dots of light here and there in the distance.

Farms, she guessed. If it came to it, she could try to make it to one of them.

Mara crested a hill and from there she saw the glittering lights of a small town not far ahead. She walked on towards it, passing a sign with a grinning family which read: *Welcome to Blue Creek.*

* * *

The dead streets and darkened homes told Mara it must be late. She wended her way along the tree-lined avenues, directionless, but wanting to keep moving. She took in details, like the picket fences and the cars in the driveway. Once in a while she'd hear a dog bark in distance or the screech of a car a block away.

Unknown territory, said the captain's voice in her head. *Stay unnoticed. Look for landmarks. Find cover and concealment if you can.*

Mara picked out distinctive houses, noted street names and intersections. She found herself on Chapel Lane and after a few blocks she came upon a church. St. Mary's, according to the sign. Next to it she found a narrow park, enclosed by a wrought-iron fence whose gate sat open. Mara slipped inside, glad for the cover of night. She found a small gazebo two dozen

31

yards in. She sat on the dry deck and let out a long sigh. The cool air against her rain-dampened pants made her shiver.

"I've been through worse," she said under her breath, thinking of the blistering deserts and sauna-like jungles of her military career. Compared to those, she hardly noticed this mild discomfort. Besides, the spring rain left the air fresh and fragrant.

She took out the captain's watch and turned it on again. The display still read:

Geo-sync update
required.
Unable to acquire
signal.
Manual? Cancel?

Mara could do a manual update if she wanted, but wondered why the watch couldn't find a signal.

"Does no one here have net access?" she asked. "No satellite coverage?"

She looked up through the tree and picked out some stars.

It's worse than that, came the captain's voice.

Mara's gaze dropped to the park, back the way she came, to Chapel Lane. In her mind's eye she saw the streets which led her here, the houses she passed and... the cars.

The cars were all wrong.

The cars were *old*.

Studebaker.

Crosley.

Muntz.

More than that, though, it was the style of the cars, all from the 1950s. Or older.

Unable to acquire signal, said the captain's voice. *You know damn well why, don't you, soldier?*

"Oh, fuck me," Mara said.

As if to underscore this, a black and white car eased along Chapel Lane, stopping at the park's gate. Mara put the watch away, but the driver held up a portable searchlight. Mara kept still.

"I thought I saw something," said one of the men in a loud voice. Red lights came on atop the car and Mara scrambled away, ducking behind the gazebo deck.

"YOU THERE!" called one of the men, spotting her.

A policeman, the captain's voice said. *Better run!*

Moving away at a crouch, deeper into the park, Mara fled, thoughts of cars and their age of manufacture pushed aside. She heard the car doors open and shut behind her and saw the weak beams of flashlights trying to cut through the blackness. Mara weaved between trees and bushes, through a flower bed and deeper still into the park.

As she ran, she wondered just how deep the park went. The answer came when she came to the iron fence at the far end. Well behind her but gaining fast, the policemen called out for her to show herself.

Amongst the shadows Mara glimpsed her only chance. A park bench sat below a tree whose branches extended almost over the fence. Not hesitating, Mara knew it was a long shot and ran to the park bench. She let her momentum take her first onto the seat, then onto its back, then into the air. She grasped for the lowest branch, hoping it was dry enough.

It was.

Her hand gripped the cold, knotted bark. The branch bowed under her weigh, but held. Mara pulled herself up, using all of her upper body, kicking her legs as the branch sprang back upwards. She found purchase on a large knot and climbed up. Rising to her feet, the branch bowed again. She climbed to the next branch, the one that would save her, and inched her way along it. She balanced herself with a lesser tree limb near her head, while under her feet the branch tapered off and bent downwards. She moved toward its tip. The smaller branches reached out like fingers in the dark above the wrought iron fence. She planned to jump out and away from the branch to clear the metal.

On the ground, yards away, the policemen cast their flashlights about looking for her. Mara tensed to jump, looking through the branches and leaves into the gloomy dark on the other side of the fence. Pale, symmetrical shapes came into view as the flashlights cross-crossed back and forth.

Headstones, said the captain.

Here's hoping I don't land on one, Mara thought.

Jumping from the branch would be like jumping from a diving board, where it bowed and flexed underfoot as the diver propelled herself off it. Bending her legs, Mara eased the branch into a rhythmic up and down motion, timing her jump.

"What's that?!" asked one of the policemen, his beam finding Mara's tree.

It had to be now, she thought, and launched herself over the fence.

"IN THE TREE!" cried the other officer.

Mara sailed over the fence, falling through the shadows. When she hit the ground, she tucked and rolled, the hard edges of the control computer jabbing into her from beneath her jacket. The stone of a grave marker broke her roll and a moment later, both officers' beams of light caught her. She didn't look back as the police ordered her to stop.

Mara could see the street at the other end of the cemetery and bolted for it, knowing the policemen would be racing to their car to cut her off. They had the advantage, they knew their town's streets, probably every back alley and laneway.

Mara reached the cemetery gate, eyes darting about her, looking for a place to flee. She saw a high stone fence across the street, too high to scale. She ran down the sidewalk lined with shops all closed for the night. She felt exposed out here, but kept moving, expecting the police car to round the corner behind her at any moment.

She heard the squeal of tires on asphalt and glanced back just as the police car swung around the corner towards her. She ran past shop after shop --a deli, a pawn shop, a barbershop-- seeing the flashing red light reflecting off the buildings around her. The blare of the siren shattered the still of the night. Mara reached a street corner and banked to her right, losing her pursuers for a moment. Her boots, practical but light, clicked on the pavement as she ran.

A vacant lot appeared ahead of her and she darted into it, staying close to the wall. She spotted a caged fire escape ladder a few yards away, the lowest rung a good six feet off the ground.

They don't want kids scaling the walls, it seems, the captain said and Mara pushed the voice away.

She jumped and grabbed the lowest rung. Hand over hand she climbed, her feet using the wall, stopping only when she saw the red light of the police car. She froze in place, pressing her body against the ladder, trying to be invisible inside the cage. She tilted her head toward the street and watched as the police car slowed next to the vacant lot. The searchlight came on and panned back and forth through the darkness of the unlit property. It hit the wall below the ladder, maybe fifteen feet from where she clung motionless to the side of the building. Mara waited. When the searchlight winked out and the police car accelerated up the street, Mara relaxed. Even when it passed out of view behind a row of buildings, she could still see the flashing red light bouncing off the storefronts. Moments later even that was gone.

Mara let out another sigh and climbed back down the ladder. Cautious as she left the vacant lot, she darted across the road and down a dark side street.

5

May 18, 1953
Blue Creek

The townsfolk considered *The Yellow Canary* a respectable establishment, with its brightly appointed décor and welcoming atmosphere to both soda fountain diners and those in search of a good, stiff drink. At one end of the long counter, they served ice cream and poured soda for the youngsters and families. Further down, the soda fountains gave way to draft beer and bottles of hard liquor. A jukebox marked the unofficial boundary where the coffee shop booths stopped and the bar tables began. Kids seemed to know not to go much past that point, despite there being no specific rule restricting them. Likewise, few adults seated in the booths near the front window ever ordered a beer, much less anything harder. When the children came of age, they saw it as a rite of passage to cross that invisible line to the back end of the bar and order a drink, a *grown up* drink, from the proprietor Fred Dooley. Fred knew just about every kid in town and knew exactly how old they were, because they held many of their birthday parties in those booths. But the ritual was the ritual and he'd take his time carding each one of them, looking over their driver's license with a sceptical eye as the initiate's friends watched in respectful silence behind him or her. Fred Dooley would let the young man or woman wait there, making them sweat a little, secretly loving the honour bestowed on him, that of granting the mantle of *adulthood* on a generation of the towns folk.

Blue Creek mourned the loss of Fred Dooley when he died suddenly of a heart attack the summer before. Few people in the history of the town commanded such respect and earned

36

such love as he had, and St. Mary's church had been standing room only for his funeral.

"Ain't it a hell of a thing?" Deputy Berger said. Berger had thin shoulders and the start of a pot belly, the kind a man gets in his thirties when his metabolism and exercise regimen both slow down while his poor diet keeps on going.

Behind the bar, Tom Dooley tried to ignore Berger, but knew that wouldn't work for very long. As Fred's only son, Tom inherited *The Yellow Canary* when his father passed away. People in town liked Tom, but he couldn't escape the stories of his father's greatness. Tom would smile and agree ("You're right, Mr Mayweather, Dad was a saint. A king amongst men!") and tried to ignore his father's long shadow as it seemed to blot out the sun.

Every afternoon shift, Berger took his usual seat at the bar and ordered the same thing, a roast beef sandwich, extra pickle, and black coffee. After the first bite, Berger proclaimed, "The sandwich of kings, just like Mom used to make!"

During the rest of his visit, the deputy pontificated about the news in that day's papers, everything from the big city headlines to the *Blue Creek Frontiersman* local news. Tom always saved some of the more involved day-to-day tasks for when Berger showed up, so he'd have an excuse to disappear into the back room if need be, leaving Berger to mutter to himself or to Betsy Parker, *The Yellow Canary's* waitress. These days, though, Tom had no Betsy to deflect Berger. In April, Betsy Parker became Mrs Harold Prince. Tom last saw her two weeks ago, when she came to pick up her final pay cheque. The *Help Wanted* sign had gone unanswered since then and Tom started to seriously consider going to the Prince house to beg Betsy to come back to work, even one or two nights a week. He'd even give her a raise.

"I said 'a hell of a thing, ain't it, Tom?'" Berger announced. Tom stopped his inventory of the liquor bottles and walked to where Berger sat with his back to the jukebox.

"What's that, exactly?" Tom asked.

Berger pointed to the headline in the *Frontiersman* which read: *LOCAL MAN MURDERS NEIGHBOURS.* Tom already

37

heard about what happened a few nights ago, the night of the big storm. Everyone in town knew by now. Berger was right, it was a hell of a thing. Not long before, Mr Tony Bullock finished a drawn out, messy divorce. That appeared to be what caused him to snap. He attacked his neighbours across the street, the Watsons, and killed three people: both Mr and Mrs Watson and their son's girlfriend, Debbie Elliot. The Watsons' son, Cal, had survived, shooting Bullock dead with a shotgun. Cal, Debbie and their friends were regulars at *The Yellow Canary*, good kids.

Bullock, on the other hand... It shocked Tom what happened, but didn't quite surprise him. Bullock had been high-strung, controlling. Mandy Bullock had had enough last year and left him. She was no saint either, but Tom wondered if beneath the man's rigidness she maybe saw the potential for murder in Tony. Maybe that's why she left him.

"You knew Tony Bullock, didn't you, Tom?" Berger asked.

"Yeah, he came in sometimes," Tom said. The bell above the door jingled and Tom saw a woman silhouetted against the bright sunshine pouring in from the front window. "I didn't see that coming, what Tony did, even after Mandy left."

"Who amongst us could see such a thing in a man? Stress does crazy things to people," Berger said and took a bite of his sandwich. Through a full mouth he continued, "Oh, before I forget, the boys and I are playing poker at my place on Saturday. Might make it a regular thing. Consider yourself invited."

"Thanks, I'll keep it in mind," Tom replied.

The woman at the door had a duffle bag and a canteen slung over her shoulder. For a moment, she reminded Tom of the service men coming home from the war years before. Her wrinkled clothes looked to Tom like she'd slept in them. Her green eyes darted about the diner, so pale as to be almost white. She picked up the *Help Wanted* sign and approached Tom and Berger.

"Who do I talk to about the job?" she asked in a soft voice, a touch uncertain.

"You talk to this man, Tom Dooley" Berger said, pointing to Tom. "Just like the song, you know?"

The woman stared at Berger and gave a nervous shake of her head. "No, I'm sorry. I don't know..."

"Oh, come on," Berger said. "It's a famous song, little lady. Grayson & Whitter. It's about a hanging."

The woman shrugged.

"Do I have to know the song to get the job?" she asked, still looking uncertain at both men.

Berger let out a hearty laugh.

"Hire this girl, Tom," the deputy said. "She's a hoot!"

"Come over here a moment," Tom said to the woman, leading her to a booth away from Berger. "Let me ask you a few questions, huh?"

They sat and Tom noticed the faint smell of smoke, like this woman had been near a campfire. He asked, "What's your name?"

"Mara Dale," she said.

"Nice to meet you," Tom said, sticking out his hand. She hesitated, then shook it. He expected her grip to be as meek as she appeared, but it was strong and steady.

"Likewise, Mr Dooley," Mara said.

"Please, call me Tom. Mr Dooley was my father," Tom smiled.

Mara smiled back, her pale green eyes fixed on his.

"Alright, Tom," she said. "Call me Mara."

"Okay, Mara, let's start with your background," Tom said and noticed her shift in her seat. She looked away, seeming to take in the red and white tile pattern on the floor. Tom pressed on, "Are you from Blue Creek? I can't say I've seen you around and I know just about everyone in town."

"I just arrived here a few days ago," Mara said, looking up at him again. "I'll be honest. I don't know anyone in town and I need a job."

Tom leaned back, stretching his arms behind his head. He let out a long exhale. It was his turn to look away uncertain.

"Well, okay," Tom said. "I appreciate the honesty."

He drummed his fingers on the table top and then returned his gaze to her.

"It's clear you need a job," Tom said. "But if I can be equally honest, if you're just passing through, that's not much good to me."

Mara's shoulders slumped and she nodded.

"Okay," she said. "Thank you for the interview."

She stood up, ran her hand through her hair and walked away from the booth. At the counter, Berger paused in his meal to watch her leave.

Tom let out a frustrated groan.

"Wait!" he said. "Come back, Mara. Sit down."

Mara stopped at the door and looked back at Tom, who waved for her to join him.

Sitting down, Mara held Tom's gaze with an expectant expression.

"The job is mainly waitressing, some bartending and working the counter," Tom explained. "You'll be on your feet a lot, especially during the busy hours."

"I understand," Mara said. "I'm used to hard work."

"Have you ever worked as a waitress before?" Tom asked.

"No, I haven't," Mara said. "But I grew up in a disciplined household. My father was in the Army. He instilled in us a strong work ethic. I'm adaptable and used to thinking on my feet."

Tom nodded, looked past her out the window to the street and considered her answer. Mara waited, patient and quiet.

"I'm going to be upfront with my reservations, just so there's no misunderstanding," Tom said, raising a finger to emphasize his point. "It's nothing personal. You seem like a good person. This job involves handling money and I have to know there's no funny business going on. I don't want to find the till short or a bill mysteriously unpaid, if you catch my meaning."

"I do," Mara said. "I have no interest in stealing from you or the customers."

"That's Deputy Berger back there," Tom said, pointing behind him. "He's a regular. So is Sheriff Meyer. So are the other police officers in Blue Creek. If I find you've stolen so much as a nickel, I won't hesitate to call them. Are we clear on that?"

"Crystal clear," Mara said.

"Before I put you on the payroll, we're going to do a trial run," Tom said. "I'll pay you at the end of your shift each day. You demonstrate you're serious about this job and we'll make it a permanent thing. And by serious, I mean being on time for your shift, in uniform and ready to work your kiester off."

Mara smiled.

"Of course," she said.

"When can you start?" Tom asked.

"Right now, if that's convenient," Mara replied, eagerness filling her eyes. "I mean, after I freshen up a little."

She's really that desperate for a job, isn't she? Tom thought.

"Alright then, Mara," he said. "We'll give it the old college try, won't we?"

"I won't let you down," Mara said.

Behind her, an elderly couple came into *The Yellow Canary* and waved at Tom. He waved back.

"Looks like the lunch rush is about to start," he said. He got up and Mara followed. "I'll take you to the back. There's a uniform and an apron there. While you're getting changed, I'm going to make a phone call."

Tom hoped the recently wed Betsy Prince would be willing to come in for a few hours to train the new girl.

6

May 16, 1953
Blue Creek

On the night Mara arrived in Blue Creek and narrowly escaped the police, two days before she walked into *The Yellow Canary* and asked Tom Dooley for a job, Mara moved along the town's dark streets. She came to a creek --the namesake of the town, it would seem-- and found it to be more like a river. It ran through the heart of the community in a shallow, narrow valley, but it offered her concealment. Mara decided to rest in a dry patch of ground under a thick cluster of trees. She sat staring up at the silver clouds and bright moon, and her thoughts returned to the larger problem.

Mara Dale was a woman out of her time.

All the evidence pointed to that, like the street lights, signs, and the models and years of the cars. It was the 1950s, Mara guessed, meaning the Breach had sent her back in time after it pulled her in. That explained the absence of a net signal and why the watch couldn't even connect to GPS or military satellites.

The realization had led to a sudden, unexpected feeling, one she wasn't use to.

Panic.

She could feel her sanity slipping as she turned the problem over and over in her head. She was trapped. She didn't know if she could open a Portal to the Breach with the broken computer. Even if she could, would it return her to her own time? The scientists at the facility studied that Portal for years. As stable as it seemed, they took no chances. They struggled with every experiment to bring it under control. They'd also tried to open a new one once and that had been a disaster.

She'd been at the facility when the volunteer, at a distant classified mountain location, had tried to create a Portal, using precise (and what everyone hoped were accurate) coordinates. For a split second, a Portal did open, then it lost stability and engulfed the volunteer. The scientist made no further attempt to open a new Portal to the Breach after that. They decided to stick with the one they had. Future tests were discussed, but the lead scientist, a handsome man named Stevenson, had emphasized more research. The team needed to learn a lot more about the Breach, but safely.

And safety takes time. He always stood by that, said the captain's voice. Stevenson, a civilian scientist brought in by the government, was very close to the captain. It wasn't much of a secret that the two were in love.

In the moonlight under the tree, Mara's panic ebbed.

He was pulled in right along with you, the captain said. *He might even be here in this town.*

"It's a long shot, but perhaps," Mara said in the darkness. "Maybe all the people the Breach pulled in ended up here."

Mara closed her eyes, meaning to rest them for only a moment, but ended up sleeping for hours.

It was not a peaceful sleep. Mara dreamed of the facility, the takeover, the shooting and being pulled into the Breach. That was frightening enough, but then came something more terrible, the feeling of being watched while trapped in that world of grey, swirling, smoked glass.

I'm not alone here, Mara thought in her dream. *There's something else. Something sees me. I can't let it find me!*

So she ran, through the grey world—-

The Breach, whispered the captain's voice very close to her ear. *This is what the Breach looks like from the inside. You saw it. Just for a moment you saw it.*

Mara ran and ran, trying to get away from whatever was watching her. The grey turned to black and she felt safe.

When Mara awoke, the morning sun lit through the mist and the trees. Without the cover of night, she felt exposed again and decided to move on. She drank from the creek and followed its path southeast as the sun climbed higher. It did not take long for the rushing water to veer away from the town. When she decided to make camp, Mara settled into a tree-lined dell. She took the control computer, the one with the cracked screen, out of her jacket and set it in the sun, hoping to dry it out, to see if it would ever work again. She took the captain's watch out of her pocket and turned it on.

It's your *watch now*, came the captain's voice again.

A jolt of pain stabbed in Mara's head. She saw the shooting of her team by the soldiers sent to lockdown the facility, heard the voice of the captain yelling for the soldiers to stop, her voice nearly drowned out by the concussive gunshots. She could smell the gun powder that hung in the air after the soldiers ceased fire.

Through wet eyes, Mara looked around.

"God," she said to herself, wiping her eyes. "I'm coming apart at the seams. What's happening to me?"

The headache eased and the shaking slowed as she took some deep breaths. She took off her leather jacket as the morning grew warmer. She rolled up the sleeves of her shirt and returned her attention to the watch.

Any applications requiring a geo-synch --such as the calendar, map and weather apps-- wouldn't work until she could determine the date. If she knew the time, she could manually adjust the clock, but otherwise those functions were useless for now. With no internet or GovNet in the 1950s, those apps were good for nothing, too. The calculator app worked fine and Mara found the game app and fired it up. The screen was a little more than an inch square. Tiny coloured figures bounced around it, waiting for her to tap the screen and kill them, but she only stared at it, feeling distant and disconnected. It was like looking through a pinhole into the future, only that future was her past. Her life before waking up on the side of the road seemed so very far away.

She turned off the watch and put it away. It hurt too much to look at it.

You're stuck here, soldier, the captain said.

No. At least, maybe not, Mara thought, fighting the growing fear. *I have the control computer. I can try to use it—!*

What, go through and come out in the Late Triassic Period? Maybe Pre-Cambrian? the captain mocked.

I'll run tests. I'll try to learn as much as I can! Mara pushed back against the fear, the *panic. I won't make the same mistakes—*

Stevenson was a brilliant scientist, but look what happened to the volunteer he sent out, the captain chuckled. *If that fellow lived, he could be anywhere. Besides, what is there to go back to? I blew up the facility on you and everyone else, didn't I? Best case scenario, you get the exact coordinates to open the Portal, you enter the Breach and it takes you back there. You emerge in the collapsed rubble of a devastated underground government research facility. If you're lucky, you rematerialize in the debris. If you're not, you're buried alive.*

Mara began gasping for air in her panic attack as it all came crushing down on her.

There was no going home.

Like on the road the night before, Mara began to giggle, then outright laugh. She didn't know why she thought the situation was funny, but it was, even as the panic seized her. Tears ran down her cheeks again and she hugged her knees, rocking back and forth.

When the fit subsided, Mara got up on shaky legs, walked to the water's edge, made sure no one was around, undressed and washed herself in the creek. As she sat drying off in a patch of sun, she decided she needed some essentials.

That meant going back into town.

* * *

Mara made her way back to town just as shops began to open and the sidewalks bustled with activity. She kept her head down, trying her best not to attract attention. Still, passers-by took notice of her, glancing sideways as she passed. With the black leather coat, the black jeans and boots, Mara thought she must look like trouble to these people.

Up ahead, she saw the tell-tale three spheres hanging outside the pawn shop. When she fled the police the night before, Mara had passed it. Now, she needed money and had very few options. She took off her jacket and carried it over her arm. The bell rattled above the door as she entered and a man came out from the back room. Shelves of books, clocks and assorted knick-knacks lined one wall. Squat, wood-framed radios lined another. Mannequins and racks displayed clothes stood towards the rear of the store, beside more shelves with shoes, boots, hats and gloves.

"Good morning," said the man behind the counter. Mara pegged him as well past middle-age, into his sixties. He had distinguished salt and pepper hair and broad shoulders. His eyes seemed to be appraising her the same way he appraised the items in his shop.

"Hello," Mara said.

The pawnbroker waited for more, but when it was not forthcoming, he spoke again, his voice cheerful, but a touch impatient.

"Is there anything I can help you with, Miss?" he asked.

Mara roused herself from her discomfort and walked forward.

"I'm sorry," she said. "I've never been in a pawnshop before."

"Believe it or not, I hear that often," the pawnbroker said. "People come in for the first time and don't know what to expect. Maybe they read too many crime novels or movies and think we're scoundrels in here, looking to fleece them. But rest assured, Miss, I run an honest business. You'll get a fair price if you're looking to part with something, and an equally fair price if you to want buy anything."

"Well, thank you," Mara said. "I'm hoping to pawn something, actually."

"And what would that be?"

Mara held up her leather jacket and draped it on the glass cabinet of the counter between them. The cabinet displayed a vast collection of jewellery, everything from rings and necklaces to broaches and cameos. The pawnbroker looked doubtful at the jacket, but picked it up and examined it.

"Supple, soft leather," he said. "Feels like lambskin."

"That's right," Mara said.

"Rider design," he went on, laying the jacket on the counter. "Strong zipper. Good for use with gloves."

He looked up at her.

"There's no maker's label or brand," he said.

"No," Mara replied. "It was custom made for me years ago. I didn't wear it often."

The pawnbroker nodded and looked back at the jacket. He checked the lining, the sleeves and details. He put his hands on his hips and stared down at the jacket for long, silent seconds before he spoke. He looked at her without raising his head.

"I'll give you five dollars," he said.

Mara blinked.

"Five...?" she asked, unsure if she heard him right.

"See, it's a custom cut," the pawnbroker explained. "I have to find a woman close to your build, which may not be uncommon, but there aren't too many girls in Blue Creek looking for this sort of thing. If I'm lucky, one of them will see a motorcycle picture up the street at *The Garden* and snatch this up. More than likely, I'll be sitting on this for six months or a year."

Mara wanted to grab the jacket and tell the man to forget it, but the captain's voice came loud and clear.

You're alone. You have nothing, remember? Your stomach was growling five minutes ago.

The pawnbroker let out a heavy exhale and said, "Tell you what, five dollars cash right now or six dollars store credit. That's the best I can do."

"Can I look around?"

"You certainly may, take your time. The offer stands until you walk out the door," the man said.

Mara browsed the items towards the back, flipping first through the clothing racks. She noted a good number of olive drab Army field jackets among the clothes each priced at a dollar. She took one off the rack and held it up. It had been stripped of identifiers and insignia, but was otherwise in good shape.

The pawnbroker's voice came from behind her.

"After the war, those jackets started pouring through here," he said. "Some are Army surplus, some from boys coming home from Europe."

"I see," Mara nodded. She hung the jacket back on the rack and spent a few minutes looking at the inventory before walking back to the counter. Seeing something in the cabinet that caught her eye, Mara stopped and bent over for a closer look.

"That's a fighting knife from the war," the pawnbroker said as Mara admired the blade. "I have more than a couple like this from folks around the county."

"I'll take this," Mara said, pointing at the knife, "and a few other things; the other half in cash, if the offer still stands?"

* * *

The bell above the door of the pawnshop rattled as Mara stuffed the remaining money in her pocket. The pawnbroker looked over her shoulder and his smile fell away. Mara turned and saw a man in a double-breasted suit and a fedora lighting a cigarette. Thin, but fit, he had a folded newspaper under his arm. Mara trusted her instincts and they whispered of danger about this man; something in the stance, the well-practiced casual air that hid a serious demeanour.

The newcomer put his lighter away, took a pull from his smoke and flicked his ashes on the floor. He looked at her, then to the pawnbroker, then back to her. With great effort, Mara turned away and packed her newly bartered possessions into the beat-up dufflebag the pawnbroker had thrown in for free ("Got one too many holes in it to be of much use to me," he'd said. "Don't go telling folks I didn't charge you for this, Miss. Can't have them thinking I'm going soft").

The newcomer approached the counter, put the cigarette back in his mouth and extended his hand to the pawnbroker.

"Parker," the man addressed the pawnbroker. His voice was neither menacing nor friendly, its dry tone seeming to suck the air from the room. Parker, the pawnbroker, had to lean forward over the counter to shake the man's hand.

48

"Mr Davis," Parker said. "Beautiful day, isn't it?"

Davis put the folded newspaper on the counter as he released Parker's hand. His eyes fixed on Mara, taking another drag of his cigarette. Mara finished packing the dufflebag and looked at the newspaper.

"Is that today's paper?" she asked, avoiding eye contact.

"Yes, it is," Davis said, letting the smoke swirl about him. "The city paper. I'm finished with it, doll, if you want it."

"Thank you," Mara said, grabbing the newspaper.

"Think nothing of it, sweetheart," Davis said, flicking ashes on the counter in front of Parker.

Mara looked at the pawnbroker, thanked him for his help and started out of the pawn shop. As she left, she heard Davis address Parker.

"My employer is not happy with your offer to renegotiate your terms of repayment," Davis said, his voice still casual. Mara sensed the chill underneath it as she opened the door. The bell clattered as Parker replied.

"I thought Mr McCabe would understand," Parker said as Mara stepped out of the pawn shop and onto the warm street. The door closed behind her with a sharp thud. She took a deep breath of the fresh spring air, then looked over her shoulder through the pawnshop window. Parker gestured and argued while Davis simply stood there smoking his cigarette.

As she left the scene, she looked at the paper and learned it was Saturday the 16th of May, 1953.

You were right, whispered the captain's voice in her head. *You're a long way from where you started.*

* * *

Mara made a few other stops that day before returning to her dell by the creek. She gathered wood from the deadfall around her and at the creek's edge pulled a dozen football-sized stones from the earth and brought them to her campsite. There, she dug a shallow six-foot trench. With half the stones, she made a ring for her campfire. At the top of the slope overlooking the dell, Mara pried loose a rock big enough to sit on and rolled it

49

down to her campsite. The earthworms squirming underneath did not go to waste either. She washed in the creek again, this time with soap bought from the drugstore, and after that, tried her hand at fishing. The fish battled the current as they headed upstream. It took an hour, but eventually she caught a decent-sized one.

As the sun set, Mara read the paper, but much of it meant nothing to her. It was practically ancient history compared to where and when she came from. She did snicker at the comics, though. It passed the time and kept her mind occupied. When she finished, she made a fire using some of the newspaper as kindling. After getting the fire high and healthy, she gently put the remaining stones in the glowing embers. As the stars came out, she scaled and gutted the fish, then cooked it. She sipped from her canteen, filled at the water fountain next to the clock tower in town. During her trip into town, Mara had found a park bench near the fountain and used the newspaper as cover as she'd manually adjusted the time and date on the captain's watch. Now she at least had an accurate clock. Before leaving the park, she noticed a pair of memorial plaques mounted to the base of the tower. The first read:

IN MEMORY OF THE 1885 EXPLOSION
OF MINE SHAFT NO. 3

At 1:27 P.M. on November 23rd, 1885, an explosion in Shaft No. 3 killed forty-two mine workers. The accident shook buildings in Blue Creek. Timber set aflame by the initial explosion was hurdled from the shaft and rained down upon the town, causing much devastation, but few injuries. Bucket brigades and snow fall saved the town from being fully engulfed by fire.

Below it, the second plaque read:

THE SITE OF THE UNITED FORTUNE MINING
COMPANY STORE

Founded to support the mine in 1850, Blue Creek began life as a company town. On this spot stood the Company Store, where employees of the United Fortune Mining Company spent their scrip (the company's own currency) to buy necessary supplies.

As you read this, you stand a few feet from where the store's front entrance was located.

In the dell, Mara thought about the mining accident as she lifted the cooked fish from the campfire. It smelled delicious. She ate half and saved the rest for later, wrapping it in newspaper. Mara wondered if the smell would attract animals. She held her new knife up as she cleaned it, letting the firelight reflect off the blade. Prying loose the stones in the fire with a couple of sticks, she put them in the trench she'd dug earlier. They steamed and the ground hissed as they hit the cool earth. Mara covered them back over with a thin layer of dirt and built a bed of branches and leaves over top of it.

As she sat back down on the rock next to the fire, using the folded dufflebag as a cushion, the captain's voice returned, whispering in her head.

You can't live out here forever, you know, she said.

"I know, but for the moment I'm okay, all things considered," Mara replied.

That jacket was a gift. An expensive one. You practically gave it away, the captain sounded more disappointed than angry.

"What choice did I have?" Mara asked. "I'm trapped in the past with *nothing.*"

You could try to use the computer to get back, the captain replied, tempting her again.

"No. It's too dangerous," Mara said, even as her gaze turned to the control computer. It sat on her field jacket next to the bed of branches, its dark cracked screen looking back at her.

When Mara at last bedded down, the heat radiating from the rocks had dried the ground below her.

The next day, Mara went back into town, only to find everything closed for Sunday. Families enjoyed the sunshine at the parks, picnicking and playing. After Mara refilled her canteen, she walked the quiet streets. She came to a diner called *The Yellow Canary* and saw the *Help Wanted* sign in the window.

There you go, whispered the captain. *You can get a job.*

"It's a start," Mara said.

The Yellow Canary was closed, with a sign on the door saying they would be back open again on Monday, but Mara peered into the window anyway, shading her eyes.

"Guess I'll come back tomorrow," she said.

Turning from the diner, Mara saw a police car round the corner ahead of her. She turned and walked back the way she came. The police car sped past her and slowed to a stop at the light. Mara couldn't tell if this was the same car she encountered two nights before, or if the occupants were the same officers, but all the same she wanted to turn around and walk the other way. She knew if she did that, if the policemen saw her, it might look suspicious, just the excuse they'd need to stop her. Mara didn't need that host of problems, so she kept on walking.

At last, the light changed and the police car drove on. Mara decided she'd overstayed her welcome in town today and headed back to her camp.

That night, the temperature dropped and even with the rocks reheated, Mara felt the chill in the air. Dreams of home, a city of light, glass and steel, made it difficult to sleep. Mara longed to be there, to walk those streets again.

That place is gone to you if you don't use the control computer to open a Portal, came the voice of the captain, clearer now, comforting despite the truth it spoke. Mara did want to turn on the computer, to find the coordinates, go to that place where a fissure ended. There she might open a Portal. Mara wanted it so badly it hurt.

But I can't! Mara cried in her dream. *I keep telling you, it's too dangerous. Besides, there's something in there.*

Longing changed to fear and Mara ran, much as she had the night she arrived in Blue Creek.

It saw you, said the captain. *Just for a moment. Just before you left the Breach and arrived in a cold, rainy 1953, HE saw you... IT saw you and you saw it. A face with no eyes... just black holes... and a gaping maw of a mouth...*

I'm safe if I don't open a Portal to the Breach, Mara said. In the dell, as the glowing embers of the campfire faded to grey ash, Mara curled into a ball, clutching the field jacket tight around her.

Are *you safe?* the captain asked. *Are you* really?

7

Men carried crates of goods out of the company store at the main intersection of town as Emery Dale rode past. A hand-made sign in the window read *Closed Until Further Notice*. She noted the store's busted windows and half a dozen men armed with clubs and guns standing guard as the crates were loaded onto wagons. Rumours of closure by United Fortune Mining reached Orchard Bend and Dale's employer, Maxwell McCabe, decided to send her to investigate.

The rumours appeared to be true.

Dale slowed in front of the company store and the guards took notice. The men with guns adjusted their grip and gave her hard stares. She tipped her hat, but their expressions didn't change. She looked around, up and down the street. Some folks were going about their business, but not seeming much in a hurry. A handful of prostitutes at the brothel across from the store watched the scene with great interest. Most of the other businesses still remained open, such as the butcher, the bar and the pawn shop.

Dale turned her attention back to the company store. The guards hadn't moved. Dale guided her horse toward them and almost at once they levelled their guns at her. A man came out of the store.

"That's close enough, Miss!" he said, a country gentleman with a bowler hat, a nice suit and a cane.

Dale stopped.

"Very wise," said the gentleman. "We've had some trouble since we announced the closing of the store yesterday. Some of our employees were overwrought, shall we say."

"I'm in the employ of Maxwell McCabe," Dale said. "I'm here in an official capacity, to assess his assets and investments. And to see if the rumblings about the company's eminent departure are true."

"Stand down, men," the gentleman said. The guards lowered their guns, but did not relax. They went on scanning the street should any of the locals get the wrong idea. The gentleman gestured for Dale to approach and she did.

She tied off her horse and joined the gentleman at the top of the steps.

"Ellwood Peachtree," the gentleman introduced himself, tipping his hat with a slight bow.

"Emery Dale," she replied.

"Ms Dale," Peachtree said. "Forgive the greeting by my men. They saw you were armed and have come to expect the worst of people of late."

Dale adjusted the gunbelts on her hips and followed Peachtree into the store, where men worked fast loading crates and pulling merchandise from the shelves behind the front counter.

"I'm used to it," Dale said.

"Under more hospitable circumstances, I would offer you a cup of tea or coffee, but as you can see..." Peachtree gestured to the workers.

"It's quite alright," Dale said. "I don't wish to keep you any longer than necessary."

"How may I be of service, then?" Peachtree asked.

"Is the mine closing?" Dale asked.

"My, you do cut to the chase," Peachtree replied. "You're aware of the accident which occurred last autumn?"

"The explosion? The one that killed all those miners?" Dale asked.

"The very same," Peachtree nodded. "This is all off the record, you understand. The company is re-assessing the long term damage to our operations as we speak."

"Why not keep the store open until a decision is made?" Dale asked.

"That was the plan, but two days ago a report appeared in the *Times* back east quoting an unnamed source who when asked about our prospects for the next year carelessly listed by name only *five* of the company's six current mining operations," Peachtree explained.

"And Blue Creek was the sixth, not on that list," Dale said.

"Exactly!" Peachtree said, sitting down on a crate. "With mining slowed after the accident, that omission was all the miners needed. We had a mob here yesterday, ready to draw and quarter us. We're now employing those armed men outside to safeguard the store and its contents as we transport the goods to a safer location."

"Mr McCabe has investments in Blue Creek," Dale said. "Not the least of which is produce and grain from the farms he owns. That feeds your workers and they buy it here. The effects of closing up shop will spread across the county like ripples in a pond."

"The company is well aware of its dealings with Mr McCabe," Peachtree said. He approached Dale and leaned close, so close his bad breath made her choke. In a conspiratorial tone he whispered, "Truth be told, the Blue Creek mine operation is proving no longer to be profitable from what I hear. Mr McCabe is a business man. He'll see the facts for what they are. It's most unfortunate that his pocketbook will be lighter after we're gone, but I'm confident his finances will right themselves in the end."

Dale started to reply, but a racket of angry voices erupted outside. As Dale turned, one of the store's last remaining glass windows shattered when a rock smashed through it. She ran to the door and saw two of the guards clubbing a man on the street. Peachtree went past her to the steps.

"What is the meaning of this?!" he demanded.

The guards stopped their assault and hauled the beaten man to his feet. One of the other guards rushed to Peachtree's side, saying, "This fella came calling for you, Mr Peachtree. We told him you were busy and he started yelling and threw a rock at the window. Then he attacked our men."

"Thank you, Johansen," Peachtree said.

Dale saw many eyes on the street watching the scene. People pointed, speaking in low, unsettled tones.

The beaten man's face swelled from being punched in the face. He clutched his gut, staring at Peachtree with undisguised defiance.

"You're pulling out, ain'cha?" the man asked. "Loading up them wagons and hightailin' it back east, ain'cha?"

A few of the bystanders drew close to the store. The guards with firearms saw this, exchanged looks with each other and backed up a step.

Peachtree descended the stairs to where the guards held the beaten man and stood before him.

"I know you," Peachtree said, looking him straight in the eye. "Your name is Winter."

"It is," Winter said. "I've worked the mine for four years. Lost good friends in the explosion."

"Indeed," said Peachtree, lowering his gaze and shaking his head. "We all lost people. The company lost good men. Hard, loyal workers all."

Winter sneered.

"Slaves, you mean!" he said through a fat, bloody lip. "You don't pay us in cash. Our scrip is only good at your store. You leave us now and it all becomes useless paper."

The gathering crowd shouted its agreement. Dale scanned the faces of everyone on the street, from Winter to the clusters of men she guessed were miners.

"Your concern is understandable, but premature," Peachtree said. "The company is not going to abandon you."

"Why are you closing the store, then?" came a voice from the crowd. Dale picked the man out. He belonged to a group close to where Peachtree and Winter stood.

"The store's operations are temporarily suspended," Peachtree said to everyone, raising his hands, still holding his cane.

The cries of disagreement all blended together in a cacophony of anger. Peachtree turned to look behind him, catching Dale's eye, but movement behind him caused her to draw her gun almost without thinking.

Winter had pulled a knife.

It wasn't a very big blade, almost a paring knife, really, but he had it out and in Peachtree's back before Dale's gun had left her holster. The guards flanking Winter were still registering what happened to Peachtree as Dale drew and fired with her right hand, hitting Winter in the right shoulder. Blood sprayed the guard next to him. Peachtree dropped to his knees, reaching behind his back for the knife still stuck there. Winter staggered back and looked at Dale, then charged forward at Peachtree.

He didn't make it another step as Dale fired again, hitting Winter square in the chest. He fell in the mud, dead. Too late, the armed guards levelled their guns to a ready position, visibly uncertain what to do next.

The crowd fell silent, but the thunder of the gunshots still roared in Dale's ears. She kept her weapon aimed at the body of Winter as she walked forward.

"Take Peachtree inside!" Dale ordered the guards. "Johansen, get the doctor!"

The guards carried Peachtree up the stairs as Johansen scrambled through the crowd.

The bystanders' shock wore off and the crowd seemed to grow as people came to investigate the gunshots.

Dale addressed the gathered townsfolk.

"All of you, back the hell up. Now!" she commanded them. "No one else needs to die today."

The people did as they were told, inching away. The remaining guards, with weapons clutched in nervous hands, backed up towards the company store. On the widening patch of ground between them, the body of Winter convulsed out of reflex. The crowd gasped and moaned in revulsion. They stared at him, at Dale, at the guards, murmuring and speaking low.

A strong voice, full of authority, demanded to be let through. It belonged to a broad-shouldered man with a few extra pounds that strained the buttons on his shirt.

"Sheriff Bell," called out one of the men behind Dale.

"What sweet smelling horseshit is this?" Bell demanded, charging forward, stepping over Winter's body without looking at it. Dale lowered her weapon, but didn't holster it.

The man behind Dale spoke up.

"Winter attacked Mr Peachtree with a knife, Sheriff!" the guard said. "She shot him dead."

Bell was tall, coming eye to eye with Dale. He fixed her a stern look.

"That so?" he asked.

"It is," Dale replied.

Bell looked down at Winter, gave the body a nudge with his boot and grunted. He then turned to the assembled townsfolk.

"Well, then," Bell proclaimed. "What's done is done. Winter never did have a good grip on his temper, did he?"

There was silence from everyone, until a few mutters of reluctant agreement came from the crowd. Bell pointed to a cluster of men.

"Abernathy. Edwards. You and your lot there come here and take Winter to the undertaker," Bell ordered. He turned to the men guarding the store. "Where's Peachtree?"

"Inside," Dale said. "I sent for the doctor."

Even as she said it, Johansen pushed through the crowd, accompanied by a man in a dark suit carrying a black bag.

"And here he comes," Bell said. "Doc Bloom, your patient is inside."

The doctor hurried past them, giving Winter a glance, and went into the store. The men from the crowd, Abernathy, Edwards and their group, lifted Winter's body from the mud. They carried the dead man away as everyone watched.

"The show is finished, folks," Bell said. "Go on home, or back to your business. Nothing more to see here."

The townsfolk started to drift away. Some onlookers remained, talking amongst themselves, but the imposing wall of bodies surrounding the store broke apart as people left.

Dale holstered her gun and went to Bell.

"Thank you for defusing that situation, Sheriff," Dale said.

"It's my job, little lady," Bell said. "The company keeps me on the payroll because I can keep the rabble in check. Well, most days, I can. Curse Winter and his foolishness. Was only a matter of time before he got himself shot."

"He was scared for his livelihood," Dale said, looking at the bloody spot where Winter fell. "Scared men do foolish, dangerous things."

"These men need to remember their place," Bell said. "This is a company town. They're employees. They can't be getting their hides up attacking company representatives."

Dale gave Bell a cold look, but Bell didn't see it as he turned to go inside the store. Dale watched him until he turned back to her.

"Are you coming?" he asked.

"I think my business in Blue Creek is concluded," Dale said. "You have everything under control here, Sheriff. You don't need my help."

"No, I don't, Miss Dale," Bell said, the good humour gone from his voice. "Go on back to Orchard Bend then. You don't want to keep *your* employer waiting."

He gave her a shooing gesture, turned and went into the store.

* * *

Riding out of Blue Creek under the clear afternoon sky, Emery Dale closed her eyes for a moment and squeezed her right hand to stop it from trembling. The soreness from the bullet wound in her arm flared up to outright pain and she focused on that. The trembling subsided and she opened her eyes.

"I was a major once," she whispered.

She flexed her hand and reached into the breast pocket of her duster. She took out a watch, not one made in this century or any before, but the one she'd been wearing when she awoke in 1879. On the small, black screen was a green circle and she tapped it. Application icons appeared and she selected the one marked Messages. The display read:

1 New Message

Device Clearance Recognized
Maj. E. A. Dale
Enter GvSci Passcode

— — — —

After seven years, Dale's fractured and fragmented memory
had not revealed to her the four digit passcode to open the
message. It could be just about anything.

Dale ran her thumb over the flat, smooth screen and then put
the watch away.

"Someday," she said. "Someday I'll remember."

8

May 21, 1953
Blue Creek

Mara knew she made a mistake in selling her leather jacket. Yes, it afforded her some supplies and her immediate survival had been at stake, but the time had come to get that gift back.

Under the overcast morning sky, Mara wondered whether the pawnbroker had sold it already.

"No," she muttered, ignoring the growl of hunger in her stomach. She packed up her belongings in the duffle bag and stowed them in the brush near the dell. "It'll be there, maybe in the window, waiting for me."

Mara followed the creek into town and climbed up the hill below the bridge. At the top, she waited for the sidewalk to clear and hopped over the rail. She crossed the bridge and headed downtown.

After two days of work at *The Yellow Canary*, Mara had some money and hoped it would be enough to buy it back, or at least enough to put the jacket on hold until she could pay the rest off.

"Parker said it would be hard to sell," Mara told herself, reaching into her pocket and feeling the bills and coins. "It'll be there."

It would probably cost her most of what she'd made so far, about $8 including the tips, but the need to get it back was not to be denied.

Mara rounded the corner, saw the pawnshop spheres hanging just ahead and started to jog down the street.

"Okay, here we are," Mara said to herself as she reached her destination. She slowed to a walk, then a few steps later, stopped altogether.

The whitewash of the pawnshop window and the closed sign told her just about everything. The rest she could only imagine. Davis, the man in the fedora with the cigarette, had said the pawnshop owner owed somebody money. Somebody named McCabe.

Mara peered into the window, trying to see through the white brushstrokes on the glass. Inside, the shop looked empty, the shelves and displays bare. Mara guessed whoever this McCabe was, he'd taken everything, including her leather jacket.

"That's just great," Mara said, letting her arms drop to her side. "Just perfect."

She hung her head and closed her eyes, fighting off the sting of disappointment. She pressed the bridge of her nose and said, "Goddammit."

"Language, young lady," said a hard old voice next her.

Mara looked up and saw a thin, elderly woman hunched over a cane. Her hard features and the scowl on her face seemed permanent.

"Really?" Mara replied, haught with indignation.

The old woman's cane came up in a flash and Mara blocked it out of pure, practiced reflex. She noted the strike to her arm would've hurt if it had connected.

The old woman let out a *harrumph* of contempt and her mouth twitched.

"You listen here! If your elders tell you to mind your language, you would do well to heed them," the old woman said. She pointed her cane at Mara, who took a step back. "Young people today need to learn respect. I learned in at home and I learned it in school. 'Learn from those who went before you,' that's what my teacher taught us and not a day goes by that I don't know it's the God's honest truth. Let that be a lesson to you, young missy."

The crone turned without another word and left Mara standing dumbfounded on the street. She looked at the whitewashed pawnshop window again and back at the old lady now crossing the street. The light changed around her, but the cars didn't advance until she reached the other side. Nobody honked and nobody called out for her to hurry up.

When the old woman was out of sight, Mara stuffed her hands in her pockets, felt the money there and thought she'd better head to work.

She tried not to think about her lost leather jacket.

9

August 10, 1886
Orchard Bend

The only way Sheriff Wilson could tell he was looking at Laura O'Malley's dead body in the tall grass was because somehow the locket had stayed on her neck. Wilson had seen Laura wearing the locket at church and sometimes around town. It had been a gift from her parents when she turned sixteen back in March. When Laura hadn't come home two days ago, her parents notified the sheriff. Her mother said she'd been wearing the locket that day. The search parties knew about it, in case they came across it while scouring the countryside. Laura and her friends had been swimming at the watering hole all day before parting ways to go home. No one had seen Laura O'Malley since.

That is until Freddy Wood came across the girl while hunting. His dog, a floppy-eared hound named Cheat no doubt smelled the blood. A horrified Freddy raced to town on foot to tell Wilson, moving faster than anyone expected of a man in his sixties. Freddy had the wherewithal to go straight to the jailhouse and hadn't uttered a word to anyone. Winded and panting for breath, Freddy told Wilson what he found and Wilson gathered up Doc Shaw. Along with his young deputy Allen Green, the four men and Cheat the hound went to the field north of town where Laura O'Malley's body lay.

Freddy Wood had an alibi, having been out to Sutter Grove with his wife, visiting her people for a few days. The Woods had returned home the day after Laura disappeared. That eliminated him as a suspect, which wasn't what Wilson considered progress in the case.

The sheriff stared at the locket in morbid fascination as Doc Shaw knelt next to Laura's body. How had the locket stayed around her neck, Wilson wondered, when her head had been chopped off?

Freddy stood with Deputy Green a few yards away, with Cheat at his heel.

"Is it her?" Wood asked. "Is it that O'Malley girl?"

Wilson gladly looked away from the body.

"I'm guessing it is," Wilson said.

Wood crossed himself, said a short prayer, then turned and started away. Wilson called after him.

"Freddy," Wilson said. "Go home. Don't tell anyone what you found here."

"I won't," Freddy said, looking back.

"If you tell your wife, make sure she keeps it to herself for now," Wilson said. "I don't want the O'Malleys hearing about this before I get to telling them."

Wood nodded and Wilson watched the man's back as he walked away from the scene through the waist-high grass. Wilson looked up to the heavens, fighting a wave of light-headedness. The clouds drifted across the blue summer sky, serene, indifferent to the sheriff and the girl's headless body. Wilson forced his attention back to the grassy field as Deputy Green approached. The young man had been told what to expect, but the sight was still gruesome. Nothing could really prepare a man to see such a thing, Wilson knew, but he was impressed Green kept his wits. The deputy did lose a lot of colour from his face, though.

"You want me to escort Mr Wood home, Sheriff?" Green asked. "Make sure he keeps this to himself?"

"No. I think we can trust Freddy Wood to keep it between himself and his wife," Wilson said. "Besides, I need you to stay with the doctor and guard the body until we can get it out of here."

Wilson started walking away and Green asked, "Where are you going?"

"To tell the O'Malleys," Wilson said.

Green looked at him a moment, then down at the body, and then out over the grassy plain, letting out a long sigh. Wilson figured the deputy now realized that staying out here with the body was the better of the two responsibilities.

He left Green and Doc Shaw, mounted his horse and rode toward the O'Malley homestead not far away.

* * *

At the bar, a tight swath of light from the oil lamp encircled the sheriff and the young barmaid.

"Oh, Clem, I can't imagine how hard that was," Irene Sullivan said. She clutched a rag to her breast and looked at him with heartfelt empathy. As hard as it was for Wilson to tell her, he had to tell *someone*. Here now, at Sully's tavern, two shots of whiskey in him, Clem Wilson had found he could open up to her.

"A duty I never care to repeat as long as I live, Irene," the sheriff said. "The tears. The questions. I had to tell them how we found her and I swear to the Lord above I thought Mrs O'Malley was going to faint from the shock of it."

Tears welled up in Irene's eyes.

"I can't imagine," she said, her voice quiet and soft. "What happens now?"

"Doc Shaw is with her, examining the..." he gestured to his neck and Irene nodded, wide-eyed. "...the *wound* to try to determine what the killer used to... to do what he did."

Wilson turned the empty glass around in his hand, looking at it, trying not to picture Laura O'Malley's dead body. The whiskey did its job quieting his nerves, but he wasn't sure anything would allow him to come to grips with what befell the girl.

Irene saw him fidgeting with the glass, took it from him and placed his hand in hers. Wilson looked at her and the intensity of her expression surprised him.

"You're going to catch whoever did this, Clem," Irene said, squeezing his hands in a way he found very agreeable. "I believe in you. The town believes in you."

67

"Thank you, Irene. I..." Wilson found it hard to put into words. "I'm glad I could tell you these things. I'm glad you were here to listen."

"Where else would I be, Sheriff?" Irene said in a matter of fact way. In the sudden heat of embarrassment, Clem Wilson regretted what he'd just said.

"No, what I meant to say was..." he stammered. "I need to... Gosh, it's not like that—"

Still gripping his hand in hers, Irene pulled Wilson to her, right off his stool so he had to lean over the bar. She kissed him, holding him there for several long, pleasant seconds. For the first time that day since Freddy Wood told him what he'd found, the sheriff was not thinking about Laura O'Malley's murder. Instead he smelled Irene's perfume, noting how it mixed with the smell of her soap and sweat from a hot summer day in the saloon. His other hand went to hers and caressed them. Their fingers interlocked and Wilson did not want this moment to end.

Alas, it did as Irene eased away. Still holding hands, the two smiled at each other before Irene spoke.

"It's late, Sheriff," she said, her fingers moving slow in between his, then over the back of his hand.

"Yes, it is," Wilson said, not wanting to let go. She slipped her hands away and picked up her cleaning rag. Wilson backed away from the bar, feeling the pleasant combination of alcohol, adrenalin and desire. The wide-eyed girl behind the bar gave him a look he'd never before received and he guessed this was something like love. A part of Clem Wilson realized he'd never been in love, not like this, and he liked it.

Wilson made his way to the door and let himself out with a wave, unable to think even to say goodnight. Irene waved back and he stepped out into the cool summer air. Wilson swayed along the boardwalk.

He saw the light of Doc Shaw's office. Knowing what the man was doing in there, examining Laura O'Malley's body for clues, sobered Wilson up a little. It wasn't quite enough to ruin the glow he felt and Wilson continued on to his rooms beyond the jailhouse.

* * *

August 11, 1886
Orchard Bend

Heartbroken.

What happened to Laura O'Malley rips at my very soul. I've known her since she was a little girl, taught her for many years. The mind reels at the news of her death. I weep for her, for her poor family and for the town. Something evil did this and that devil must be found and punished.

I would do well to rein in this rage. I know that's what I feel presently, Lord forgive me.

Sheriff Wilson came to my cottage as I made breakfast and broke the devastating news. He had told Laura's family yestereve and expects word will spread today. Deputy Green and Doctor Shaw were careful to bring Laura's remains into town without arousing notice. The doctor is seeing to her in an effort to find evidence of what happened and who might have done this. And that was the reason for the sheriff's visit.

"Was Laura sweet on any boy at school?" Wilson asked. "Were any of the boys showing her affection?"

"Not to my knowledge," I told him.

"Any advances spurned?" he asked.

I gave the question due consideration. Laura was a kind girl and friendly to everyone, quick to trust, honest and open, but I had to tell Sheriff Wilson that I had no knowledge of any unrequited affection. There are times I do learn of a boy's interest in a particular girl, and of a girl smitten with a certain boy, but of Laura O'Malley I could offer nothing.

Sheriff Wilson, I could see, was hoping I had a name to give him, someone he could pursue. Without that, he was left with little, I expect.

Before leaving, he asked me to think on it more, that if any notion came to me about Laura's personal life to inform him without delay. I promised to do just that. He nodded, took his leave and I was alone with the terrible news. I wanted right

69

there to give in to sorrow, but held off. The sheriff had instructed that the school be closed to-day, for fear that the predator might still be lurking in the countryside. He had told me a handpicked number of men were stationed along the roads to instruct the children to go back to their homes. I was to wait the morning at the church schoolhouse should any child arrive in spite of those efforts. The children were to stay until an escort took them home.

I had no appetite, but ate my breakfast lest it go to waste. I went to the schoolhouse and awaited my pupils. Some of the boys and girls did arrive and I told them that school was suspended. They were to wait there with me for the sheriff. At my desk, my heart bled as I looked at Laura O'Malley's vacant seat. The children asked what was wrong, some asking if it had to do with Laura. I said it did, but gave no further details. They would find out about their schoolmate soon enough.

After Deputy Green and his posse came to escort the children to their homesteads, I walked back to my cottage, my head abuzz with troubled thoughts and grief. Had I missed some small detail? Did Laura know her attacker?

Oh and what befell her.

Awful. Horrible. Evil. No word is sufficient to describe such a sickening act of violence. Worse still, they recovered Laura's body but not the... rest of her.

While it is regular that I miss Emery during her absences, I do long for her companionship now. I do hope Laura's autopsy can provide information to both Doctor Shaw and Sheriff Wilson on the identity of the one who did this, so that her soul may be at peace.

And to think, this morning my thoughts were occupied with—

* * *

A knock came from the cottage door and startled Rose from her journal.

She stood up from the table where she had been writing all afternoon, pausing only to use a handkerchief. Partway through putting her thoughts down on paper, her emotions had gotten the better of her and she'd allowed herself to shed tears of grief over Laura O'Malley's murder.

Rose smoothed out her dress, adjusted her blouse and took off her reading glasses, setting them by her journal as she closed it.

"I'll be right there," she said. Taking a deep breath, she walked to the door then stopped. A terrible thought slipped into her head.

What if it's the killer?

She shook the thought away as nonsense, but a chill seemed to fill the little cottage. Rose went to the window and peaked out. She let out a relieved sigh at the sight of Gertrude McCabe. Rose opened the door for her friend at once.

"Rose!" said Gertrude. "I came as soon as I was able!"

"Gertrude, how sweet of you to stop by! Please join me for some tea," Rose said. Beyond the picket fence, she saw Gertrude's oldest son Henry in their wagon, holding the reins. He tipped his hat and Rose gave him a wave. "Does Henry wish to come in, also?"

"I asked Henry to return in an hour's time, if that's alright?" Gertrude said.

"Quite alright," Rose replied.

Gertrude gave Henry a wave and said, "One hour, Henry."

"I'll be here, mother," Henry replied. He gave a crack of the reins, barked a command to the team and drove away. The ladies watched him go then stepped inside.

"I hope I didn't catch you at an inopportune time," Gertrude said, removing her coat and hat.

"I was writing in my journal," Rose said as she took Gertrude's apparel and hung it by the door. "It helped me put some order to the... *madness* of the day."

Gertrude took Rose's hand and squeezed it. Her sympathetic smile made Rose want to cry again. She could feel her face flush and her eyes getting wet.

"I'll make some tea," Rose said, starting toward the kitchen. She dabbed her eyes in private and prepared the hot water. She heard Gertrude's soft footsteps moving about in the next room.

"My, what a lovely photograph of Emery," Gertrude said.

"It has a remarkable story," Rose called back from the kitchen. "Sadly it's linked to another tragic day for this town. That sad day of the shooting, Sheriff Wilson found the plate still in the camera in Mr Jackson's studio. You see, Emery was tracking one of the outlaws. She followed him into the studio, which was dark, and it seems the man tried to distract her or blind her with the camera's flash powder. The plate was exposed, capturing her image. The sheriff had it developed, going all the way to Sutter Grove and the studio there. He had hoped for a photograph of the outlaw, thinking the late Mr Jackson might have taken his likeness before his murder. I think the sheriff was a little disappointed. He gave Emery the photograph and she gifted it to me for my birthday before she departed on business for your husband."

"How thoughtful of her," Gertrude said.

Rose put the kettle on the stove and joined Gertrude, who held the photograph in her hand. She placed it back on the shelf as Rose sat on the sofa. Gertrude looked around the room, walked to the nearest window and spread the curtains wide. She unlatched the lock and slid the window open. Rose closed her eyes as the sunlight washed over her face and the fresh air filled the room. She smiled, but just as quickly it was gone.

"It isn't right," Rose said, opening her eyes. "That God should give us beautiful weather on such a day as this. It seems cruel somehow."

Gertrude sat next to Rose on the sofa.

"When my home was attacked," Gertrude said, "when my sons and I were threatened, I asked God *'Why?* Why us? Why did the good man Mr Miller have to die trying to save us?' I had so many questions and I was filled with anger and guilt."

"Guilt?" Rose asked.

"Guilt that I survived and he didn't," Gertrude said. "What I learned in the days and weeks ··and even *months* afterwards·· was that the questions don't always have answers. Sheriff Wilson will find the man who did this, but whatever his motive was committing such an act, that's only a small part of it. The unanswered *'Whys?'* will never entirely add up when placed against the tragedy as a whole.

"Right now, the sun is shining," Gertrude squeezed Rose's arm. "You are allowed to enjoy it, even amidst this great sorrow."

Rose hugged her friend and wept. Gertrude held her.

When the kettle whistled, Rose composed herself and left the room to retrieve it.

* * *

Leaving his mother at the schoolteacher's cottage, Henry McCabe didn't hurry as he made his way to Anderson Street (he still thought of it as Main Street, though, because some habits were hard to break). In the hot sun he thought maybe they were due for rain soon. Henry's rolled up sleeves exposed the tan borne from spending his days outside.

"You're a young man now, son," his father Maxwell had told him. "Soon you have to stand up and take on some responsibility in the family businesses. There are colleges back east. You'll get a degree, come back and help me run things. Someday, I'll retire and you'll take over."

That was the plan.

And Henry didn't much care one way or the other. It only really mattered so far as it freed him to pursue his own interests, chief among them (eclipsing all others, one could say) was wielding the Power of Life and Death.

Henry knew no one in town suspected the truth. He himself was only vaguely aware that his sanity had cracked, the way a dog that has lost its tail might dimly understand that part of itself is gone, though it doesn't really seem to matter. Much like that, some part of Henry knew he was insane, that something was gone, but since he seemed to function well without it, the matter was neither here nor there.

Henry waved at passersby as he rode the wagon through town. He nodded to the new sheriff as he passed the jailhouse, where Wilson stood talking to Doctor Shaw. Turning the wagon onto the road along the river, Henry saw an old man fishing on the boat landing not far from the McCabe Mill. The old man's dog watched Henry pass and barked. The man turned to his pet.

"Cheat! Settle down, boy. You're scaring the fish," the old man said.

Cheat the dog never took his eyes off Henry as he passed. He fidgeted and his tail was still. Over the rumble of the wagon, Henry thought the dog might be growling.

Leaving the landing and the mill behind him, Henry rode on under the late afternoon sky. At the top of a hill he parked the wagon where the train tracks met the road and took in the view. He could make out the streets of the town as they criss-crossed each other. People went about their lives looking so insignificant and small. The Town Hall neared completion, something his father was very proud of. Fields and farms surrounded Orchard Bend, dotted with trees, homesteads, ponds and small lakes. Henry turned and looked west along the railroad tracks. He picked out the edge of trees hiding the swimming hole the children in town liked to use. A hot, dry summer plagued them this year, but the swimming hole remained a refuge for many.

Henry smiled.

Henry remembered.

Killing Laura O'Malley with his bare hands had been unlike anything of his previous experiences dispensing death. For years, he'd toiled with merely executing small animals, then this last Hallowe'en he'd burned down the Reed's storehouse with Mr Reed inside. That's when he felt something more, something greater, a rush in his very blood. He knew as he walked home that night that he now possessed the Power of Life and Death. He guessed the Angel of Death himself felt much the same way. If Henry ever met him, he planned to ask.

The idea made him giggle.

Mr Reed the Store Owner had had it coming for getting too personal with Henry's mother. Mr Reed had burned for that, of course. Gertrude shed tears for her lover, but only when her husband Maxwell was not home. Henry would hear her alone in the parlour or in her bedroom. This continued until almost

Christmas. The tears turned to quiet moments staring out the window. On her lap sat the ledger she used as a sketchbook, a pencil in her hand, but no drawings glided froth from the lead. Gertrude had simply stared, watching the snow. She would shake herself out of her reverie when her boys came to her. Owen would scamper into her arms and Henry would hang back. Boys his age getting on towards manhood didn't hug their mothers, though he'd let her steal some from time to time. She was one of the good ones, after all, one of the ones worthy of life. Many in Orchard Bend weren't, but they were simply too pathetic to be bothered with.

By spring, Gertrude got over Reed's death and that made Henry glad. She was in better spirits, even when her friend the Dale woman got hurt in that gunfight. At the wake for Sheriff Anderson and the Photographer Man (really, so many names in town Henry didn't give two shakes about), Henry had stepped outside Sully's tavern and found a group of two boys and two girls around his age talking amongst themselves. Henry would've called them his classmates if he attended their school, but his mother taught both he and Owen at home, so while he recognized them from around town, he'd had little interaction with them.

When Henry saw the group outside the tavern, he went in the other direction.

"Hey there!" one of the girls then called out. "You're Henry McCabe, aren't you?"

Henry stopped, but didn't turn around.

"It's him," said one of the boys. "Let him be. He's probably got important stuff to do."

Henry took a deep breath and turned around.

He smiled at them.

"Nah," Henry said. "Nothing that important."

The group watched him.

Henry stepped forward, hand extended to the nearest boy. Henry recognized him as being a few years older than the rest them.

"You're Sam O'Toole, aren't you?" Henry asked.

"I am," Sam replied, slow to take Henry's hand. When he did, Henry gave it a firm shake.

"I hear you saved Miss Dale," Henry said.

Sam looked away, letting his hand fall away from Henry's.

"That's right," Sam said.

"Sammy's a hero!" said the other boy. Henry thought his name was Billy Howard.

"No," Sam said, looking at his feet. "I ain't a hero. I did what I had to do."

"You saved Miss Dale," Henry said. "But I bet it's hard to think about it. Sorry I brought it up."

"It's alright," Sam shrugged, trying to smile.

The girl wearing the dark red dress gave Sam a hug while looking at Henry.

"He doesn't like to talk about what happened," she said.

"Believe me, I understand," Henry said.

"We were going to go for a walk," said the other girl, who wore a smart but drab beige dress, "Over to the cemetery. You know, before everyone else gets there. Want to join us?"

"Sure," Henry said.

The group walked down Main Street, turned onto Wood Street, then onto Church. Henry stayed at the rear of the group and for the most part listened to the others chattering on. They talked about people and events he didn't know, like funny things that had happened years ago in Miss Adelaide's class and one Hallowe'en when the boys got caught soaping store windows.

"Sheriff Anderson was none too pleased that night," Billy Howard laughed. "Nor was my pa. I was cleaning out the barn for weeks after that!"

"I reckon I'll miss the sheriff," said the girl who invited Henry along, the one in the beige dress. She was pretty in her plain sort of way. As they arrived at the cemetery, Henry saw she'd fallen in step beside him.

"I suppose you're right," Billy said. "He was tough, but he kept us safe."

"I overheard my father say Deputy Wilson is getting promoted," Henry said. "The Council of Aldermen met last night."

"That makes sense," Billy nodded.

"He'll need to hire a new deputy," said the girl next to Henry. He couldn't help but admire the locket around her neck.

"Sammy, you up for the job?" Billy laughed.

"Billy!" said the other girl, whose name Henry picked up was Rebecca. She walked next to Sam, who gave them an awkward smile.

"I'm kidding with you, Sammy, you know that!" Billy said, looking innocent.

They stopped at the fence surrounding the cemetery next to the church that doubled as their schoolhouse. They said nothing for a long time as they beheld the two open graves. Soon, the funeral procession would start from Sully's tavern, where the dead lay in their coffins at the wake, and it would make its way to those empty plots. The weight of it, of death and its permanence, unnerved Henry. He didn't breath as memories overtook him, of nearly being murdered by a madman years before. The Dale woman had been there and so had the Prisoner. With her sword, Dale had beheaded him--

The girl with the locket took Henry's hand and he gasped.

"You looked as though you were about to faint," she said. Henry felt dizzy and leaned against the fence.

"I'm fine, really," Henry said. "It's just so..."

"Difficult to put into words," she said.

Henry looked to the others, to Sam, Billy and Rebecca and they were nodding.

"Exactly," Henry said. He felt lightheaded, but more than that, his body felt free of a weight inside him. It was as if he could float. He held the girl's hand tight and she smiled at him and he smiled back.

"Here they come," said Rebecca behind him.

They all looked down the road and saw the funeral procession approaching, the newly appointed Sheriff Wilson among those leading the way. The girl let go of Henry's hand and he looked at her.

"I should be with my family," she said. "It was nice meeting you, Henry."

"I'm sorry," said Henry. "All this time and I didn't get your name."

"Laura O'Malley," said the girl.

Now sitting on the hill overlooking the town, Henry knew that had been when he began to lose himself, when he nearly lost control. Laura O'Malley became important to him after they met at the funeral. She occupied Henry's thoughts. He saw her at church every Sunday and she smiled at him. He'd smile back, but with everyone around it felt like the entire town was watching him. It unnerved Henry, made him doubt himself, so he said nothing to the girl on Sundays and tried to distance her from his musings.

In June, Orchard Bend held a town picnic, an annual event, where families gathered outside the church and broke bread together. There was a mass and later there was music, sometimes well-rehearsed, more often put together slapdash by anyone who brought an instrument and could play it. The adults talked, the children played and a good time was often had by all.

In past years, Henry hated the picnic. He didn't know the other children and he kept to himself. This year, no sooner had he arrived than Billy and Rebecca found him and invited him to join their group of friends in the shade of some Atlas Cedars. Henry hoped to see Laura there, but she was not with them and Henry couldn't find the courage to ask after her. He was pleased to be greeted by Sam O'Toole, who introduced him to their other friends (whose names now escaped Henry months after the fact). They were nice to Henry and Henry was amiable. When Billy and Rebecca went off for a walk and the conversation shifted way from things Henry could relate to, he got up and went for a walk himself.

He didn't get far. It was humid for a June afternoon and when he found a shaded patch of his own, he lay under the cedar and dozed.

"Wake up, sleepyhead," a pleasant voice said and Henry opened his eyes to behold Laura O'Malley. She knelt next to him as he sat up. "You missed mass, you wicked boy."

Henry looked around.

"What time is it?" he asked.

"About half past two," she answered. "I looked for you there, like I do every Sunday, and you weren't to be seen. As soon as Reverend Thomas blessed us and bid us a fair day, I looked around for you. I saw your parents, so I went searching and here I find you practically dead to the world."

"I was hoping to see you, too," Henry said.

"If it's not too forward, Mr Henry, I must say I think about you," Laura said. "Often. Sometimes you're all I think about. I know we only had that one afternoon before the funeral, but..."

"I think about you, too," Henry said. "And 'Mr Henry'? I like that. It makes me sound like a character in a book."

"You think about me, as well?" Laura's eyes were wide, her cheeks flushed.

"I'm sorry I can't bring myself to speak to you at church," Henry said. "I don't know why, but it's difficult when others are around."

"I was afraid you thought me too brazen. Or maybe too homely," Laura looked down, her voice soft.

"I think nothing of the sort!" Henry said. The more he spoke to her, the more the giddy sensation filled him. He wanted nothing more then but to be with her forever, to set still this time and place. "You're pretty and kind and I really like you."

Laura looked back up at him, grinning.

Henry went on, "I can ask my parents to invite your family to tea. My mother loves to entertain. They can all get to know each other."

Laura's grin faltered.

"That... that might not be the best idea," Laura said. "Not yet, I mean."

"Why not?" Henry asked.

"My father and mother don't believe I'm ready to court yet," Laura said. "They don't know how I feel about you. Honestly, they don't know about you at all. They think I'm picking flowers right now and I really should be getting back soon."

"Oh," Henry said.

"Give me time to ease them into it," Laura said. "They will soften and come around."

"Alright," Henry said. "If you think that's best."

"I do," Laura said. "I know it complicates things, but give it time. And until then, I think it best we not be seen together like this."

"I saw some flowers beyond the cedars over there," Henry said, pointing to the edge of the trees. "That way you'll have some to show your parents when you get back."

"Don't pout, Henry McCabe," Laura said.

"I'm not pouting," he said. "But you should go. I don't want you getting in trouble for being gone too long."

Laura gave Henry a kiss on the cheek and hurried off to the flowers. He watched her go, rubbing his cheek. When she was out of sight, he waited a few more minutes to be sure she was gone.

Henry was shaking by then. He bent down, picked up a broken branch and held it so tight his knuckles were white. There was no thought, just spiralling emotions, chief among them rage and disgust. He couldn't make sense of what had just happened. He liked Laura O'Malley. She seemed to like him, yet she'd turned him down, told him to wait, told him they shouldn't be seen together. So what if her parents thought her too young? They should be ecstatic that Henry McCabe, son of the richest family in Orchard Bend, wanted to court their daughter.

A bird flew low out of the tree and Henry spotted it from the corner of his eye. In a split second, he pivoted and swung the branch at it, swatting the bird from the air in a mass of feathers. It hit the ground and a distant part of his mind noted the bird was a mourning dove. He stood over the injured bird as it fluttered useless on the ground. Disgust turned into exhilaration. He'd killed animals before, but never a bird, never taking it right out of the air like that.

Henry bashed the bird to death on the ground, dropped the branch and walked back to the picnic. The lightness of the past few weeks was replaced with the renewed sense of self. He'd forgotten for a time exactly who he was.

Henry McCabe was the Master of Life and Death. Of course he was.

* * *

The hour passed as Henry sat on the hill with his memories. When he returned to pick up his mother, she wasn't waiting for him in front of the cottage. He knocked on the door and Miss Adelaide answered. She invited him in, but he politely refused and returned to the wagon to wait.

Gertrude and the schoolteacher said their goodbyes and Henry drove them east to the outskirts of town, up the hill to their large, gated estate overlooking Orchard Bend. After dropping his mother off at the steps of the front porch, Henry brought the wagon around to the stable, unhitched the team and gave them some water in their pen. He walked around to the side of the barn and shielded his eyes against the descending sun. With daylight becoming shorter, autumn would soon be upon them. The trees of the McCabe Orchard cast long shadows and in the next week or so, they'd begin harvesting the apples. Henry made his way down the hill, past the orchard to the tree line near the edge of the McCabe property and through the woods there, stopping for a moment at the train tracks. He looked back and forth along the rails and began walking west. The sun continued to descend, but he didn't have far to go. If he kept walking, just about to the other side of town, he'd be near the swimming hole where Laura O'Malley was last seen alive by her friends. Instead, Henry stopped at the low trestle bridge spanning the east river, knelt and looked down at the rushing water. After a time, he stepped off the tracks, back into the underbrush and came to a large rock. Looking around, he spied no signs anyone had been here. With both hands, he rolled the rock over and exposed the small, shallow grave. He scooped out handfuls of earth until his

81

fingers hit something harder. A bit of white poked out of the dirt. He cleared more away, unearthing his prize. After a few more moments he was staring at her pale face.

Without thinking, Henry leaned down and kissed the lips of the severed head of Laura O'Malley.

10

August 15, 1886
Orchard Bend

The daily cacophony of birds woke Emery Dale in the hour before sunlight broke the morning. Lying on her bed in the one-room cabin in the ravine west of town, she sat up and looked at the pocket watch on the table next to her bed. Squinting in the dark through sleep-blurred eyes she saw it was five-thirty, too early to get up on a normal day, but Dale's sleep had been restless and tense. She threw back the bed sheet and sat up, her feet sinking into the coarse rug spread on the floor. She stretched and felt joints pop and crack. Sitting on the edge of her bed wearing only her nightshirt, she looked at her left leg, at the scar above her knee. Her fingers traced the healed tissue. She pulled up the sleeve of her right arm to expose her bicep and looked at the scar left by Daniel Underwood's bullet. It was ragged and tight, especially as she twisted her arm this way and that. The mark on her leg didn't bother her as much as this one did. Part of her supposed she should be lucky she still had use of the arm. Any deeper and the bullet would have done greater damage, but that was a small comfort.

Dale got up and lit the wood stove. She prepared a kettle, dressed in her lightest clothes, visited the outhouse, returned and made her coffee. She sat on a chair outside her front door and sipped it black. The sky alit gold and orange on the clouds and despite the ceaseless noise of the birds, serenity filled the ravine.

When she finished her coffee, Dale began her stretching regimen, warming up her muscles and joints as the blue-grey sky brightened. Then she unsheathed her sword, set the scabbard against the stone foundation of the cabin and walked the short distance to the river's edge. She stood in a wide open space looking east over the water and through the tree tops. They began to glow bright as the sunlight hit them. One by one, the higher branches lit up, followed the branches below, and the next below those. Dale closed her eyes and waited. She could feel the world illuminate around her. The air heated up. She inhaled the thick woodland smells with each long breath. When the rays of sunlight spread upon her cheeks, she raised her sword and looked down at it through the hazy shafts of summer light. She watched the sky's reflection in the forged steel. Her fingers flexed against the leather bands of the hilt. With one hand she turned the weapon over with her wrist and dropped into a comfortable stance. A western meadowlark fluttered by and she waited for it to perch on a branch across the river. It sat on the branch for a second before taking off again.

Dale began her drills with the sword, taking precise steps as she moved the weapon through long-practiced positions. She knew her movements lacked fluidity after all the years since she took up her sword, but it felt good to wield it again. She wondered why she had let it go so long.

I wanted to fit in, she thought. *Out here, in this time, people don't carry swords.*

Seven years ago, Dale awoke upriver in this very ravine, with little more than her knives, this sword and the clothes on her back. It didn't take long even with her memories and identity shattered to figure out she was trapped in the past. After acquiring her guns, she'd begun to leave her sword on the wall of her cabin, thinking it impractical, something which drew attention she didn't like.

And how is that different from now? she asked herself.

Truth be told, it wasn't much different, even after all these years. She was an outsider then and just as much an outsider now.

I have Rose, she told herself, *and a friend in Gertrude.*

Dale made a mental note to remind Rose of Gertrude's invitation to tea, made at Sheriff Anderson's wake. It was long overdue, but Rose had a lot on her mind these days with the death of her student.

The *murder* of her student.

Something was wrong in Orchard Bend. She felt it. When she'd returned from Blue Creek, Rose told her what happened, about Sheriff Wilson's visit and the whispers spoken in town. No one knew *who* the murderer was, but that didn't stop the theories, such as Laura O'Malley having a secret lover. Dale found that idea one of the more sane rumours. At the other end of the spectrum, talk turned to a demon roaming the countryside seeking the heads of its victims. The more paranoid in town were loath to let their children travel alone. Few folks ventured out after dusk.

As she walked through the drills one by one, her muscles remembered the familiar rhythms. The sword's blade moved up and down, through sweeping curves and arcs. She found herself wishing she had someone to practice with, to spar with.

With no warning, pain ripped through her mind, blinding and hot. Dale couldn't remember the last time she'd felt a migraine this bad. It must have been years. Just as she thought it was too much, Dale saw something through the pain, beyond it.

A girl stood in front of her, her blond hair in a tight bun, barefoot, wearing white. The girl, in her early teens, swung a long wooden practice sword at Dale. Dale's own hand moved to block it with her own wooden sword.

And just like that, the memory ended.

Another memory! her mind screamed through the residual pain in her head. Dale realized she'd dropped to her knees, palms on the cool dirt, and she opened her eyes and saw her sword on the ground next to her. She picked it up and rose to her feet, breathing hard, her head swimming. She took care to not lose her balance as she walked back to her cabin. She sheathed her sword and went to the barrel of water by the door. She splashed her face and wetted her hair. The chill of the water brought focus to her spinning thoughts. She moved her chair to a shaded patch and sat down.

"A memory," she whispered.

Dale sat there a long time that Sunday.

11

June 6, 1953
Blue Creek

The late Fred Dooley's old Birch portable record player lived behind the counter at *The Yellow Canary* and Mara Dale thought she'd figure out how to operate it. The only customer at the moment was Ray Turnbull. Ray's routine when he visited *The Yellow Canary* was to park himself on a stool and wait for Tom Dooley to put a cold bottle of beer in front of him. Ray would say nothing as he downed the first beer in a succession of long swallows. He'd ask for another and Tom would oblige. Mara had been working when Ray first dropped in. He was from out of town, but personal business brought him to Blue Creek. It wasn't until his second visit, three beers in, that Ray opened up to Tom.

"Estate business," Ray said. The man didn't look at Tom, keeping his eyes fixed on the bottle in his hand. "My sister and brother-in-law both passed away. Maybe you knew them. The Watsons."

With the diner quiet that night, Mara listened to the conversation from behind the counter as she cleaned up.

"Murdered," Ray said. "By their neighbour, who you may also know. Bullock."

Tom nodded.

"It's a sad story and you have my condolences, friend," Tom said, putting a glass of water next to Ray's bottle.

Mara didn't hear the rest of the conversation as some teens piled into a booth and she went to take their orders. By the time she returned from the kitchen, Ray downed the last of his beer. He got up, leaving the water untouched, paid his bill and left.

"Unbelievable, if you ask me," Tom said, shaking his head. "The man loses his sister, he and his wife have to take in his nephew, and now he has to deal with the estate and the house and all that. No wonder he needs a drink or two to get through coming here every few days."

"The Bullock murders, right?" Mara said.

"That's right," Tom said. "Happened a few days before you walked in here asking for a job."

Mara poured the teens' sodas as she spoke.

"I read about it in the paper," Mara said. "It really is awful. Something like that affects a whole town."

"I knew the boy, the Watsons' son," Tom said. "Not all that well, but he came in with his friends pretty regularly. Todd King, Freddie the Fish, that crowd."

"Those were his friends?" Mara said. She knew that group by sight. They were loud, fun and the one nicknamed Fish made no effort to hide the fact that he enjoyed checking out Mara's legs below her uniform skirt whenever he could.

Tom nodded, pouring Ray's untouched glass of water into the sink. And so Ray's visits went on like that every four or five days for that last three weeks.

Now, Ray sat nursing his third beer as Mara took the old record player off the shelf and examined it. The old Birch looked sort of like a compact suitcase. Ray watched her as she opened the lid and peered inside.

"You crank the arm in front," Ray offered. A lever protruded from the front of the player and Mara looked at it, uncertain.

"Go on," Ray said.

"I don't want to break it," Mara said with a giggle.

Ray shrugged and went back to his beer.

Mara gave her own shrug, gripped the crank and turned it. The mechanisms inside resisted, but it turned. She felt the tension build up in the motor, like a big wind-up toy, then stopped, not wanting to overstress it. Who knew when this was last used?

She lifted the arm and thought maybe that would start the turntable spinning, but nothing happened.

"I have to get on home," Ray said. "Long drive to Orchard Bend."

"That'll be two dollars for the beer," Mara said, taking his empty bottle from the counter.

Ray paid his tab, put on his hat and coat and started for the door. He stopped, straightened his tie and said, "The release latch is under the arm."

"I beg your pardon," Mara said, watching him.

"The record player," Ray said, half turning. "The latch is under the arm. It'll start the thing spinning."

He demonstrated by making a flicking motion with his hand. Mara looked down at the record player, lifted the arm and saw what might have been the release lever underneath, next to the turntable. She fiddled with it, pushing it one way then another, and it clicked as it let go. The table spun.

"Well, look at that," Mara said, smiling.

"Have a good night," Ray said as he walked to the door.

"You, too, Mr Turnbull," Mara said with a wave.

The bell jingled over the door as Ray departed and Mara stood looking at the spinning turntable. With the diner empty, she looked at the clock. It read 9 PM. The movie theatre down the street would let out soon and *The Yellow Canary* would be packed.

Mara clicked the latch back in place, closed lid of the player and put it back on the shelf. As she did, the bell clattered above the door and Mara called out, "Be right with you. Take a seat wherever you want."

Behind her, a man's dry voice replied, "I'm okay to stand, sweetheart."

Mara didn't move. She knew that voice. Her muscles tensed as she turned to see Mr Davis at the end of the counter, newspaper folded under his arm. He tapped a cigarette out of the pack in his hand, put it to his mouth, flicked the lighter open and lit it. When his eyes returned to her, she saw them narrow with recognition.

"Well," Davis said, "ain't this unexpected? You work here now, doll?"

"Yes," Mara said.

"I'm here to see Dooley," Davis said. "He around?"

"No," Mara answered. "He had business out of town and will be back tomorrow."

"That so?" Davis said. He took a drag from his cigarette and asked, "How long have you and Dooley been fucking?"

Mara blinked.

"What?"

"Dooley wouldn't leave you here by yourself if he didn't trust you," Davis said. "The only way I can see you gaining his trust so fast is letting him visit Cupid's Alley."

"You're disgusting," Mara said.

Davis gave a subtle shrug that said *Yeah, you're probably right, but you've got bigger problems right now, sweetheart*. He puffed his smoke and asked, "Can I trust his bed buddy with a message?"

"Sure," Mara said.

"Tell him the rent's overdue," Davis said, the cigarette flapping between his lips as he spoke.

"Anything else?" Mara asked.

Davis took the newspaper from under his arm and put it on the counter.

"You want this again?" Davis asked, nodding to it. "The city paper's always a good read."

Mara said nothing.

"Come out from behind the counter, sweetheart," Davis said, taking the smoke from his mouth and flicking the ashes on the floor.

Mara didn't move. She crossed her arms and clenched her jaw.

Davis rolled his eyes, throwing his head back in mock weariness.

"Don't make me ask twice," he said.

Mara shook her head, gave a strained little laugh and stepped out from behind the counter to face him.

"That's what I thought," Davis said. "You do look good in that uniform."

Mara laughed again to keep from crossing the room to kill this toad of a man. She had the idea that killing him might not be so easy. She spied the shape of a gun under his coat, but more than that, he'd probably put up a decent fight. And killing him wouldn't end Tom's troubles with Davis's employer; it would only make the situation worse.

Davis tipped his hat to her and turned to the door, saying to himself, "I *do* like a woman in uniform."

When he was out the door, Mara looked down at her waitress uniform and immediately wanted to change out of it. She also wanted to drive Davis's face through the plate glass of the diner window.

Steady now, whispered the captain. *Davis isn't important. His message is. Tom owes money and they're looking to collect.*

Mara took the city newspaper off the counter just as the bell rang over the door. Three laughing, chattering teen girls came in and grabbed a booth. Mara waved and said, "Be right there."

She looked at the newspaper, then tossed it in the garbage.

* * *

Just before midnight, Mara heard the jingle of the diner's door bell.

Tom's back, whispered the captain.

"Yes, he is," Mara said.

She sat on the edge of her bed on the second floor above *The Yellow Canary,* in the cramped rear storeroom. Over the past two weeks, Mara had tidied up the place enough to call it liveable. She planned to get her own place when she saved up enough rent money. For now, though, it was better than sleeping outdoors.

The footsteps reached the top of the stairs. There came a knock and a muffled voice.

"Mara?" Tom asked, "It's me. Are you decent?"

Mara got up, still in her waitress uniform and opened the door. Tom smiled, his hands stuffed in his jacket pockets.

"How was the city?" Mara asked.

"Fine," Tom said. "May I come in?"

"It's your storage room," Mara said, waving him in. "Let me take your coat."

90

"Thanks," Tom said, slipping out of it. He parked himself on the bed, laid down and stretched out.

"By all means," she said dryly, "Make yourself at home."

"Any problems today?" Tom asked. "Didn't burn the place down, I see. That's always good."

"No problems," Mara said. "But you had a visitor."

"Oh yeah?" Tom asked.

"Davis," Mara said. "I think that's his name. He works for someone called McCabe."

Tom sat up on his elbows, the humour gone from his face.

"Davis came *here?*" Tom said.

"Looking to have a word with you, yes," Mara said.

Tom dropped back down on the bed with a groan.

"He said to tell you the rent is due," Mara said.

"Shit," Tom said. "Did he say anything else?"

"Only that I look good in a waitress uniform," Mara said. "So you owe someone money?"

"I don't want to talk about it," Tom said. "I'll handle it. No need to worry yourself."

Mara sat back on the bed next to Tom.

"Just be careful, okay?" she said.

Tom's hand moved to Mara's leg and he began caressing her thigh, sliding her uniform skirt up her leg.

"I missed you," he said. "Next time I go to the city, you're coming with me."

Mara took his hand, intertwined her fingers with his and leaned over him.

"Won't *that* be a scandal!" she smiled. "People are bound to talk."

"Let them," Tom said and pecked a kiss on her lips.

Mara climbed on top of him and began undoing his pants.

"You are the most amazing woman I've ever met," Tom said, closing his eyes.

* * *

June 7, 1953
Blue Creek

91

The next morning, Mara woke up alone on her thin, hard mattress, the sheets still smelling of sweat and sex.

It beats sleeping outside, whispered the captain.

"Yes, it does," Mara said.

Better freshen up before work, the captain's voice told her and Mara got up, walked naked to the bathroom and made herself presentable. She stood before the mirror and looked herself over. She turned to her right and the tattoo on her deltoid stared back at her. It depicted a sword impaling a skull.

It was my idea to get that, remember? the captain said. *The rest of the unit just had skulls done, but you needed to be special.*

Mara grinned, then giggled.

You're probably the only woman in this rinky-dink town with ink on her, the captain laughed.

"This town's not so bad," Mara said.

You don't belong here and you know it, the captain said, her voice stern, unrelenting. *You feel it, everyday, that urge to run. This isn't where you belong.*

"Enough!"

The captain didn't reply, but Mara knew she wasn't finished.

Mara washed up and dressed back into her uniform. She slipped a hand into her pocket and felt the piece of paper in there. She took it out, sat on the edge of the bed and examined the ticket for the horserace. She'd taken it from Tom's jacket when he handed it to her last night. Mara put it in the pocket of her jeans on the floor, straightened her uniform and went downstairs to start her shift.

12

June 7, 1953
Orchard Bend

Davis got out of his car and breathed in the heady evening air. Row upon row of headstones and monuments spread out before him. He saw the boss's empty car up ahead, but not the man himself. Davis adjusted his fedora against the setting sun. He took out his pack of smokes and his lighter and started on between the columns of graves as he fired up a cigarette. The overgrown remains of a footpath led from the driveway, the flat stones broken and twisted. Davis watched his step. A man could turn his ankle on one of the hidden chunks of stone.

Past larger monuments which marked some of the oldest graves in the yard, Davis saw the heavy wrought iron fence separating the McCabe plots from the rest of the deceased townsfolk. Inside lay generations of the family going back all the way to Liam McCabe, one of Orchard Bend's founders. The gate stood open and Davis saw his boss standing beyond, his back to the world. Another man stood at the open gate. Davis recognized him as Tyler Brand, the reporter, one of McCabe's local *employees*. Brand appeared deep in thought.

Before Davis drew any closer, he paused and looked around. A few other families milled about, visiting their dearly departed way off among the newer plots. Davis took a few quick pulls from his cigarette, put it out on his shoe and tucked the butt back in the pack. Any other day, in any other place, he'd find a trash bin or ash tray, or just flick the butt on the ground, but standing here surrounded by the dead, Davis kind of thought that would be disrespectful. He personally didn't give a shit, but he knew Mr McCabe would care and in a job like his, you did the little things to keep the boss happy.

Davis passed Brand as he moved through the gate and caught the unmistakeable whiff of alcohol on the reporter. He also looked like he needed a good night's sleep and a shave. Brand only glanced up as Davis passed him, then resumed staring at the ground. Davis made up his mind to suggest Brand be excused from this gathering. Something was off about the reporter, his head wasn't in the game. Davis noted the grave of Gabrielle McCabe, the recently deceased granddaughter of his employer Owen. Patches of grass grew on it, but no headstone marked her final resting place. From the tall grass beyond the boundary of the cemetery, crickets began their evening chirping. Davis, not a man prone to impatience or fidgeting, contented himself with the serenity of the graveyard that Sunday evening. He watched a pair of birds (he guessed them to be mourning doves) land on a headstone outside the fence. The male began a courting dance, turning this way and that, and the female bobbed up and down before taking off. Davis nodded to himself as the male flew off in pursuit.

His attention turned at the sound of a car approaching. He saw it crawl along the driveway toward them. The gravel crackled under the tires. Davis eyed it as the vehicle parked behind his own car. A man got out and hitched up his belt, then started along the same path Davis walked to get here. Halfway to the gate, the man's foot snagged one of the broken pieces of flat stone. He tripped and almost planted his face in the grass if not for catching hold of a gravestone to break his fall. The man straightened himself and adjusted his belt with both hands, then pressed on. He reached the gate and entered. Davis didn't recognize him. He noted the man's narrow frame and the fledgling potbelly under his suit jacket. There was something else, too. The way the man had twice fixed his belt, first when getting out of the car, then after tripping on the path. Davis wondered if this man was a cop. Sure, it wasn't much to go on, but still Davis had an inkling.

The two men waited.

When Owen McCabe turned around it wasn't the slow shuffle of a man in his seventies. He spun around and Davis thought him rather spry. In one hand, McCabe clutched his black,

94

leather-bound ledger. Not for the first time did Davis wonder what exactly was in the thick, well-worn book. He would not find out today, nor did he ever expect to.

McCabe looked past both Davis and the newcomer, zeroing in on Brand.

"Ty, you can wait at the car," McCabe said.

Brand looked at the other men one at a time, then walked out of the gated area and down the path to McCabe's car. The three men watched him go. Davis admitted some relief that he himself didn't have to suggest dismissing Brand. He was prepared to, but it would have been awkward to say the least.

Owen wasted no time, his attention now on the newcomer.

"Tell him," Owen said to the potbellied man, gesturing to Davis.

"Tell me what?" Davis asked.

"Shut up and let the man speak," Owen barked at Davis.

Davis waited as the man shifted on the balls of his feet, his anxiety palatable.

"Well, like I said, Mr McCabe, sir," he stuttered, "He got back just in time for our Saturday poker game last night. He said he'd been in the city..."

Davis put his hand up and the man stopped.

"Who are we talking about?" Davis asked.

"Tom," the man said. "Tom Dooley."

"Finish your fuckin' story, Berger," McCabe said.

Despite the warm spring sunset around them, Davis felt a chill in the cemetery.

"At the end of the night, Tom said he'd met up with some people. Some *really important* people, those were the words he used," Berger continued. "He said he'd finally taken care of business. I didn't know what or who he was talking about, but when I got his coat for him, I found a phone number in the jacket pocket, along with a horserace ticket. I think that's where they met up, Tom and these 'really important people.'"

"What was this phone number?" Davis asked, growing impatient.

Before Berger could answer, Owen was at Davis, moving so fast Davis almost tripped taking a step back. The old man's

95

boney hand grabbed the lapel of Davis's trench coat and pulled him within whispering distance.

"The Assistant District Attorney," Owen growled low. "That goddamn piece of shit is ratting us out."

The words hung there as McCabe let go of Davis with a jerk of his hands.

Davis looked at his boss, stunned. He looked over at Berger, who nodded.

"He saw what happened to Parker, the pawnbroker," Berger said. "He wasn't happy and he knew it could happen to him, too."

"He met them at a racetrack, right?" Davis asked, pointing at Berger. The man nodded.

"Near as I can figure," Berger replied.

"At a racetrack," Davis repeated. "*Not* at a police station. That means he talked to them, but didn't give them a formal statement. He's testing the water. It's bad, but it's not the end of the world. The D.A. can't do anything without a formal statement."

"I'm not taking that chance," Owen said. "That's why *you're* here, Mr Davis."

Owen looked Davis square in the eye.

"You're going to take care of this," the old man said.

13

June 8, 1953
Blue Creek

Mara dropped the needle on the record and the crackling hiss from the old Birch portable record player was replaced by a rapid fire banjo backed by acoustic guitar. Tom leaned against the jukebox, listening with great interest as Mara smiled at him from across the counter. She turned up the volume as the harmonized vocals came in singing about the titular condemned criminal who shared Tom's name.

"Is this the same song Deputy Berger was talking about?" Mara asked.

Tom exaggerated self-consciousness as he smiled with his hands up.

"Yes, it is," he admitted. "But the lyrics are a bit different. I haven't heard this version before."

"I found it at the record shop," Mara said. "I wasn't even looking for it. I was just flipping through the albums, looking at song titles, and this one had it."

She held up the record sleeve and showed him.

"*American Folksay*," Tom read aloud.

"The notes say this actually happened?" Mara asked. "This man Tom Dooley was really hanged?"

"That's the story," Tom said, "stabbed his girlfriend and was hanged for it back in the 1860s. Now it's a murder ballad."

Mara hummed along with the final chorus and the song came to an end. She lifted the needle from the vinyl and turned off the record player.

"You figured out how to use the old Birch, huh?" Tom asked, setting the sleeve on the counter and looking at his father's record player. "We used to take this contraption everywhere.

My dad loved it. When he died, I sold most of his records to the Watsons. Cliff was a collector. I figured they should go to someone who'd love them as much as Dad did. To his dying day, Dad said he never made the connection with the song when he and mom named me. I guess I believe him, but it's a heck of a coincidence."

As Tom spoke, a group of teens came into *The Yellow Canary* and took their regular booth. Mara recognized them as Todd, his girlfriend Katy and Freddie the Fish. The Fish stole his usual glance at Mara's legs while listening to Todd.

"...I'm telling you, I can get the car and we can head over there," Todd said, more serious than Mara normally saw him.

"I say we do it!" The Fish said, turning his full attention to his friend.

The conversation stopped as they noticed Mara waiting to take their order.

"How's everyone today?" Mara asked.

"Good. Great," Todd said. "A round of milkshakes, I think."

The other two nodded in agreement.

"Coming right up," Mara said and left them to their conversation.

"It's a long drive," Katy said as Mara moved out of earshot. "I don't know if my parents will let me go."

The elderly couple two booths down waved at Mara and asked for a refill of their coffee. Behind the counter, Tom put the Birch record player back on the shelf and turned to Mara.

"Say, um, how would you like to go see a movie one of these days?" Tom smiled. "We've been getting to know each other in, well, *other* ways, but I think it would be swell to, you know, get some fresh air."

"Are you asking me out on a date?" Mara said quietly. "Dinner and a movie, that sort of thing?"

"Hey now," Tom said, shaking his head. "I said 'movie,' you're the one adding 'dinner' to the equation. That's a big step and I'm not sure I'm ready."

Mara gave his arm a playful punch.

"Is that a yes?" Tom asked.

"I think I can fit it into my busy schedule," Mara replied with a wink. She took the coffee pot from the maker and headed for the elderly couple's table. As she poured their refills, Todd slid out of his booth.

"It's too quiet in here, Mr Dooley, don't you think?" Todd asked.

"That's why it's there, son," Tom said, pointing to the jukebox

"Katy, I'm playing our song!" Todd called back to the booth as he dropped a coin in the machine.

"I'm not dancing, not in a diner," Katy called back. "No offence, Mr Dooley."

"None taken," Tom smiled.

Todd made his selection and walked back to the booth, where he stood with his hand out, inviting Katy to join him.

"Doesn't look like you have much choice," the Fish laughed.

The 45 dropped and the piano triplets of "Lawdy Miss Clawdy" filled the diner. Katy put her hands over her grinning face and groaned.

"Don't leave me standing here, doll," Todd said.

"Alright, alright," Katy relented as she slid out of the booth. "This is *so* embarrassing, Todd King."

Empty coffee pot in hand, Mara grinned as she watched the couple dance. Katy's awkwardness fell away as she put her arms over Todd's shoulders. At the counter, Tom set the three milkshakes on her tray and she walked over to get them. Before Mara could pick up the tray, Tom took her hand. Out of reflex she almost pulled away. Tom stepped out from behind the counter and in doing so raised her arm over her head. Mara smiled as she twirled. Tom took her other hand, wrapping his fingers around hers, both of them now gripping the coffee pot's handle. Mara laughed at how absurd they must have looked. She could see the Fish laughing at both couples, shaking his head and slapping his knee.

When the song ended, Mara sat on one of the stools at the counter. Tom delivered the milkshakes and Mara overheard the Fish say, "Nicely done, Mr Dooley."

"Thanks, kid," Tom said.

Don't let him fool you, the captain's voice whispered. *He's a good man, but he has problems. Remember the visit Davis made? He's into something or owes them money. So did the pawnbroker and look what happened to him. And what was Mr Wonderful doing at the horse races in the city? Gambling? Trying to get the money he owed?*

Mara clenched her jaw to keep from audibly telling the voice in her mind to shut up.

Davis will be back, the captain told her. *You'd better be ready. I doubt he'll be in the mood to give Tom any breaks.*

"Enough," Mara muttered, rubbing her temples. The headache coursed through her brain and she shut her eyes.

"Don't swoon on me, sweetheart," Tom said as he passed her and went behind the counter.

"Mind if I take five?" Mara asked. "I think I need some air."

"Yeah, go ahead," Tom replied. "Take ten. You earned it."

Mara got up and went through the kitchen to the alley out back. There, she stood in the chilled spring air. A wooden milk crate sat next to the door. Tom Dooley employed it when he needed a cigarette away from the clamour of the diner on busy nights. Mara used it now, leaning forward with her elbows on her knees and rubbing both temples. She closed her eyes and focused on the quiet. The headache eased. When she opened her eyes she decided to stay out here a few minutes longer. She let her eyes wander over the contents of the alley. A single old tire leaned against the wall across from her, next to some rusted chain-link fencing and discarded paint cans. Beside her was a stack of newspapers bound by twine. Tom had just put the papers out earlier that day. Mara noticed the one on top was not the *Blue Creek Frontiersman* but rather the *Orchard Herald*, the local paper from Orchard Bend. Ray Turnbull must have brought it with him on one of his visits and left it here. The date read *May 20, 1953*, and the headline read: *STORM TOPPLES TREES, CAUSES DAMAGE COUNTYWIDE.*

Go ahead and read it, whispered the captain.

Mara hesitated for the briefest second and then pulled the paper out of the stack. She skimmed over the story of the storm that hit on May 14th.

The storm that brought you here, the captain observed.

"Yes, it was the same storm," Mara said, not realizing she's spoken aloud. "The night of the Bullock murders, too."

She flipped to the second page and continued the article. It told of trees coming down on roads and a lot of property damage, but nothing too severe. No injuries or fatalities reported.

Mara started to put the paper back on the pile so se could return to work when a smaller second page headline caught her eye.

UNIDENTIFIED REMAINS FOUND!
by Tyler Brand, Sr. Staff Reporter

On the afternoon of May 16, unidentified human remains of two individuals were discovered in a disused building on the property of William Hansen by his two children. Police are investigating and are unable to comment. An anonymous source within the Sheriff's Office says the remains, two human skeletons, appear to have gone undiscovered for approximately sixty years.

At once, Mara felt lightheaded. Dread filled her, along with the feeling of being watched. She glanced over her shoulder, despite knowing full well no one was there.

"I can't let it find me," she whispered.

The back door flung open and Mara dropped the paper.

"Break's over, good-lookin'!" Tom smiled. "We're swamped in there now."

"Right. I'm sorry, Tom," Mara said, getting up.

"You can make it up to me later," he winked.

Mara smiled, but the dread lingered and she couldn't shake the thought of the two skeletons.

* * *

Todd, Katy and Freddie the Fish hadn't intended to close *The Yellow Canary*, but when they realized how late it was, they paid and rushed out the door. Smiling and shaking his head as he watched them go, Tom hoped they didn't get in too much trouble from their folks. It wasn't uncommon for parents to call after their children at the diner and tell them to get on home, particularly on a school night. It was exam time, though, and none of the teens' parents had elected to ring *The Yellow Canary*, so he guessed the kids would be fine.

Tom wiped down their table and walked back to the counter. His thoughts turned back to Mara and how she had just left in a hurry at the end of her shift. She often hung around the diner after work or went upstairs to the privacy of the storeroom where Tom let her stay. He'd always drop by and visit, see if she needed anything. More often than not, they'd have what he considered mind-blowing sex, which sometimes even exceeded his wildest imaginings. Tom's list of previous romantic partners was a short one. First, his brief steady in high school, Betty Lou Romaine. He'd barely got to second base with her, behind the gymnasium during the Sadie Hawkins Dance. A week later she dumped him for a linebacker. Senior year, he hooked up with Clara Tucker. After a few weeks they finally did it in the back of his dad's Studebaker. But Clara was in a rebound from her previous boyfriend. As hot and intense as it all was, their fling together ran its course, burning out not with the fireworks of a dramatic break up, but in the cool realization that he and Clara had little else in common apart from sex. They called it quits just before they went off to their respective colleges. There had been no one special in college for Tom, but a few parties had led to pleasant, empty encounters. He moved back to Blue Creek after college and since taking over the diner after his father passed away, there had been nobody at all, not that Tom noticed much. Running the business took up most of his time and when it didn't, Tom was happy to see a movie by himself or go for a drive. He hadn't planned on hooking up with Mara Dale when she walked into *The Yellow Canary* looking for a job. It was the furthest thing from his mind. Imagine his surprise when she started getting fresh and friendly with *him*. It started with flirting, the way she smiled at him and the way she spoke. Even now, he couldn't quite put his finger on it.

During her interview for the waitressing job, she'd seemed so meek, almost squirrelly. He half gave her the job out of sheer pity and he expected she'd last two days, maybe three, then he'd have to give the poor girl her walking papers. At Tom's request, his former waitress Betsy Parker—

Prince, he corrected himself again, *Betsy Prince. She's a married woman now.* Tom recalled the embarrassing moment when he introduced Mara to Betsy, calling her by her maiden name.

—Anyway, Betsy *Prince* came in for a few hours to show her the ropes, but Mara had not needed much hand-holding.

"Where did you find her?" Betsy had asked in a hushed voice that first day. She sat at the counter sipping a cup of coffee, watching her trainee take the orders of a family crammed into their booth.

"She just walked in this morning asking for a job," Tom said.

"She's a bit on the... *kooky* side, isn't she?" Betsy said.

"How do you mean?" Tom asked.

Betsy thought about it a moment and said, "I don't know. I can't put my finger on it. This is going to sound nuts, but she kind of acts like a soldier."

"She said her family was military," Tom said.

"If I didn't know any better, Tom, I'd said *she* was military," Betsy said. "Not an army brat, but actually *served* in the military."

"Maybe she worked in a VA hospital or something," Tom said.

"Maybe," Betsy nodded. Tom could tell she wasn't quite convinced, but she let the matter drop when Tom asked how married life was treating her.

"Off to a rockier start than we planned," Betsy sighed. "Dad had to close the pawn shop. There were bills and... Sorry, I'd rather not get into it."

"Yeah, I saw the shop was shut down," Tom said, patting her hand. "I hope it all works out."

"Thanks, Tom," Betsy said. "I suppose we'll see."

After he and Mara had become intimate, Tom had reason to consider her past again. He learned first hand that she talked in her sleep. She didn't do it every night they were together, but the few times he caught her, he picked up words like *facility*, *orders* and *captain*.

That's when Tom took his deductive musings a step past Betsy Prince's. If Mara Dale was somehow in the service, he wondered if she was on the run, AWOL. He didn't want to believe it, of course, but the argument could be made. She shows up in town without a penny to her name, with a service background and one that hinted at something very bad having happened very recently.

And earlier today Tom had heard her out back on her break, talking to herself while reading an old newspaper. Tom had gone back to get her as the diner got more busy and heard her say something like, "I can't let him find me" or "I can't let *them* find me." The more Tom thought about it now, the more he didn't like it. It meant she was in trouble and he had a feeling it was the kind of trouble that was hard to outrun.

Tom walked through the dark kitchen to his office. Before he could turn on the lights, the ember of a cigarette glowed in the gloom. Davis sat in the shadows at Tom Dooley's desk, the cigarette lighting pinpoints of red in his eyes.

"Mr Davis," Tom said, mustering all his willpower to speak in an even voice. "I didn't hear you come in."

"No," Davis said. "You didn't."

"Hey, I've got your money," Tom said, backing away without realizing it.

"Have a good day at the track, did you?" Davis asked.

Oh, Christ, he knows, Tom thought, but his expression never waivered. *Somehow he knows.*

No, he doesn't, growled his father's voice of reason. *There's no way he can know.*

McCabe was a powerful man, but surely he couldn't know the moment by moment goings on at a city race track, right? That would be absurd.

"Yeah, wouldn't you know it!" Tom said. "A few of my ponies came through for me."

"That's peachy, Tom," Davis said.

"Look, I'm sorry it took a bit longer to get it to you," Tom said. "I threw in a bit extra. You know, for the delay."

"That's awfully thoughtful of you," Davis said and took another puff.

"The money's in the top drawer," Tom said. "It's locked, but—"

"Not anymore, it's not," Davis said. In the darkness, Tom saw him pat his breast pocket. "Oh, you're gonna need a new lock for that drawer. Sorry."

"Don't worry about it, everything's a-okay," Tom said, relieved.

Yeah, he doesn't know about the meeting with the D.A. Tom realized. Davis wouldn't bother telling him to replace the lock if he intended to kill him. Tom relaxed, at least as much as anyone could around Davis. The man had a way of just making a person nervous. Tom felt confident he was going to get out of this meeting still breathing.

* * *

Mara watched the sun set from the bridge over the creek as cars past behind her. In the distance, a train whistle carried on the wind. With her attention elsewhere, she did not notice. After her shift at *The Yellow Canary*, Mara changed out of her uniform, told Tom she was going for a walk and left the diner before he could ask what was wrong. She walked for several hours around the town, aimless and angry and scared.

Something was wrong.

The dread from reading about remains found in Orchard Bend made no logical sense, yet she couldn't shake it. The thought persisted that she was being watched somehow.

No, not watched, said the captain in her thoughts.

"Then what?" Mara asked.

She didn't notice the couple with a stroller glance at her as she spoke, then hurry on with uncertain looks.

Something is out there, the captain said. *It saw you while you were in the Breach.*

"How is that possible?" she asked.

It appeared the captain had no answer.

"Maybe I'm going mad," she told herself.

She left the bridge, but was not ready to go back to *The Yellow Canary*. She twisted and turned about the streets as the sky darkened. The streetlights winked on one at a time as she walked with her head low.

Something is out there.

"But what? What is out there?" she mumbled.

It saw you...

"Does it see me now? That's the question," she mumbled on.

"Evening, Miss Dale."

The voice so startled Mara that she jerked out of her reverie and spun around, muscles tense as she dropped into a fighter's stance without thinking. The voice belonged to Deputy Berger. He had pulled up behind her in his squad car without her realizing it. She relaxed her stance almost as fast as she'd taken it, but Berger was watching her with a look of amused curiosity.

"Sorry to take you by surprise just now. Everything alright?" he asked.

"Yes," Mara replied. "Long day at work. Clearing my head with a walk."

"Looks like you got a lot on your mind still, if I do say so myself," Berger smiled. "Whatever it is, I reckon you'll worry your pretty little head off thinking too hard on it."

It was Mara's turn to give him a curious look.

"I'll try not to do that," Mara said, flashing a smile to mask her contempt at being patronized. "Thank you, Deputy."

"You have a good night," Berger said, tipping his hat to her. "If you want a quiet place to think, the library is around the corner to your left."

"That's a good idea, Deputy," Mara said with another fake smile. She punctuated her next words by waving a pointed finger at him. "Aren't you just *full* of helpful notions this evening? Thank you, again."

"My pleasure, ma'am," Berger said and pulled away in his squad car.

Mara found the library right where Berger said it would be, a squat building fronted by tall, narrow windows. The lights cast a warm glow and Mara went inside. She found the smell of the books comforting somehow. At desks and in well-worn chairs, people sat reading. At a table nearby, two students studied with books and paper scattered about them.

A woman --the librarian, Mara guessed-- came out from behind the counter and approached her. The woman's eyes darted about Mara, taking in her attire. Mara hadn't updated her wardrobe much in the few weeks since she'd been here. Leaving her storeroom apartment earlier, she'd grabbed her army field jacket without thinking much about how it made her stand out.

"Excuse me, but we will be closing in about twenty minutes," the librarian said.

"Sure," Mara said, nodding. She stepped away, looking at the tall shelves lined with books, feeling the dread that had plagued her all afternoon slipping away. It wasn't gone entirely, but at last she could shut it away to a corner of her mind and relax.

The librarian gave a sharp cough and Mara looked at her. Outside came the sound of a siren, faint, but growing louder.

"Young lady, I think it's time you leave," the librarian's eyes were levelled over her horn-rimmed glasses, fixed on Mara. Past the librarian, Mara saw a squad car tear down the street, siren blaring and red lights flashing.

"Deputy Berger suggested I drop in and—"

"Deputy Berger does not run this library," the woman said. "I do. I'm asking you to leave."

"Why?"

"Do you intend to take out a book? I highly doubt you have a library card, because I've never seen you here before," the librarian said.

"I can't just sit and—?"

"No. You're causing a scene now," the librarian gestured to the nearby patrons and Mara saw some were looking at her. "Leave and do not come back."

It felt like all eyes in the library were on her and Mara needed no more prompting to turn and leave. As she reached the door, she heard the librarian give a *tisk* and mutter, "Shameful."

Mara stopped.

Are you sure you want to do this? asked the voice of the captain.

"Yes, I am," Mara said.

She turned and levelled her own piercing gaze at the librarian. The woman took a step back. Just about everyone was watching her now and Mara didn't care. A rotund man standing in a row of bookshelves not far away started forward, intending to put himself between Mara and the librarian.

"Look now, Miss," the man said. "You were asked to go on your way—"

"Be silent," Mara said with icy quiet. Her gaze never left the librarian, but she noted the man stopped, mouth agape. The dread was gone, the lingering paranoia replaced with anger and focus.

Let'em have it! the captain cheered.

"Oh, I will," Mara said. "You bet your ass I will."

Through her fear, the librarian gave Mara a look of utter confusion.

Mara took another step towards the librarian. She pointed to the cowering woman.

"*You* have NO idea what you're—!"

The door behind her slammed open, cutting Mara off. As she spun around, a boy in a letterman jacket ran past her and stopped in front of everyone.

"FIRE!" he yelled. "There's a fire downtown!"

The boy stood there, expecting more of a reaction than the stunned silence that greeted him. He threw his hands up and said it again.

"FIRE! For Pete's sake!" he looked at everyone as they came back to their senses. The boy pointed out the window. "*The Yellow Canary* is on fire!"

14

The wind rattled and shook the trees surrounding the dell on the shore of the creek. The sliver of the moon at midnight offered very little light. Mara had the captain's watch out, its flashlight app casting a pale beam as she worked.

First she dug up her battered duffle bag then set about making camp once more in the privacy of the dell. The stones she'd left weeks before remained untouched, so she rebuilt her fire pit with them. Before leaving the dell to take up residence in *The Yellow Canary*'s storeroom, Mara had stocked the duffle with some canned food and filled her canteen with water. She ate stew from a can that night without much thought. Everything since the library had been without much thought.

Mara had been the first person out the library door when the boy announced *The Yellow Canary* was on fire. She'd run the half dozen blocks to the center of town and found a crowd gathered around the building. Violent flames ripped through the ground floor. Onlookers gasped and screamed as the plate glass window shattered. Deputy Berger and the other officers kept everyone back. Mara tried to get to him, but the fire trucks arrived and the police pushed everyone back even further down the street.

Mara left the crowd and went around the block to where Tom parked her car. Mara hoped Tom was somehow lucky enough to be in it, perhaps blissfully unaware of the fire, but the car was empty.

Mara knew Tom sometimes walked home. It was a good hike, but on a nice night like this, maybe... just maybe. Mara jogged most of the way and found Tom's house dark. She pounded on the door, still hoping against hope. When no response came, Mara sat down on the steps of his front porch.

"There's still a chance," she whispered, her voice sounding not unlike the captain. "He could've taken the long way home. Or be out at the movies. He likes the movies."

Hope rose again as a man rounded the corner a half dozen houses up from her. She stood up and walked down the steps to the short path across Tom's tiny lawn. The man stopped and Mara knew it wasn't Tom.

Under the streetlight, the fedora hid the man's face, but when he took the cigarette out and flicked the ashes on the sidewalk, Mara knew in an instant who it was.

"Davis," she said under her breath.

There was no way he could've heard her, but Davis turned on his heel and started back the way he came. Mara crossed the lawn and hit the sidewalk running. Davis rounded the corner and disappeared from view.

"Shit," Mara said under breath.

She heard a car starting up from around the corner. Adrenalin surged and she rounded the bend at a sprint, runningout into the street. She was within inches of the car as it screeched away. It widened the distance in no time, but that didn't stop Mara from giving pursuit down the next street and across several lawns. A man on his porch yelled at her as she leapt over his low hedges and into his neighbour's flower garden, but she did not let up. She lost ground, but continued the pursuit for another two blocks and around corners. Davis's car then sped up ahead of Mara, racing to the bridge that spanned the train tracks which bisected the north part of town.

Mara finally gave up the chase at the bridge, winded and gasping. She watched Davis disappear into the night.

"Goddammit!" she yelled, her voice hoarse and weak after her sprint. As her burning muscles cooled down, Mara walked in circles around the bridge, then leaned on the railing, pulling in air in deep breaths. She wanted to sit, but decided to head back to Tom's house. Maybe there was a clue to Davis's visit. If she could break in unnoticed, perhaps she could find something.

That plan collapsed when she arrived and found a squad car parked in front of Tom's house, its red lights flashing. As Mara approached, she saw a deputy she didn't recognize coming out of the house. He had a piece of paper in his hand and read it solemnly. Mara stopped on the sidewalk when another squad car pulled up and Sheriff Meyer climbed out. Dale knew him from the diner. The deputy met Meyer at the foot of the steps and handed him the paper. The sheriff read it and handed it back to his deputy, saying, "Keep that, it's evidence."

Mara moved forward and called out, "Sheriff Meyer!"

He look up, his weathered face grim.

"Miss... Dale, right?" he said.

"What's going on? Is Tom okay? *The Yellow Canary...*" Mara trailed off as the sheriff put up his hand.

"I really shouldn't be telling you this, but it's going to come out anyway, I guess," Meyer said. "Looks like Tom Dooley killed himself. Burned his diner down with himself inside it."

"How do you know?" Mara asked. She'd already guessed the answer, but she wanted to hear him say it.

"He left a note," Meyer said. "I've already said too much, I think. It's a sad night and we've got a lot of work to do. I'm sorry."

Meyer left her on the sidewalk and went inside. Mara stood there in disbelief for several minutes before walking away, her mind spinning.

It was midnight when she returned to the dell for the first time in weeks. After she ate, she busied herself by the firelight preparing her bedding of branches, leaves and heated stones.

Davis killed him, whispered the captain.

"I know," Mara said, staring at the sky. The horror of it came in flashes. She could almost see it and very much didn't want to. Her mind conjured up the images nonetheless. She saw Davis there in *The Yellow Canary*, come to end Tom.

He probably made Tom write the suicide note and gave it to the police, the captain said. *That might even have been why he went to the house before you chased him away. Leave the note, nice and tidy.*

111

"That means the police are in on it, too, some or all," Mara said. "We can't trust any of them."

No, but they aren't the real problem, are they? the captain asked.

"No," Mara replied. "It runs deeper."

You know who you have to find.

"McCabe."

* * *

The next morning, Mara could see the burnt out remains of *The Yellow Canary* from the phone booth across the street. The phone book provided the information Mara needed, listing only one Parker. A visit to the post office and an examination of the town map on the wall told her where to find the street. She adjusted the strap of the canteen across her chest and it bounced on her hip as she strode to the pawnbroker's home. A *For Sale* sign mounted on the lawn eliminated any doubt that this was the place. Seeing no doorbell, she gave a measured knock and waited. From inside she heard the din of a radio so she knocked again. Footsteps followed and when the door opened, it was Betsy Prince who answered. When she saw Mara she blinked out a tear from her bloodshot eyes.

"Mara, I..." Betsy said, fighting to get the words out. "It's so awful! Poor Tom."

"I know," Mara said. "I can't believe it either."

"Please come in," Betsy said and ushered her inside. "Can I get you a drink?"

"No, I'm fine. Thank you," Mara replied, looking around. Boxes filled the foyer and the living room, leaving walls and bookcases bare.

Betsy nodded, then paused, looking at Mara.

"How did you know I was here?" Betsy asked.

"Um, I didn't," Mara said. "I actually came to speak to your father. He ran the pawnshop, didn't he?"

"Yes, I did," said Parker, who appeared in the kitchen doorway.

"What's this about?" Betsy asked, looking from Mara to her father.

"I remember you, young lady," Parker said. "You bought that jacket and canteen from me, and a few others things, too."

"Can we talk in private, Mr Parker?" Mara asked.

"Anything you can say to him, you can say to me," Betsy said.

"Betsy, it's fine," Parker said, waving a dismissive hand.

"Dad, I don't like being left out," Betsy said. "After what happened to the shop, we're in this together. We promised each other."

Parker sighed and gave his daughter a mere look. It was enough and Betsy deflated a little.

"Fine. Alright," she said. "I'll be upstairs."

Mara and Parker watched her leave and then Parker led Mara through the living room to the back porch. He dusted off some weathered lawn furniture and carried them to the shade of a low maple in the middle of the yard.

"This whole business with the fire is terrible," Parker said, more wary than sorrowful. "Suicide, they're saying. It has Betsy all in a tizzy. Tom Dooley was a good man. Took after his father, God rest them both."

"You're selling your house, too?" Mara said.

"Betsy's mom passed in 1950," Parker said, looking at the house. "She's married now, Betsy is, to a good man who'll take care of her. We had her late, you know. I was almost 40 when God blessed Sue and me. Happiest day of my life. I figure it's time to enjoy my golden years while I still have some spring in my step. I don't need an empty house to rattle around in by myself."

"McCabe," Mara said.

She didn't entirely believe the wistful look on Parker's face as he waxed nostalgic and at the mention of McCabe's name, it vanished in an instant.

"I figured that's why you were here," Parker said.

"Davis came to see you that day I was shopping," Mara said. "He came to see Tom, as well."

113

"Betsy told me a new girl was waitressing at *The Yellow Canary*," Parker nodded to himself, still not looking at her. "That was you, huh?"

"Yes," Mara said. "Davis paid Tom a visit just like he did you. I know you got deep into something, debt most likely, and that's why you had to close the pawnshop. I'm guessing that's the real reason you're selling your house."

Parker said nothing and Mara waited. The breeze carried the pleasant fragrance of the flowers blooming in the garden. The leaves above them swayed and their shadows danced on Parker's face as he sat thinking.

"You should let it drop," Parker said. "There's no outcome where you find any sort of peace looking into Owen McCabe."

"You've already figured out what really happened to Tom," Mara said. "You know how serious this is."

"I'll keep my thoughts to myself," Parker said, "for Betsy's sake. And for yours."

"I'm sorry to bother you, then," Mara said and stood up.

"Leave Owen McCabe in his ivory tower in Orchard Bend and get on with your life. That's my advice," Parker said.

Mara looked at him, eyes narrow. She stuffed her hands in her pockets, turned and walked away from the pawnbroker.

"Tell Betsy goodbye for me, if you would," Mara said as she reached the gate.

"Wait, young lady," Parker called out. Mara's hand was on the latch. She looked back at Parker, who rose from his chair. "Come with me a moment."

The garage sat adjacent to the house, with a door leading in from the backyard. Parker opened the door and pulled a string dangling from the ceiling. A single bulb came on, offering little light in the gloom, but enough for him to start rooting through the boxes there. Mara watched him from the door and breathed in the musty air.

Parker rearranged a dozen boxes in quick succession before he found the one he was after. He opened it and pulled something out. When he turned to her, she saw it was a large package, wrapped in plain newsprint.

"Here," he said, walking to her and holding it out.

Mara took the package and unwrapped it. Her jaw dropped when she unfolded her leather jacket.

"You deserve to have it back," Parker said. "I'm sorry I can't help you any other way. Take it, leave Blue Creek and start another life."

"Thank you," Mara said, running her fingers over the supple leather. She wrapped it back up and tucked it under her arm.

"Good luck," Parker replied.

* * *

No help from Parker, the captain whispered.

"No," Mara agreed.

The firefighters had finally doused the last of the flames in the earlier morning hours. All the details were in the newspaper. Mara figured the *Frontiersman* had run late to get the edition out by the delivery time that morning. Townsfolk gathered at the site, standing at the barriers blocking traffic. Mara herself leaned against a lamppost not far away watching the men sift through the rubble. The building was all but gone, the inside a charred mess, the roof having collapsed and burned. Much of the fire department's work the night before was focused on the neighbouring structures, soaking them in an effort to keep the entire block from being lost. The damage was extensive regardless.

People passed Mara without looking at her, lost in their own thoughts and conversations. Some wept, some stared in morbid fascination at the carnage.

The newspaper said they'd found Tom Dooley's remains in the kitchen. Dental records would confirm, reported the sheriff, but the presence of a suicide note at his home wrapped the case up tight as far as they were concerned. Meyer's comments on the record were of the tragedy in losing a pillar of the community and thankfulness that no one else had been hurt.

Meyer is very likely in McCabe's pocket, the captain said in her mind. *If he's not, someone in his command is.*

"True again," Mara said.

If McCabe is prepared to murder his enemies and the law is not on your side, your options are very limited, the captain added.

"There's only one option," Mara replied. A woman passed by with her stroller as Mara spoke and she gave Mara a confused look. Mara didn't take any notice as she spoke to the captain, "Leave Blue Creek."

* * *

Mara restocked on some supplies and was back at her dell a short time after noon. She made a fire, cooked some stew and ate it. As she packed her belongs, she pulled out the broken control computer and considered getting rid of it. It would do her no good, non-functional as it was now. It was only extra weight, but somehow it felt wrong to leave it behind. Not only could it be found out here, a relic out of its time that could cause a host of problems, but it was also a link to her old life, a reminder of where she came from.

She stuffed the computer in her duffle bag, along with her supplies, her gear and her leather jacket, still wrapped in paper. She cleaned her camp, leaving little trace that anyone had been there. With the duffle slung on her back, her canteen bouncing against her hip and an apple in her hand, Mara left the dell and walked along the edge of the creek. She didn't stop when she reached the bridge into town, but kept going until see saw the train bridge. She took her last two bites of the apple and tossed the core into the brush. She climbed up the steep bank, through tall, scraggly grass and paused at the top.

Orchard Bend, she learned in the last three weeks, lay west of Blue Creek. It felt right to go in that direction, in part because she now knew Owen McCabe lived there, but also something deeper seemed to pull her in that direction. Keeping her eyes and ears alert for trains, Mara began walking.

* * *

The night she left Blue Creek, Mara made camp a dozen yards from the tracks, in a picturesque wooded glade. After the day she'd had, Mara was beat. The golden spring sunset rippled through the branches and she thought it all quite beautiful. The shafts of light picked out fluttering moths. She soaked it in, the crackle of her fire, the sweet-smelling air. When the image of Tom burning in *The Yellow Canary* rose up in her mind unbidden, Mara nearly vomited. The nausea passed, but Mara couldn't seem to catch her breath. She curled up on the ground and hugged her knees, shaking, gasping for air. Images flashed through her mind of Tom writing the suicide note and Davis holding a gun to his head (*that's probably how he did it*, Mara told herself, *making Tom write it at gun point, the monster. What must Tom have been thinking in those last moments? Was he begging for his life? Was he thinking of her?*). An almost shapeless evil seemed to lurk everywhere. The vision of two skeletons uncovered after sixty years came to her. So did memories of the facility with two sets of soldiers about to fire on each other. The captain had surrendered, turning over her weapon to the major, then the screams and the explosion that followed...

It all came crashing in on her and Mara cried out, wept and screamed herself until there was nothing left but a mostly hollow shell and the need to keep going. She didn't think she could eat that night, but cooked a chicken broth and was surprised when her appetite awoke at the smell. Her canteen was a third full after dinner and in the dying blue sunlight, Mara found a stream. She used her empty cans to boil the water and refilled her canteen. The stars twinkled when she finally settled in. She let her tired brain simply stare at the fire as she rested against her duffle at the base of a tree. A song came to her. Though she didn't remember all the words, she hummed it and sang the chorus about the poor man hanged for murder those many years before.

* * *

117

June 11, 1953
Orchard Bend

Mara Dale passed the sign for Orchard Bend around mid-afternoon two days after she left Blue Creek. It stood overgrown at the side of the tracks. The tall trees flanking the rails obscured any view of the town until she reached the low trestle bridge, where the landscape stretched out before her. In the afternoon sun, Mara picked out the town's water tower and the criss-crossing streets interwoven with three rivers, including the one the trestle bridge spanned. She hurried across it, hoping a train wouldn't arrive right while she was in the middle of the bridge. No train came and she continued at a walk. On the other side, a road crossed the tracks, heading south in the direction of the town, but it didn't feel right to go that way, so she pressed on along the rails. After another forty minutes, the tall trees on either side of the tracks gave way to smaller ones and the telltale signs of human development. She passed a cemetery and a smattering of homes. Ahead she saw what looked like a freight yard, with rusted out railway equipment, rundown boxcars and several one-storey buildings on the verge of dilapidation. The tracks ran parallel to a road at the top of the south bank. Thirsty and wary from the day's walking, Mara scaled the north bank and sat in the shade. She sipped from her canteen and let her back and legs relax. Cars passed on the road on the opposite side. Further down, beyond the freight yard, a wooden bridge stretched over the tracks. Cars zipped back and forth in either direction. The bridge made her think of the one in Blue Creek, where she'd given up her pursuit of Davis two days before.

Mara hummed "Tom Dooley," sitting on the north bank and sipped from her canteen. She saw a teenage boy walk up the tracks the way she'd done earlier. He didn't look like he'd come all the way from Blue Creek as she had, though. He climbed the south bank and walked along the road, pausing to look in her direction. Mara hummed low, looking up and down the tracks. She took another sip of her canteen. The boy moved on down the road away from her and she watched him go, then

118

capped her water and stood up. Her joints gave a healthy round of pops and snaps as she stretched. Gathering up her duffle bag, Mara walked to the wooden bridge on the other side of the freight yard and climbed up to the road. From there, she made her way into town.

* * *

Owen McCabe was not listed in the phone book.

Mara closed the book, replaced it in the phone booth and stepped back out onto the sidewalk. The park bustled as Mara crossed the gardened lawn next to the Town Hall. It was bigger than Blue Creek's municipal building by far. Everything about Orchard Bend seemed bigger, as small towns went. She found a seat on a bench, took off her jacket and set her duffle bag at her feet. It appeared the local teens were just getting out of school, probably writing exams, same as the kids in Blue Creek. Mara thought of Todd King and his friends in *The Yellow Canary*. It didn't seem real that it was gone. Or that Tom was gone—

Murdered, the captain corrected her.

—or that just a few days ago she'd been working in that diner.

Out of the corner of her eye, Mara saw a teenage boy and girl walking down the path in her direction. They veered onto the grass and away from her. A sudden headache made her jaw clench. She rubbed the bridge of her nose and waited for it to pass. Mara took a gulp from her canteen and decided to keep moving. She wanted to find a place outside of town to make camp, and a feeling in her gut told her to head west.

* * *

It wasn't a dell she found in which to set up camp, but a ravine near a long neglected bridge west of Orchard Bend. Following along the river bank, Mara came across the stone foundation of a long ago structure and beyond it a grove of white aspens. Anywhere in the ravine would make a good place to set up camp, but Mara kept walking deeper into the quiet grove, captivated by the stillness and shafts of light cutting through the late afternoon haze. As she moved between the graceful white of the aspens, she lost her footing on a stone. Her duffle slid from her shoulder and hit the ground. She recovered at once, but left the bag and continued onward, almost mesmerized.

Coming here was the right thing to do, came the captain's voice.

"Yes," Mara agreed. "It certainly was."

At last she stopped, not really knowing why. Mara looked around at the trees, which glowed in the patches of sunlight. She looked up at the canopy and the blue-white sky above, turning as she did. Her foot kicked loose a stone. When she brought her gaze back down, she saw the carving in the tree.

A flower.

Mara went to it, leaning in close, admiring the work, simple, but clearly a rose. She straightened up, turned to retrieve her duffle bag and saw the other carving in the tree opposite the flower. To the uninitiated, it might look like an "L" growing out of the side of a "P," but Mara knew this symbol.

"The Fighting Dragons," she whispered. "Breathe fire and kick ass."

Recollections both hazy and indistinct swam to the surface. Mara had heard of Fort McDaniel, the home base of The Fighting Dragons, an elite division. She herself had never been there, but she'd know the symbol anywhere, even this crude carving.

Mara caught movement out of the corner of her eye and spun around, her hand dropping to the knife on her hip. Her eyes flicked about, scanning, but she saw only underbrush in the grove. She relaxed and lifted the canteen from over her shoulder. She drank the last of the water, making a note to refill it from the river. Casting a glance at the carvings once more, Mara went to retrieve her duffle bag. She walked a short distance from the grove to make camp at the bottom of a low hill. The storm a month earlier had left deadfall everywhere, most of it dry. The grove in the ravine felt even more secluded than the dell back in Blue Creek and Mara found a small

120

rivulet near her camp. She bathed nude in the water, scrubbing off two days of steady foot travel and then washed her hair. The cold water felt wonderful in the warm air. Refreshed and clean, she wrapped herself in a towel and rung her hair out on the shore.

Again, she spotted movement not far away to her right, a person standing there watching her. In a swift movement she unsheathed the knife lying on top of her clothes, but no one was there. Now Mara didn't doubt her senses. Someone *had* been standing there, looking at her. She surveyed her surroundings, knife tight in her grip. She listened for footfalls or snapping twigs and heard nothing. She waited, her senses keen. Minutes passed. At last she dressed, figuring whoever was out there would see what they'd see. Only it didn't feel like she was being watched anymore, despite what her eyes insisted they'd glimpsed. When she had her boots on, she made her way to the spot where she saw the figure and found no trace. No footprints, nothing disturbed, no evidence anyone had stood there. To be thorough, Mara scouted the area, working her way to the old stone foundation and back through the grove. Other than her, it didn't look like anyone had come through this area in a long time.

Back at her camp, she prepped her fire and filled her empty cans with water to boil, then started the fire and cooked a can of spaghetti. She boiled the water as she ate, watching the sun descend in the sky. Thoughts of Tom and her brief time in Blue Creek seemed distant now and she was grateful for that. The only feeling that hadn't changed was her desire to find Owen McCabe. It might take some doing, but he was here and Tom Dooley's murder would not go unanswered.

In the failing light of dusk, Mara once more hummed the murder ballad "Tom Dooley" and poured the boiled river water into her canteen. When she finally climbed into her sleeping bag, sleep took her faster than it had in days.

***

June 12, 1953

121

Orchard Bend

Mara dreamt of skeletons.

Someone whispered to her.

You've come at last, said the feminine voice, soft, airy, like a spring breeze. Mara thought she sounded sad.

The skeletons lay in a dark place, one Mara could not quite make out. She saw shapes in the shadows, what looked like a chair lying on its side and a potbelly stove. The skeletons were long dried, covered in rags that had once been clothes, both lying on the floor, one missing its head and an arm. The other sat across from its grisly companion, its skull on its lap as though it had rolled off its neck.

Where am I? Mara asked.

The place we all come to, eventually, the voice said.

Mara looked around for the source of the voice and found herself standing in the grove at sunset, next to the tree with the crude Fighting Dragon "L-P" carving on it. With a pen knife, a dark-haired teenage girl carved on the tree opposite it, her face as if in a trance. Mara looked closer and saw the girl's delicate fingers guide the blade to etch the shape of a flower into the bark. When the girl finished her task, the voice told her "Thank you." The girl put the knife away, lay on her back on the ground and closed her eyes. Mara thought she looked peaceful and serene as she slept there in the hazy summer light of the grove.

Without warning, the girl's body turned black, charred flesh covering her bones. Mara wanted to cry out at the awfulness of it, but no sound came out. The body, moments ago lovely and peaceful, crumbled and decayed into the ground. Mara turned away to see the translucent, spritely apparition of the girl standing next to her, watching what had once been her earthly vessel collapse into dust. This dark-haired ghost looked up at Mara, gave a bright smile and skipped away through the trees. The girl's spirit seemed happy, but Mara watched her with sadness.

Around Mara, the very air began to brighten, the light grew cold and the grove disappeared, replaced with a clinical-looking room. The two skeletons from the dark place lay side by side on adjacent tables, one skeleton still incomplete, missing its arm and its skull. Mara looked around and saw no one, but heard the distant sound of two male voices. The willowy spectre came into view and stood between the tables where rested the skeletons. The spectre's fair hair was much lighter than the teen girl's and it blocked Mara's view of the apparition's face. She stood taller than the spirit of the teen girl and Mara moved to her, around the tables on which lay the remains. At Mara's approach, the fair-haired spectre spoke and Mara realized it was the same soft voice she'd heard before in the dream.

Stop him, the spectre said. *He's a prisoner who cannot be allowed to escape.*

Mara halted, looking at the slender apparition. Again the scene shifted, moving through a grey world all too familiar to Mara. It lasted only a moment, but Mara had to fight down the raw panic at seeing the Breach. When she found herself in a dimly lit, barren hall, with the grey vision of the Breach gone, Mara's panic was replaced with horror. The scene was like a tableau, with Mara standing behind a blonde gunslinger who knelt over the body of a man on the floor. His chest had been blown to pieces. The woman's left thigh was bloody and her right arm hung limp at her side; the ghastly aftermath of a battle between the dead man and the lady gunfighter. Mara wasn't sure how she knew that, but she was certain it was accurate. However, the truly horrible part came in the form of the thing standing over both of them. Whatever had been human in this creature had long ago withered into a grotesque echo of a man. Mara had trouble making out this dark inhuman form, but there was no mistaking the gaping holes where eyes ought to have been, or the terrible gap where she expected to see a mouth. Mara could also make out its scraggly, thick beard and ragged hair. What Mara could discern of its clothes spoke of a ratty combination of flak gear and an improvised collection of animal skins.

As if in slow-motion, the tableau began to move. The woman looked up from the dead body on the floor. Two men approached her, both armed, one with his shotgun trained on the dead man. The muffled sound of voices came again as the men spoke, but it was the woman Mara concentrated on. She looked not at the men, but at the thing staring down at her.

"I know you," the woman said.

"Major, it's me," the thing replied.

As the woman collapsed, the dream broke apart. Mara awoke in the predawn darkness, looking up at the stars glittering in the deep blue sky. Where often her dreams became little more than images, thoughts and feelings after she awoke, fragments really, this one remained vivid, especially the hideous dark thing with holes where eyes should have been. The thought of him, of it, gave Mara a chill. She curled her sleeping bag around her.

* * *

With his flashlight picking out the way, Tyler Brand moved between the cemetery's even rows of marble and stone. He caught the odd name here and there. *Cooper. Smith. Anderson. O'Malley.* He moved past gravestones so faded with time he could no longer read the names carved into them. When he came to the wrought iron fence surrounding the McCabe plots, Brand threw his coat over the top to protect him against the sharp points. He set his flashlight down and scaled over. Inside, he reached through the fence, retrieved his flashlight and walked to Gabby McCabe's unmarked grave. Brand suspected that if Owen McCabe could have his way, he'd see to it his granddaughter's grave went unmarked for the rest of time.

"Hi, Gabby," Brand said. "I hope you're proud of me, babe. I did it. I stole Owen's ledger. I dropped it off at the sheriff's doorstep. Owen's days of freedom are numbered. When Sheriff Thorn reads it, when he reads Owen's confession about having your parents killed, that will be it. When he reads Owen's mad ramblings about a shadowy *prisoner* killing you, they'll lock him up and throw away the key. Well, that's if they don't decide to execute him for murder instead. Either way, he's done. I just wish you could've lived to see it."

Brand looked up at the stars through his wet eyes.

"I miss you, Gabby. I'll always miss you," Brand said. "I wish I could stay, but I can't. After Owen's long gone, I might come back. I can't stay because if he figures out I took the ledger, I'm a dead man. I'm sure he'll put it together in the morning, that it was me who took it. But I'll be in the city by then, on a plane, headed far away. I'm not even going home tonight, it's too dangerous. He has a cop on his payroll, Lieutenant Pine. On the chance Owen is wake now, sicking that lapdog on me, going home would suicide. I've got money and the clothes on my back. It will have to be enough."

Brand looked back down at the grave and touched the cold earth.

"I love you, Gabby," he said. "Visit me in my dreams, okay?"

Brand rose, turned away from Gabby's grave and walked to the fence. He climbed back over, retrieved his coat and headed between the rows of gravestones to the entrance. He walked down the road, got into his car and drove away from Orchard Bend. He did not look back. His life in the small town was done. In the morning, when Brand didn't call or show up to work, his editor at the Orchard Herald would wonder where he was, but wouldn't raise a stink, at least not for another day or two. Brand wouldn't even be in the country at that point.

Ty Brand drove past the sign saying *You Are Now Leaving ORCHARD BEND. Safe Travels!*

"Bye, Gabby."

15

The Orchard Herald, October 25, 1886
THE CASE OF LAURA O'MALLEY STILL UNSOLVED
By Thomas Buchanan, Editor

The case of Laura O'Malley looms like a thundercloud over Orchard Bend, its shadow seeming to engulf the light of the town's very soul.

"No stone will remain unturned," said Sheriff Clem Wilson, speaking from his office at the jailhouse. He declined to comment further when asked about details of the case.

The mourning of Laura O'Malley by her dearest friends has abated little in the eleven weeks since her death.

"She was a joyous soul and a good friend," reflected a teary-eyed Miss Rebecca Clarke, who with Master Billy Howard had known the victim since they were young children. "It's awful that no one yet knows what happened to her."

"I think about her every day," Billy told the Herald. "I have faith Sheriff Wilson will bring Laura's killer to justice."

* * *

October 30, 1886
Orchard Bend

Rose Adelaide, along with a good many of the townsfolk, walked the streets of Orchard Bend that evening in her finest attire, the dress she reserved for only special occasions. She received compliments from passersby and complimented others in return. She made her way to where the crowd gathered outside the now-completed Town Hall. The stone and brick edifice stood two impressive storeys high, capped with a decorative steeple-like lantern pointing to the sky. It glowed high above the people, golden against the cold blue dusk. When Maxwell McCabe put forth the idea of a Town Hall a year ago, Rose had hoped to dissuade the Council of Aldermen and argued in favour of building a new church-schoolhouse, one large enough to house the growing population. Her efforts failed. Now she stood in the cool air duly taking in the imposing monument and reflected that it really did speak of status and vision. The town seemed bigger now, more important. She didn't know how much of that was an illusion cast by the mere spectacle of the structure, but the town had indeed grown over the years and would continue to grow. The Town Hall seemed to declare that intention with great volume.

"It's quite a sight, wouldn't you say, Miss Adelaide?" asked Dr Shaw, sidling next to her. He looked smart in his top hat and overcoat.

"I cannot disagree, Doctor," Rose replied.

"A thought occurs to me," the doctor said, "and it's perhaps my age talking, but..."

He trailed off, looking at the Town Hall with an expression Rose couldn't read, something between sadness and contentment.

"Do go on, Doctor," Rose said, taking his arm in hers and giving him a pat on his sleeve. He looked at her with a smile.

"Well, Miss Adelaide, as I look upon this grand achievement, my thought is that I gaze upon something that will outlast us all," Shaw said, wistful in his musing. "We are being given a glimpse into the future, to a point in time beyond all of us here. It might simply be the size, but I look at this structure and I feel myself a wee bit smaller. One day I'll be dead and buried, but this will remain."

"Goodness, Dr Shaw," Rose said, letting her surprise show, "such a perspective in this time of celebration. I'm not sure many here wish to be reminded of mortality."

Shaw put his hand on hers, their arms still locked, and looked around them.

"No," he said, "I don't believe they do."

127

Silence descended between them with that sobering thought. They moved together with the rest of Orchard Bend to the front steps of the Town Hall. When they got closer, Rose spotted Maxwell and Gertrude McCabe greeting townsfolk along with other prominent citizens. The schoolteacher guided the doctor towards the wealthy couple.

Maxwell shook the hand of Reverend Thomas as Rose and Shaw reached the top of the stairs. Gertrude saw them first and her face lit up.

"Doctor, Rose, how wonderful to see you both!" she exclaimed.

Shaw tipped his hat.

"Mrs McCabe, it is always a pleasure," he said.

"I must say," Rose admitted, "even as I've watched this project come to fruition almost daily, to at last see it completed, well, it is impressive."

Gertrude took Rose's free hand.

"I promise, Rose, I'll speak with my husband about directing his attention to the needs of the school now that work on the Town Hall is concluded," Gertrude said.

"What's that you say, my love?" Maxwell now turned his attention to his wife as the Reverend went inside. "About the completion of the hall? There is much to do yet filling its grand interior with municipal agents, chief among them a mayor. We must set up an election board, among other things."

"I was saying to Ms Adelaide, Maxwell, that the school is overdue for consideration in matters of increased funding."

"Quite right, my dear," Maxwell said, looking from her to Rose. "Draw up a list of needs, both immediate and long term, and I'll see to it the aldermen give it due consideration at our next meeting. But do let me personally thank you for all your hard work over the years teaching our children, Ms Adelaide. I expect we'd be lost without you."

"Mr McCabe, I strive only to do my very best in the eyes of my Lord and my employer. Your words mean a great deal to me, as does your support," Rose said, looking him straight in the eye.

"How about we head inside, Miss Adelaide?" Shaw suggested, looking past them into the hall.

"Do go inside," Gertrude said, her eyes alight. "You will be doubly impressed!"

"We'll speak more, Gertrude," Rose said as she stepped away from them toward the door, with Dr Shaw in tow.

"Yes, we will, Rose," Gertrude replied with a wave.

As they walked through the doors and into the foyer, Rose found several of her older students tasked with taking the guests' coats. She handed hers to Rebecca Clarke, along with her bonnet, while next to her Dr Shaw gave his overcoat and top hat to Billy Howard.

Rose heard music coming from the grand assembly hall beyond, upbeat and energetic. A buzz filled the air, the way it did at weddings or the annual town picnic. Rose couldn't help but smile. Inside, ribbons and flowers decked the hall, adding a touch of colour to the otherwise bare interior. The tall, imposing wooden columns ran the length of the room, from the main entrance where Rose and Shaw stood, to the wide stage at the far end. The five piece ensemble consisted of two women and three men. A banner above the stage proclaimed them to be the Blue Creek Family Jug Band. As they brought the song to a rousing finish, applause rippled through the hall. They then started in on the next number, a rollicking piece Rose didn't know. Dr Shaw, grinning from ear to ear and clapping along, went to retrieve some cider. The rich smell of the hot apple drink filled the air as much as the festive atmosphere.

From her hand bag, Rose produced a small notebook and a pencil. She wanted to capture the moment.

The town needed this, she scribbled. *After such a horror we experienced so recently, so many unanswered questions, the grip of fear and paranoia at last seems to abate, if only a little. That small relief is welcomed by all.* When she returned to her cottage later that night, she would transcribe the scribbled thoughts into her diary. Still beaming, she slipped the notebook and pencil back into her handbag.

Rose made her way slowly down the great hall, taking it all in. The carpentry and masonry were fine and understated. The wood glowed from the light of the many lanterns about the room.

"Miss Adelaide!"

Rose turned to see Irene Sullivan coming toward her, with Sheriff Wilson following a few paces behind.

"Irene," Rose smiled, "please call me Rose. It's been some years since you were my student."

"Rose," Irene said, as if testing it out. "Thank you."

"Miss Adelaide," Wilson said, "I was wondering whether you knew if Ms Dale would be here tonight. Mr McCabe said she was due back in town today."

"I had heard that also, Sheriff," Rose said. "Alas, I have not seen her."

Wilson frowned, looking back at the entrance to the hall, probably hoping Emery Dale would appear. Instead, he saw someone else, Thomas Buchanan, editor and owner of the Orchard Herald newspaper. Wilson went to him. Buchanan did not see the sheriff approach, so engrossed was the editor in jotting down his notes. Rose and Irene watched as a heated Wilson engaged the newspaper man as Dr Shaw returned with the cider.

"The article Mr Buchanan ran in the paper the other day has stuck in Clem's craw," Irene said, shaking her head. Her eyes shot daggers at the editor as Wilson gave Buchanan a piece of his mind. "Did he really think Clem needed a reminder that poor Laura's killer is still at large?"

Buchanan, for his part, did not take Wilson's words lying down. In the din of the assembly hall, Rose could not hear the exchange, but Buchanan responded, gesturing and pointing around the room as Wilson stood with his hand on his hips. When he finished having his say, Buchanan turned and walked away, neither withered, nor put out by Wilson's criticisms. Wilson watched him, shaking his own head. Irene started toward him, but Dr Shaw stopped her.

"Let me talk to him," Shaw said. Irene balked.

"I'm perfectly capable of comforting him, Doctor," she said.

"Yes, I have no doubt," Shaw replied. "But please trust me, *as a doctor.*"

Though she didn't like it, Irene gestured him forward and Shaw went to where Wilson stood brooding on the far side of one of the columns.

As much as Orchard Bend needed this celebration of the new Town Hall, Rose guessed the sheriff would find little comfort in it. Shaw put a hand on the man's shoulder and said something to him. Wilson nodded. Shaw led him away and Rose turned back to Irene.

"I think this place needs some paintings on the walls," Irene said, attempting to change the subject. "Isn't that the thing they do in important buildings?"

"Yes," Rose said. "Some of them."

"I hear they plan to move the post office from Anderson Street to here... Oh, no," a look of concern swept over the young barmaid's face and Rose followed her gaze to the entrance.

In had walked Frances O'Malley, mother of the late Laura O'Malley, dressed all in black and clutching her small gold cross. She stood out like a thin, shadowy void in the colourful mass of people. They stepped aside as she passed. She walked down the center of the assembly hall, setting her own pace. Matilda Clarke, mother of Rebecca, went to her.

"Frances," Mrs Clarke said, "I came by your farm the other day--"

"Step aside, Matilda," Mrs O'Malley said, neither slowing nor looking at her friend. Matilda did as asked and watched her go by, standing helpless as her husband came to her side. Mrs O'Malley kept walking, looking at no one, her fingers moving over the crucifix in her hands. Rose saw the mud caked on the grieving mother's boots and the fringes of her dress.

She walked all this way from her farm, Rose realized, wondering how many miles that was.

Through all this, the band had played on, but the townsfolk grew noticeably quieter as they watched Mrs O'Malley cross the room.

"What is she doing, Miss Adelaide?" Irene asked.

Before Rose could answer, Mrs O'Malley stopped in the center of the hall and stood very still. The band's song came to an end and Rose heard one of the lady singers ask, "Is everything alright out there?"

In the hush that followed, Rose —only a few feet from the woman in black— could hear her speaking low. It took a moment for the teacher to make out the Lord's Prayer coming from Mrs O'Malley's lips.

Rose wanted to go to her, to try to speak to her, perhaps take her to a less conspicuous place. Then Frances O'Malley let out a shrill scream that ripped the air. Throughout the hall, hands covered ears against the piercing sound. When she stopped, the echo hung in the vast chamber a chilling second longer, before at last dying away.

When she spoke, Mrs O'Malley's once demur, airy voice growled and croaked as she addressed the room.

"Look at you," Mrs O'Malley said. She began to turn and those she faced backed away from the slight woman. The grieving mother seethed, "You gather here tonight and imbibe drink and fill your guts with slop. Sinners! All of you!"

"That's enough, Mrs O'Malley," Sheriff Wilson said as he pushed through the onlookers. He cast a glance to Irene and that was enough for Mrs O'Malley.

"Too interested in that painted Jezebel to solve my little girl's murder, aren't you, Sheriff?" She pointed the cross at him as she levelled her accusation. "Does she spread for you? Is that why you're too busy to find Laura's murderer?!"

"Now, listen here," Wilson said, taking Mrs O'Malley's arm. She yanked it away and pointed to Irene, who stood stunned and embarrassed with her hand over her mouth. Rose put an arm around her.

"A wretched evil lives in Orchard Bend and unless you wish your own head taken from your body like my Laura, you best mind what I say, harlot!" Mrs O'Malley lowered the cross, but kept her veiled stare fixed on Irene.

Wilson and Dr Shaw each took an arm and this time Mrs O'Malley did not resist. As they led her off, Irene pulled away from Rose.

"YOU HAVE BECOME A VILE, DISGUSTING THING, MRS O'MALLEY!" Irene screamed, her body shaking with fury. "LAURA WOULD BE ASHAMED OF YOU!"

Rose rushed forward and took her former student's hand, but Irene shrugged it off.

"I'm alright," Irene said.

Rose handed her a handkerchief and Irene used it to dab away the tears in her eyes.

"I'm sorry, Miss Adelaide-- I mean, Rose," Irene stammered. "I shouldn't lose my temper, but she has trespassed in our tavern once too many times, causing a ruckus, hurling other such obscene accusations, mostly at Clem for not solving Laura's murder."

"Her grief has consumed her," Rose said.

After a moment more of awkward silence, the band played on.

* * *

Rebecca remembered the quiet, kind, introvert of a woman Laura's mother had been. Laura's upbringing was pious and her parents strict, but they were warm and welcoming to others. Mrs O'Malley's appearance tonight, however, just about made Rebecca want to hide under a table. The grieving mother had swept through the foyer without a word or a look in their direction. Rebecca could almost taste the dread at seeing Mrs O'Malley appear at the celebration, the same woman who, in the wake of her daughter's death, took to raving in the street and shops about Laura's case. And when she screamed in the assembly hall and berated Sheriff Wilson and Irene Sullivan, everyone could hear her, even in the foyer. As Sheriff Wilson and Dr Shaw led Mrs O'Malley away, Rebecca mourned the loss of the good woman this mother had been. Then Irene Sullivan yelled her retort at Mrs O'Malley. That's when the veiled head of the woman turned and Rebecca thought she was looking into the eyes of madness. Mrs O'Malley, still being led out of the building, said something that chilled Rebecca to her core.

"She will feel great pain before she dies, the harlot," Mrs O'Malley spat.

In the hour that followed, Rebecca replayed the heart-wrenching scene over and over in her mind. At last, she forced it away and picked up a discarded newspaper sitting on a table near her, unfolded it and gazed at the piece about Laura. Mr Buchanan had quoted both her and Billy. Not for the first time did Rebecca feel some shame about it. The way Mr Buchanan had used what she said made it sound like she and Billy were criticizing the sheriff. Her mother and father had almost not allowed her to come to the grand opening tonight and Billy's parents had expressed similar displeasure.

Rebecca put the newspaper down.

With the flow of people now little more than a trickle coming into the new Town Hall, Rebecca took Billy's hand as they sat in the foyer.

"I don't think Mrs McCabe would mind if we went inside," Billy suggested. "That apple cider smells really nice."

"It's so crowded, though. I'd rather stay out here," Rebecca said. She batted her eye lashes and gave Billy a doe-eyed look. "You could run in and get some cider for the both of us."

That was all it took for Billy to jump from his seat.

"Absolutely! I'll be right back, don't go anywhere," Billy said as he crossed the foyer and pushed through the throng of people to get into the assembly hall. Rebecca got up and stretched.

When a small figure crashed into her leg, Rebecca spun around in surprise. The young boy landed on his bottom in the sitting position, laughing as he looked up at her.

"Sorry," said the boy.

Rebecca knelt down and patted him on his head.

"What's your name, young sir?" she asked.

"Owen McCabe," he replied.

"Oh, is your brother Henry?" Rebecca asked.

"Yes," Owen answered, his attention now drifting to the toy horse in his hand.

"There you are!" said Henry to Owen, appearing from the assembly hall. "Hi, Rebecca."

"Hi, Henry," Rebecca smiled. "Your little brother's adorable."

"Yeah, he is," Henry said, reaching down and picking the boy up from the floor with an exaggerated growl that made Owen and Rebecca laugh, "when the little Puck isn't up to no-good. Run away from me, will you? We'll see about that!"

Henry held his brother up in the air and Owen giggled. When Henry put him down, Owen tried to run, but Henry caught him again.

"Henry, good to see you again" said Billy as he approached with two mugs of apple cider.

"Hi," Henry said.

Billy gave Rebecca her mug and she sipped the steaming, fragrant liquid.

"Sorry, I only have the two," Billy said to Henry, indicating his drink.

"Oh, I get my fill of cider at home," Henry said with a shrug.

"You must get mighty tired of it," Rebecca said.

"Henry, Owen," said Gertrude McCabe as she approached. She saw Rebecca and Billy and smiled. "Oh, and Rebecca and Billy, my I nearly forgot. It seems most of the guests have arrived. Thank you for organizing the coats. Do enjoy the rest of the evening."

She slipped the two a dollar each and picked up Owen, who squirmed but let himself be held.

"And you, my little prince," Gertrude said to Owen, "our chariot awaits."

"Going home, mother?" Henry asked.

"Yes, it's well past Owen's bedtime," Gertrude said. As if to underline this point, Owen had draped himself on her shoulder and his eyes were half-closed. "Your father is inside giving a speech and I expect he'll socialize for some time yet." She headed for the door and waved at the kids, "You children have a pleasant evening."

Rebecca and Billy thanked her and Gertrude carried Owen from the foyer.

"How about we go outside," Billy said, taking Rebecca's hand. He scooped up their coats and led her out into the cool night air. Henry followed. They sat on the steps, listening to the music from inside, watching Mr Burke drive Mrs McCabe and Owen off home.

"My father says they're going to plant trees all out here, all over the lawn," Henry said.

"Is that so?" Billy asked, giving Rebecca's hand a squeeze. She looked at him and he gave a wink.

Henry continued, "And maybe even a flower garden, too, and—"

"Laura loved flowers," Rebecca said under her breath, looking up at the sky.

Henry gave a sound like he choked, then he coughed and fell silent, staring into the night.

"Want to go for a walk?" Billy asked Rebecca.

"We mustn't stray too far, Billy Howard," Rebecca smiled, "My parents are fond of you, but not so much as to allow that."

As Billy and Rebecca started down the steps, Henry followed, hands in his pockets. Billy squeezed Rebecca's hand and when she looked to him, he gave another wink. They stopped and he turned to Henry.

"You're going to catch your death, Henry," Billy said. "You should go get your coat."

Henry nodded.

"Yes, you're right," he said. "I'll be right back."

Henry jogged back up the steps and went inside. Billy gave Rebecca a fiendish grin and though she knew it was something of a mean trick to abandon Henry, she let Billy lead her away from the Town Hall steps, around the corner and down the dusty, shadowed side street.

"I think we can steal away a few minutes alone, don't you?" Billy said, holding Rebecca close. She answered with a kiss, hoping Henry wouldn't be too upset to find them gone.

* * *

After her tirade at the Town Hall, Wilson placed Frances O'Malley under arrest and both he and Dr Shaw took her to the jailhouse. She offered no struggle, but did not stop muttering her fevered displeasure. Wilson hoped she'd quiet down and sleep the episode off once in her cell, much like the drunks he sometimes had to escort from Sully's tavern. That was not to be. In fact she only became louder and more profane.

"I'm on to you, Sheriff," Mrs O'Malley proclaimed. "YOU are the wretched, Godforsaken monster who murdered my Laura! It's the only explanation. You murdered her, cut her fucking head from her fucking body and of course you're not going to turn *yourself* in. You Goddamn fucking DEMON SPAWN! MY DAUGHTER IS DEAD AND MY HUSBAND HAS ABANDONED ME AND IT'S ALL YOUR DOING!"

Shaw had seen enough and left the jailhouse. He returned soon after with his black bag and from it produced a bottle of laudanum. It took both men to get Mrs O'Malley to swallow the alcohol-morphine mixture. Mrs O'Malley struggled at first, driving an elbow into Wilson chest before he could lock her arms under his own. Then she refused to open her mouth. With Shaw's help, Wilson held her hands behind her back with one hand and applied pressure under her jaw with two fingers as Shaw poured the laudanum between her pressed lips. She sputtered and resisted, but eventually swallowed the liquid and the men let her go. She cursed them as they left, but soon lay on the bed. Though still muttering, the steam had gone out of her. Shaw stayed a while at the jailhouse to watch her, and when she fell into a deep, exhausted sleep, he left, promising to check in on her in the morning. Wilson saw the doctor out, then returned to his desk. Mrs O'Malley began to snore and Wilson sat thinking about Laura's case.

Dr Shaw's report sat on Wilson's desk. The old man had been thorough. Laura had suffered no apparent assault on her chastity. Her head had been removed with either an ax or a hatchet, but the doctor didn't think that was what killed her. Despite the damage where the head was severed, Shaw had picked out bruising around the neck and was positive it came from hands which strangled her first. The cartilage in her neck under the bruised area was also crushed.

Likely grabbed from behind, Doc Shaw had said. *The killer might even have dazed Laura with a blow to the head before strangling her, because there was no evidence she gave up much of a fight. Without the head, though, it's impossible to know that for sure.*

Wilson unlocked the desk's top drawer and took out Laura O'Malley's locket, holding it by the chain in the lantern light. It had been around her neck when Freddy Cook and his dog Cheat found the body. Wilson pressed the lock and opened it. Inside were two pictures, one of her father and one of her mother. Wilson looked from the photograph to Mrs O'Malley asleep in her cell and back again. The Frances O'Malley in the photo, the one with a daughter and a husband and a happy (if strict and pious) life, was hardly the same woman he'd jailed tonight after her outburst. The woman in the photo had everything to live for back when Mr Jackson took the photo at his studio. Now that woman's life was gone. And so was Jackson, for that matter, killed along with Sheriff Anderson.

Wilson sighed and closed the locket, putting it down on his desk. He unpinned his badge, the one that had belonged to Sheriff Anderson, and ran his thumb over the metal.

"What do I do that I haven't done already, Sheriff?" Wilson asked. He put the badge down next to the locket and watched the play of flickering light on the surface of each. The badge was flat and dull compared to the shine of the locket. Filled gold, Mr O'Malley had told him before the man left town and his wife. It had been within their price range, but the two parents still had to save to buy it from a catalogue at Reed's Store.

Wilson picked up the locket again and a thought occurred to him.

"Why didn't the killer take it?" he said out loud.

Wilson already had the notion that the killer knew Laura O'Malley, which ruled out any passing vagabonds or travellers. He'd looked into that angle anyway, to no avail, checking with Sully and Trask, who both rented rooms at their establishments. He'd also asked around the farms if anyone had hired an out-of-towner or had seen anyone about the countryside who wasn't local (or even anyone who *was* local). Now drifters or day labourers seemed to pass through Orchard Bend around the time of her death.

138

So why leave the locket?

The obvious answer was so as not to get caught with the evidence, but the killer had taken her head, which was still missing. That suggested the killer was interested in a trophy, perhaps, but not valuables.

Wilson dropped the locket on the desk as his tired brain slammed a memory into his mind in vivid detail.

It was April, the day they buried Jackson and Sheriff Anderson. At the front of the funeral procession, Wilson's emotions threatened to get the better of him. His eyes stung with tears that day, but he'd held them back. He was the new sheriff in Orchard Bend and couldn't start off weeping like a child, no matter how overwhelmed he felt. As the procession approached the small cemetery, a gathering of young folk was already there. Sammy O'Toole was among them. And Billy what's-his-name. And the Clarke girl.

And Laura O'Malley.

Sweet Jesus, Lord above, how had he forgotten that?

And there had been another boy there...

Henry McCabe.

Wilson felt dizzy. He put his head in his hands and squeezed his eyes shut. It made no sense, yet it made perfect sense.

Wilson had asked Miss Adelaide if Laura had any suitors and the schoolteacher didn't know. Of course she wouldn't know if Henry and Laura were friendly because Henry was schooled at home by his mother.

The McCabes were the wealthiest family in Orchard Bend, so Henry wouldn't need to steal the locket for its material value.

Laura had been decapitated with an ax, something every farm had, but something the McCabe Orchard would have, too.

And Henry had been there, at the cemetery, with Laura, the day of the funerals.

Wilson needed some air, so went outside, checking first that Mrs O'Malley still slept soundly. Standing on the boardwalk, Wilson turned the details over and over in his head. Doubt started to sink in. It was *possible* Henry McCabe was the killer, but there was no evidence.

"Evenin', boss," Deputy Green said as he rode up on his horse.

"Green," Wilson said with a nod. Wilson had been so preoccupied that he hadn't noticed Green's approach down the street.

"Something wrong, boss?" Green asked, climbing off his horse. As he tied the mount to the post in front of the jailhouse, Wilson didn't answer, lost as he was in his own thoughts. Green shrugged and pulled a small sack from his saddlebag. "Well, it's my shift, Sheriff, so you can head on home. Or back to the party over at the Town Hall."

Again, he didn't reply to Green, but stood with his hands on his hips, deep in thought.

Green took the notice off the door, the one directing visitors to the Town Hall. Wilson had placed it there as no one was on shift at the jailhouse during the party. In his haste dealing with Mrs O'Malley, Wilson had forgotten to take the notice down.

"Okay," Green said, heading to the door, "you have a good night, boss."

"Oh, Green. Mrs O'Malley is locked up in there," Wilson said. "She got to spraying fire and brimstone at the Town Hall tonight, real bad. Doc Shaw and I brought her here and gave her a shot of laudanum. If she's back to her right mind in the morning, or at least not cursing up a storm like she does, you can send her home. If you need the doctor, I think he's back at his rooms."

"Got it, boss," Green said and went inside.

Wilson stared at the closed door then turned and walked back toward the Town Hall.

* * *

Billy and Rebecca weren't around when Henry came out of the Town Hall. He'd only been gone a moment to retrieve his coat, so from the steps he looked for them around the front lawn. They were nowhere to be seen and Henry thought maybe they'd gone around the side of the building. Seeing no one there, Henry turned and found Sheriff Wilson approaching.

"Young Mr McCabe," Wilson greeted him with his hand out.

"Evening, Sheriff," Henry replied with an awkward smile. He cast about again for Billy and Rebecca as he shook the sheriff's hand. Surely they were around there somewhere.

"That's a mighty strong handshake you have there, son," Wilson said. "A strong handshake says a lot about a man."

Wilson adjusted the buckle of his gun belt and Henry continued looking around for his friends.

"Lose someone, Mr McCabe?" Wilson asked.

"I was to meet some friends out here," Henry said.

"And who would that be?" Wilson asked. "If I see them, I'll say you're looking for them."

"Billy Howard and Rebecca Clarke," Henry said. "They were right here when I went to get my coat."

"I see," Wilson said. "It stands to reason they're around here somewhere."

Henry stuffed his hands in his coat pocket. Had they tricked him? Surely not. They were his friends, why would they do that?

"They were friends of Laura O'Malley, too," Wilson said. Henry tensed, but continued to look up and down the side of the building. Wilson kept on, "I read what they said in the newspaper. Made me look right incompetent."

"Her death has hit this town hard," Henry said.

He knows! cried Henry's panic, but a stern voice imposed itself, crushing the fear.

No, he doesn't. He can't know, said the voice belonging to the Master of Life and Death. It was *his* voice, Henry's true voice.

Wilson nodded.

"That's true, Henry," Wilson said. "Did you know her? Laura O'Malley, I mean."

He does *know!* cried his panic.

The Master of Life and Death said nothing. He didn't have to.

"We'd met," Henry said, still not looking at Wilson.

"She was close to your friends, Billy and Rebecca," Wilson said with a heavy sigh. "I know it's hard on them that her killer is still out there. They said as much in the newspaper. What keeps me up at night is—"

141

Henry was fast. To Wilson's credit he'd expected he might get a reaction. Wilson's draw was quick, but not quick enough. Henry slammed Wilson into the wall with a backhanded punch to the man's chest. Henry grabbed for the sheriff's gun and Wilson pulled away, gasping. Henry recognized the sound of a man with the wind knocked out of him and drove his body into the sheriff's, pinning him against the wall. The gun hit the dirt and Henry staggered to pick it up. Wilson was heaving in gulps of air, clutching his chest, but still he came at Henry, who froze.

For a long time after, he thought about what happened next. Panic seized him and he couldn't think as he held the gun and saw Wilson charging him. Then the gun rose and Wilson's hand reached for it. The sheriff's mouth was open as he pulled in a gulp of air like a drowning man. Henry pointed the barrel of the gun at Wilson's gaping jaw. Then Henry, Master of Life and Death, squeezed the trigger.

Wilson was dead before he hit the ground.

16

October 28, 1886
Ashleyville

Residents of Ashleyville knew the sound of whistling when it came from Lake's Mercantile. Chester Lake whistled when he was in a bad mood and whistled louder when he was in a good mood. He'd sing when he was downright merry, his voice loud and a touch off key, but this was not one of those days. When the door of his shop opened and the little bell jingled, Chester looked up from his inventory log and his contented whistling came to an abrupt end.

"Oh, it's you," he said, with surprise and a touch of fear. "I wasn't expecting you today."

Emery Dale stood with her gloved hands behind her back, looking at him from under the brim of her hat. Chester waited for a reply and when none came forth, he coughed and put down the ledger.

"Yes, right," he said. "I have Mr McCabe's payment, plus interest. Last one, I reckon."

Dale waited for him by the front door as he went into the back, still rambling.

"Don't take this the wrong way, Ms Dale, but as grateful as I am to Mr McCabe for this loan, I'll be just as grateful to be finished paying off this debt," Chester said. When he returned, he had a cheque in hand. Dale saw his hand tremble a little as he handed it to her. It was like that with him every time she came through town. She took the cheque, examined it, then tucked it into her wallet.

"Is there anything else I can help you with?" Chester asked. With the final payment made, some of the nervousness left his voice; some, but not all.

"No," she said and turned to the door.

"Well, then, it was a pleasure doing business with you. And with Mr McCabe, of course. If you find yourself in need of anything, don't hesitate to come in."

The bell jingled as Dale opened the door and stepped outside. She stood on the boardwalk and adjusted her gloves before walking to where her horse was tied to a post, drinking water from a trough. She glanced in the window of Lake's Mercantile and stopped. With a wry smile she went back inside.

Clearly, Chester was not expecting to see Emery Dale again so soon.

"Um, welcome back, Ms Dale," he stammered, eying her now with a mix of suspicion and fear.

There was always a little fear, Dale mused, and probably always would be.

"How much for the picture frame?" Dale asked.

"The one in the window?" Chester asked in return.

Dale nodded and Chester retrieved the ornate frame for her. He read the price tag on the back.

"One dollar," Chester said. "It's a fine one, straight from New York City. But, um, seeing as we go back a ways, professionally, that is, well, I'd be happy to sell it to you for fifty cents."

"I'll take it," Dale said, taking out her wallet. She pulled a dollar and put it on counter. "For a dollar."

Chester looked at the bill, then to her, then back at the money like he didn't know what to do with it. Then he picked it up and rang her transaction through. That completed, he looked at her, still a little stunned, as if waiting for something to go wrong. Dale tucked her wallet back in her duster and put her hands on her hips, resting them on her gunbelts. Chester saw the guns and went pale, but still didn't move. Dale rolled her eyes and broke the silence.

"Here's a thought!" she said, "How about you wrap the frame and I'll be on my way before the Second Coming? I have other things to do today."

Chester jerked back to his sense and nodded.

"Yes. Yes, sorry," he said, picking up the frame and putting it on the stack of plain wrapping paper at the end of the counter. Nervous or no, the shopkeeper made quick work of the wrapping, finishing it with a bit of string tied around all four sides. When he gave her the frame, his hand was shaking again, subtle, but there. Dale took the package, thought about saying something but didn't, tipped her hat and left.

Outside, Dale put the frame in one of her saddlebags, and then walked around to the other side of her horse. The slender scabbard of her sword jutted from the other saddlebag. She undid it and lifted the sword and scabbard out, looped it over her shoulder and adjusted it until it sat just right on her back. A couple walking with their young son passed her on the boardwalk and did a double-take before hurrying along on their way. Dale watched them go, not bothered now by their fear. With the next part of the job, fear was the right response.

* * *

The watering hole on the other side of the tracks didn't have a name. It wasn't the sort of establishment that needed to advertise. The sorts of people who drank in places like this had no problem finding them. It lay at the end of a narrow, muddy corridor that could by a stretch of the imagination be called a street. The ramshackle structures, an assortment of tents and lumber assembled in vague approximation of habitable dwellings, were homes nonetheless. Dale passed these without affording them a look, but she could sense the eyes of a dozen onlookers watching her. Her boots sank in the mud with each step and she strode on without wasting any time. When a man sporting an eye patch stumbled from his humble abode and into her path, she stepped aside, but it wasn't enough. Before he ploughed straight into her while adjusting his trousers, her gloved hands grabbed the ragged, stained collar of his long johns. She used his momentum to hurl him into the adjacent wall. That the wall absorbed the blow without collapsing impressed Dale to no end.

145

"Hey, watch it, ya no-good..." cried the one-eyed man, but his voice trailed off when he saw her. Or rather when he saw she was armed. "Beggin' yer pardon, Miss. Lost my footing, I dare say. I blame the eye patch."

He gave the leather pad covering his eye socket a tap and straightened himself up. Dale left him without a word and continued on to the watering hole.

A cloth hung over the doorway in the absence of an actual door. Dale moved it aside and entered. She stamped the mud from her boots and peered through the murk that filled the room. The dive had no windows, just cracks of light seeping in between the mismatched boards that constituted the walls. A simple bar stood at one end, with a lantern hanging above it. The patrons, appearing content to remain in the shadows, sat on old crates at boards propped up as tables. Nearest to her, a few looked up from their drinks then went back to their business. Dale could also make out a card game at one table, but didn't see the man she came here to find.

Mr Eye Patch stumbled in behind her and made his way to the bar. The bartender leaned his rotund form on the warped wooden countertop and it bowed under the weight.

"You mind yourself, Black," the bartender warned.

"I have taken a vow, my good man," said Black. "I will bring no further ill upon your fine establishment. I swear."

Black crossed himself and put a coin on the table. The bartender poured him a shot and Black picked up the glass. Before he could down it, Dale's gloved hand clamped his wrist.

"Come now, Miss," Black grumbled. "I apologized for before!"

"I'm looking for someone," Dale said.

"If you're in the habit of preventing people from enjoying their refreshments, this someone may not want to be found by you," Black said.

Dale snickered and let go of his wrist. Black took the shot before anything else could stop him. Dale took out her wallet and put a few more coins on the table.

"The next two drinks are on me—"

"Bartender!" Black called out. "I'll have another."

"...*After* you answer my questions," Dale finished.

"You drive a hard but fair bargain," Black said. "What would you like to know?"

"You acquainted with a man named Cavanaugh?" Dale asked.

"Quick Harry?" Black asked.

"That would be him," Dale nodded.

"What would your business be with the fellow?" Black asked, his eye narrowed. "If I may ask?"

"He has information," Dale said.

"I reckon your association with Quick Harry has concluded," Black said as the bartender poured his next shot. Black gulped the drink and let out a satisfied gasp.

"Why do you say that?" Dale asked.

"The man is going to hang by week's end," Black replied.

* * *

The size of the train station told everyone who saw it where the power lay in Ashleyville. In its three storeys it housed the Central United Continental Railroad Company's regional offices and it dominated the view of everyone who set their gaze in that direction. Even with its imposing size, the station carried a beauty and elegance of design, from the rich timber to the fine masonry. In stark contrast, however, the squat single storey of the Railroad Police station across the street, with its dull grey stone and utter lack of ornamentation reminded visitors that this railroad town favoured law and order. Despite having escorted Maxwell McCabe to the CUC's offices several times over the last seven years, Emery Dale had not once set foot in the police station.

Until today.

Dale climbed off her horse, tied it up and stepped inside. Where the Orchard Bend jailhouse had only two cramped cells and only enough space for an office, the Railroad Police station sported an impressive, wide front hall. Photos of noteworthy captures and arrests decorated the walls, as did the CUC emblem. A mannequin stood blank-faced in the corner wearing the distinctive blue and gold Union uniform from the war. Unlike the empty holster, the scabbard still bore its sabre. A voice began to sing down the hall behind her and Dale turned. The hallway led to the holding cells and Dale counted a half dozen individual ones and two larger pens at the end. Imprisoned men occupied three of the cells and what appeared to be a couple of tramps lay curled up on the floor of the larger cells. From one of the solitary cells came a man's deep voice singing of someone named Henry Lee. Dale knew that voice.

She turned and saw a tall, well-groomed man in a trim uniform crossing the hall in her direction.

"Ah. You would be Emery Dale, is that correct?" the man asked. Dale put him at approaching fifty, but still fit enough for the job.

"Yes, I am," Dale said.

The man offered his hand and Dale shook it.

"I'm Lieutenant Harper," the officer said. "I run this station. I supposed it was only a matter of time before I'd see you here today."

"You were expecting me?" Dale asked.

"I've been aware of your presence in town, as is my job," Harper said, leading her away from the cells to the large back office, the walls replete with wanted posters and similar documents. The tidiness of the space served as another reminder of how far she was from Orchard Bend. At their desks, two plain-clothes officers paused in their conversation to watch her go by, one with red hair and one blond. Dale tipped her hat to them and they returned uncomfortable nods. Harper saw this and stopped.

"Ms Dale, might I introduce two of my officers," he said. Both men stood up straight, almost at full attention. "This is Officer Byrne..."

"Ma'am," said the red-haired policeman.

"...and Officer Rogers," Harper said.

"Pleased to meet you, Ms Dale," said the blonde.

"As you were, officers," Harper said, leading Dale away.

When they came to Harper's office door, he said, "Join me in here, if you would."

Harper held the door open and gestured her inside. Dale slipped the sword off her back and set it against Harper's desk

148

as she sat down. Harper took his seat and glanced at her sword.

"Charming weapon, Ms Dale, I must say," Harper smiled. "I'm an admirer. Do offer correction if I'm in error, but you carry a curiously designed hand-and-a-half sword. It's shorter than one would think standard, but I attribute that --and I mean no disrespect-- I attribute that to arm length. It must make the sword easier to draw from the back, yes?"

"It does," Dale said, her eyebrow raised.

"I was new to this post when I first heard your name," Harper said, leaning back in his chair. "You single-handedly killed the notorious Underwood Gang in 1879. Did you know they held up a Western Star stage on the outskirts of town that spring? That was my first case as the head of this station. A CUC official was aboard the stagecoach, along with one of our undercover officers. Both were killed, along with the driver. They let the woman live and I thought it was a sign that despite their violence Ernest Underwood and his gang had a line they wouldn't cross. Women. Likely children, too."

Harper shook his head and leaned forward, fingers intertwined on the desk.

"Turns out, I was wrong," he said. "In Orchard Bend, Ernest shot a schoolteacher and almost shot a boy. And they were stopped. By you."

Dale said nothing, waiting for him to get to the point.

"Anyone is capable of anything, Ms Dale," Harper said. "That's what I learned those first weeks commanding in Ashleyville. The Underwoods taught me that. You taught me that in your own way. And Quick Harry Cavanaugh taught me that when he conspired to steal horses and supplies from the CUC. Somehow, he convinced the right person to give him a job standing watch at the railroad stockyard. He had nearly unimpeded access to everything, so he gathered up some new friends and put together a plan. Too bad for him, one of his new 'friends' worked for me. This time, Harry won't be quick enough to escape the noose."

Dale nodded.

"You have him in a cell," Dale said. "I heard him singing."

"Yes, he does have that habit," Harper said. "I expect now you're going to ask to see him, correct?"

"Yes," Dale said.

"There's a judge set to arrive in the morning," Harper said, standing up. "I expect the trial to be quick. This judge is familiar with the CUC. We have a good rapport."

"You have the three men out there dead to rights, it would seem," Dale said. "I only need a minute."

"Since I'm such an admirer, Ms Dale, you can have two," Harper said with a wink. "After that, perhaps you would join me for a meal at the Clementine."

"That sounds delightful, Lieutenant," Dale smiled.

He led her back through the office area and the two plain-clothes officers watched her pass, exchanging a look between each other.

"You'll have to leave your weapons here," Harper said. "Can't have the prisoners trying to make a grab for them, you understand."

"Of course," Dale said. She took the sword from her back, unholstered her guns and unsheathed her knives, putting each on a table. Harper put his own six-shooter down next to her weapons and the two continued to the cells. The plain clothes officers, Byrne and Rogers, never took their eyes off her.

As Harper led her through the foyer, he pointed to the mannequin.

"Didn't know what to do with the old uniform after the war," he said. "It's travelled around with me in a trunk. It's been a lot of places. Chicago, Springfield... Then, we came by the mannequin on a case and wouldn't you know it, a match meant to be. Perfect fit."

Harper chuckled to himself and Dale flashed him another smile. He continued on to the cells and Dale turned her attention to the prisoners. In his cell, Quick Harry lay on his bed singing about a man named Tom Dooley who was going to hang. Dale stopped as a deep headache went through her. She shook it off and rubbed her temples.

"You feeling unwell, Ms Dale?" Harper asked.

"It's nothing," Dale said. "The day has been a long one."

150

"They don't seem to get any shorter, do they?" Harper mused. He walked up to Harry's cell and said, "You have a visitor, Cavanaugh."

Harry stopped singing and sat up on his cot.

"That's Quick Harry to you, you Pinkerton!" Harry said.

"Watch it, son, or I'll change my mind about letting her see you," Harper said.

Harry put his hands up and said nothing.

Dale looked back towards the office space and saw the two officers trying to look inconspicuous as they watched her.

"Two minutes, Ms Dale," Harper said.

"If you could afford us some privacy, Lieutenant, I would be much appreciative," Dale smiled.

Harper looked at Harry, then back at her.

"As you wish," Harper said. "Don't approach close to the cell, don't hand anything to the prisoner and if the prisoner attempts to hand you anything, do not take it. Understood?"

"Yes," Dale said.

"Very well," Harper said. "Two minutes."

Harper went back to the office area and Dale watched him for a moment before turning to Harry.

"You alright?" she asked him.

"Nothing a good drink wouldn't cure," Harry said with a humourless laugh. "I am a might glad to see you, Ms Dale."

"Indeed," Dale said. She produced a key from her pocket, a large one that she slipped into the cell's lock. She turned it and the mechanisms inside clicked and rattled. The door sprung open with a creak.

"Hey! Stop what you're doing!" Harper ordered when he turned and saw Dale freeing his prisoner. The plain-clothes officers rushed forward as Harper reached for the gun that wasn't in his holster. He called out over his shoulder, "Sound the alarm!"

"That won't be necessary, Lieutenant," said the blond officer, Rogers. He had his gun drawn and levelled at Harper.

"Rogers, you better explain yourself, son," Harper said in a quiet voice that did little to hide his rising fury. Dale, with

Harry behind her, reached the end of the cells near the front hall and moved past Harper toward the front door.

"You're under arrest," Rogers told his lieutenant.

The crack of a gunshot startled the four of them. In the sudden haze of black powder, Rogers looked down at the exit wound in his shirt and the red stain spreading out from it. He looked back up at Dale in disbelief and fell to the floor. Behind him, the red-haired officer, Byrne, looked to Harper, sharing almost the same look of disbelief his victim had. His gun wavered as his hand shook.

Dale saw this and moved, crossing the half dozen feet to Harper as he turned to her. With a second to react, Harper threw a punch which Dale blocked without thought. Harper was not inexperienced and let loose a flurry of jabs and punches. He was sloppy, but strong and fast. Dale was faster, her hits connecting as Harper flailed. When she heard Byrne's gun cocking, she yelled out, "Harry! Outside! Now!"

Harry ran to the door and the officer fired. Harry cried out in pain. Byrne swung around, bringing his gun to bear on Dale as her fist connected with Harper's face. She felt his jawbone break under her gloved knuckles. Byrne cocked the gun and fired, but Dale was moving again, flanking him. The bullet ripped through her duster. Her foot found the seat of a chair as a step onto a desk. Byrne swivelled, firing again and again at his moving target as she got behind him. The acrid smoke from the gun clogged the room. Out of ammunition, the red-haired officer dropped to his knee and grabbed Rogers' gun.

By now, though, Emery Dale had her sword.

The officer didn't get off a single shot before Dale sailed over a table, her duster flying about her. The blade of the sword slashed across the man's chest.

From outside, Dale heard fists pounding on the front door. She looked up, eyes burning from the gun powder in the air. Harper had barred the door with a heavy wooden beam. Clutching his broken jaw, the lieutenant crouched like a dangerous cornered animal. Harry lay in a bloody mess at his feet, gasping and clutching his chest.

"It's over," Dale said, tense and on her guard.

Harper stumbled to the mannequin that wore his old Union uniform and Dale realized too late what he was doing. She charged, but Harper had the sabre unsheathed in time. He dropped into a ready position and parried her attack. Their blades rang with each slash, thrust and parry. Harper knew his way around his weapon, the sabre slicing her duster, first once, then again. Dale's sword found his cheek and left it split, but he found an opening and his blade cut her abdomen. The wound was not deep, but it bled. Dale retreated a few steps and Harper grinned through his broken face, his jaw hanging open at an unnatural angle. Dale waited, blade ready, both hands tightening on the leather grip as she brought it to her own ready position. Harper held his sabre in one hand, crouched, poised to attack. Dale watched her opponent, focused on nothing but his stance, looking for a weakness, trying to anticipate his next move. His only way out of this was to kill her and Quick Harry. No witnesses against him. The prisoners in their cells could not see what was happening, but that wasn't stopping them from banging on their bars and shouting in confusion. Harper meant to go through her. It was his only chance.

There came a crash of breaking wood somewhere beyond Harper's office and Dale saw in the man's expression that those outside had broken through a back door. Harper knew he had to strike now.

* * *

He was faster than Dale thought possible.

* * *

When the four police officers stormed the room, they found carnage. Harper lay dead, still clutching the wound where Dale impaled him through the stomach. Dale herself knelt next to Quick Harry on the floor. His eyes appeared to regard her with soft affection, but she knew no life resided behind them. She

153

closed his eyes and closed hers as she let her head hang low over his body.

"Jesus, Mary and Joseph," muttered one of the officers.

"They're all dead," said another, "except her."

"Mr Beech is not going to like this," said a third.

Dale heard the steady click of footsteps from down the hall and opened her eyes when they stopped.

"What in the name of the Holy Goddamn Trinity happened here?" Beech gasped, taking off his smart, stylish bowler hat. "Miss Dale, explain this! Harper was to be taken alive."

Dale rose to her feet and faced the head of the railroad office. She fought down the urge to drive a fist into his salt and pepper moustache and break his teeth. She spoke low, her voice even and cold.

"That *was* the plan," she said, pointing to the body of the red-haired officer, "until this man decided to change it."

"Byrne?" said one of the officers, a man whom Dale thought might be handsome if not for the ugly scar on his cheek.

Dale looked Beech square in eye.

"You had this outfit under investigation personally," Dale said, clenching her fists to hide their trembling. "How did you not see he was in with Harper? This man, Byrne, killed Rogers and tried to kill me. Harper was not prepared to go quietly. And because of your shoddy intelligence, Mr Beech, Quick Harry is dead, too."

"Who in the hell do you think you are talking to, young lady?" Beech said, stepping forward, hands on his hips. "Our investigation was *thorough*. There was nothing to suggest Byrne was among Harper's circle of traitors. We vetted him. He passed every loyalty test."

"Until he gunned down a police officer in the back," Dale retorted.

Beech sneered.

"Remind me, Miss Dale," he said, "who came into my office telling me it was time to spring the trap on Harper, that he had your Quick Harry and was going to hang him? Oh, never mind, it's all coming back to me now. It was *your* idea. Well done, you executed your plan to perfection."

154

Dale fumed, her gloved hands now flexing.

"Maybe if we hadn't rushed into this endgame, your informant or friend or *lover,* whoever he was to you, wouldn't be lying dead over there," Beech growled.

"Harry made your case for you. He was worth a thousand of you, you disgusting shithole," Dale shot back.

Beech's open palm flew at her face, but her own gloved hand caught his wrist. In a quick motion, she twisted his arm at an unnatural angle and did not let up. Beech cried out in pain and looked over his shoulder at the nearest officer, the one with the scar.

"You there, arrest this woman!" Beech ordered him.

The scarred officer looked from Beech to his fellow officers, then shook his head.

"No, sir," he said. "I don't think that will happen today."

Dale let go and Beech clutched his wrist, staggering away. She picked up her sword and nodded to the officer with the scar. No one said anything as she gathered up her possessions. Donning her hat, she addressed the men.

"Make sure Harry is taken care of properly or we'll have words," Dale said. "A nice headstone and all, a full funeral, you follow?"

"We'll make sure it happens, won't we, Mr Beech," said the scarred officer. Beech muttered under his breath.

Sword in scabbard, Dale looped it over her shoulder and walked to the front door. Giving Harry a last look, she lifted the beam barring it closed and left the police station.

17

October 28, 1886
An Island

Rain, fog and hundreds of people filled the darkness of the park. Few took notice of the man who stumbled about in the murky gloom. His world had been reduced to a dozen feet in any one direction. He clutched a small computer with a spinning red circle displayed on the screen. It dangled from his hand and came close to dropping to the ground as he swayed across the grass. The man didn't notice the display change, the spinning red circle replaced by a blinking gold rectangle. Seconds later, the rectangle blinked off and the small computer went dark.

Moving through the steady drizzle, men in top hats and bowlers cast him fleeting glances. Ladies in ornate bustled dresses tucked themselves beneath the umbrellas held high by their male escorts. To the lost man, these people seemed to have come alive from an old photograph. Husbands and wives hurried past him. He found a tree and leaned underneath it, watching them. Ragged groups of families huddled close, weighed down with a burden of earthly possessions. They muttered in tongues the man thought were maybe Germanic or Slavic. The better dressed avoided these strangers and the man avoided everyone, watching their forms be consumed by the fog as they journeyed away into the night.

"This isn't the Breach" the man said. "What is this place? Where am I?"

He patted his body, reassured to feel himself real. He stared at the blank computer in his hand for many seconds, then undid a cargo pocket of his uniform pants and tucked the computer inside. He ran both hands over his close-cropped matted hair and gave his attire a cursory inspection. The light rain soaked his grey uniform. He straightened it without thinking, all the time looking around.

A gentleman and lady came out of the fog along the path like apparitions and stopped beneath the weak glow of a solitary lamp. The man beneath the tree listened.

"Such is the pity," the gentleman said, handing the umbrella to the lady. He did up his heavy coat as he went on, "For days, the men were rigged all about Bartholdi's statue. Did you see the picture in the *Illustrated?*"

"No, I didn't," the lady replied, her eyes scanning, trying to cut through the fog.

"The workers appeared the size of insects, dangling from her shoulders on lines, like sailors from the masts of ships," the gentleman said. "The view just now must be nothing compared to standing at her feet and gazing upon her colossus."

"Shades of 'Ozymandias,'" muttered the lady. She jerked to her left as harsh laughter came from the shadows not far away. The man under the tree could not see the source either, but remained on his guard.

"Come now, dear. As they say, she *enlightens* the world," chided the gentlemen, taking the umbrella. "Or she *will* when they at last set her alight out there. The ships were an impressive sight, nevertheless. The harbour must be chaos now, more so than is often the state of things."

The two made to leave and the man under the tree darted forward. The couple stopped, the gentleman gasping in surprise. The man halted a few feet from them and asked, "Where am I?"

The gentleman looked uncertain and switched the umbrella to his other hand, putting his free arm around his lady.

"What's that you ask?" said the gentleman. "Are you lost?"

The man looked around them.

"I *am* lost. What is this place?" he asked.

"The Battery," the lady answered.

"The Battery?" the lost man asked, looking to the ground.

"Forgive us, good sir," the gentleman said, "but we must be on our way. Foul weather and all. We do hope you find your destination."

"The Battery," the lost man said as if not hearing the gentleman. Undaunted, the gentleman and lady scurried off, vanishing in the gloom. The lost man mouthed the words and began to walk the path, leaving the glow of the lamp behind. As the brume enveloped him, the world turned grey and hazy. Everything became indistinct once more, even the looming collection of girders and supports reaching above him over the tree line like a great arm through the fog.

Fear sank in, soaking him much the way the rain soaked his clothes. There came the sound of footsteps behind him, shuffling and uneven, but moving in haste. The lost man turned, twisting his body and craning his neck.

A figure lurched its way along in his direction, a black silhouette whose distorted form caused the lost man to stop in his tracks.

"The Prisoner!" gasped the lost man. The shadow drew closer and the lost man stood frozen in horror, his mind racing. Any moment now this approaching abomination would look up. The lost man would see the horrible gaping eyeholes and disturbing maw where a mouth should be.

"Everything alright then, sir?" said a deep, male voice and the lost man spun back around. There stood a man with a heavy, black moustache, wearing a dark uniform. The two columns of buttons and the badge told the lost man this was a police officer.

"I am being followed!" the lost man said, stepping forward. The policeman stopped him, bringing his nightstick up to the man's chest.

"Followed, you say?" the policeman asked. "Followed by whom?"

The man turned and pointed back into the fog.

"There!" said the lost man, but the dark shape was gone.

"Can't say as I see anyone in particular," the policeman said.

"It was there! Behind me. Following me again," the lost man insisted, his voice shaky, his hands wringing together. He turned back to the policeman, who shrugged.

"I believe you, but whoever it was is gone," the policeman said. "The Battery is fit to rupture tonight with all the gawkers come to see the statue out there on Bedloe. And there are always meanderers from Castle Garden. Seems like the whole city came here to look across the bay, just to see that lady come alight. All for naught in this weather. Can't say I'm at all surprised some snotter had his eye on you. This cursed pea soup makes my job a damn sight impossible. Can't see much of anything more than a dozen paces on."

"The Prisoner moves still through the passages of the Breach," the lost man said to himself as he ran his fingers through his short wet hair.

The policeman gave him a quizzical look.

"That a bit of poetry, then?" the policeman asked.

The lost man looked at him and smiled.

Poetry, the lost man mused. *Yes, it almost* was *poetic, wasn't it?* The rest of his unit would've found it just as funny. Holtz would say he had a way with words. Dale would've told him to knock it off and get his head back in the game.

"Something like that," said the lost man, finding his voice clearer now, more certain. He straightened up his stance, squared his shoulders and tugged at his sleeve.

"What's your name, stranger?" the policeman asked.

"Liszt," the lost man replied. He tugged at his other sleeve first once, then again, turning his arm this way and that. Then he held out both arms and compared them. The first was still off. He tugged at it again.

Better, Liszt thought, giving a satisfied nod. *The captain would approve.*

"You don't say?" said the policeman as Liszt fussed with his uniform. "Like the composer?"

Liszt looked at the policeman, eyes wide, but with a smile inching at his lips.

"Yes," Liszt said, "just like the composer."

"I have a friend who works at the Old Yellow Brick Brewery, as we call it," the policeman smiled. "He sometimes let me sneak my mother inside to hear the music. She enjoys the 'Hungarian Rhapsodies.' Why it was almost a year ago to the day, last November, that she last heard one there. Poor old Liszt died not three months gone now and it breaks my mother's heart."

Liszt regarded him with an impassive stare. A glob of water dropped from the tree above and landed right on Liszt's forehead. It trickled down his brow and the side of his nose and Liszt didn't blink. He did not even notice. The policeman waved his baton at Liszt's attire.

"That's a curious outfit, Mr Liszt," he said. "I've seen just about every stitch on the travellers coming out of Castle Garden, but I don't recognize yours. The pattern, for instance..."

Liszt looked at his uniform, then to the policeman.

"It's camouflage," Liszt said.

"Is that supposed to be a Sergeant's rank there?" the policeman asked, pointing to the patch on Liszt arm. Liszt's head began to pound and it got harder to focus.

"Yes," Liszt said. "Sergeant Wilhelm Liszt, United States Army—"

"You'll forgive me, sir, but what sort of uniform *is* that?" the policeman asked, making little effort to hide his disbelief. "I ain't seen a uniform by that like in all my days on this job. And believe me, in this city I've seen some of the most—"

"This city!" Liszt interrupted, his eyes fixed unblinking on the policeman. "What city is this?"

The policeman shook his head.

"A few barrels have come off your wagon, haven't they? I can see it now," policeman said. "You spend time on Ward's Island?"

"Ward's Island," Liszt muttered, drifting back into his own thoughts. He tucked at his sleeves again, ran a hand through his hair a couple of times and rubbed his temple. "The Battery...?"

160

"Right then, fella, you and I are going to take a walk, see about getting you home," the policeman said, tapping his nightstick in his hand.

"Home," Liszt said, still deep in his own mind. He reached down, touched the cargo pocket with the small computer in it and gave it a little pat. The policeman watched him, cautious and tense. Then Liszt came out of the torrent of his mind and looked around. "You called it Castle Garden... This place, The Battery... Battery *Park!*"

"Yes, you're in the Battery park, on the island of Manhattan," the policeman said. "Geography not your strong suit, was it?"

"It started *here!*" Liszt said, looking this way and that, casting about for a direction in the fog. The policeman could only shake his head again.

"Seeing ghosts now, are we?" the policeman asked.

"Castle Clinton, Castle *Garden,* which way is it?" Liszt asked.

"What business do you have there this time of night, fella?" the policeman asked. "If you had family coming in, I expect you'd already know where it was."

"Maybe I can get back," Liszt said. "If I can find the Portal to the Breach, the one the scientists were studying, maybe there's a way in. It's frequencies and harmonics. Stevenson tried to explain it to me. It was under Castle Clinton, don't you get it? That's where it is. That where I have to go!"

"Settle yourself, fella. I assure you the outcome won't be to your liking if you don't," the policeman said, pointing his baton at Liszt. "I don't know what you're on about, but you're not getting into that immigration depot. There ain't nothing under Castle Garden but dirt and rocks and more dirt. And no one's called it Castle Clinton in years, not since it was a fort."

"Show me," Liszt said. "Do me that much."

"You keep from going off the rails, I'll take you there," the policeman said. "Not inside, mind you, but you'll see for yourself from the gate."

The policeman gestured back to the way Liszt had come and the two men walked through the deepening gloom.

"What day is it?" Liszt asked. "What's today's date?"

"October 28th," the policeman said.

161

"In the year...?" Liszt asked.

"Heaven help me, you don't know the year?" the policeman balked. "You really *do* need help, fella. It's 1886, not that it'll mean much to you shortly. Not much call for keeping the calendar straight out there on Ward's Island, I suppose."

"What's your name?" Liszt asked, "If I may ask?"

"Cochran," the policeman said.

There came a clattering rumble behind them and Liszt turned to see the boxy shapes of train cars rolling along the elevated tracks atop the girders and support beams he'd seen earlier.

"Just the Ninth Avenue Line, fella," Cochran said as the train disappeared into the darkness. "Another one will be along any moment. You want to see Castle Garden or stand here gawking?"

Liszt waited as the second train lumbered through the fog going in the opposite direction. Cochran spoke, but Liszt didn't hear him in the noise of the train as it passed. It didn't matter much what he said anyway, because Liszt killed him seconds later. The sound of approaching voices pulled Liszt back to himself and he gazed down at Cochran's body, flexing the hand that had snapped the man's neck. Liszt dragged the officer from the path and waited in the shadows as a chattering immigrant family went by.

When he stepped back onto the path wearing Cochran's ill-fitting uniform, the drizzle of rain had abated. He passed another couple, both well-dressed and talking in hushed voices. They nodded at Liszt and he smiled back, tipping his policeman's hat to them.

After a few minutes, it became clear the fog was thinning out. The Battery still lay cloaked in a deep void of black shadows, broken here and here by lamp posts which did little against the darkness, but visibility had improved. Further along the path, families sat clustered under trees. The cries of babies and the voices of men and women carried through the night. Some groups sat around meagre campfires and with wary eyes watched Liszt as he moved past.

It didn't matter, though. All that mattered was finding the Portal to the Breach. After what felt like a nightmare of years, of decades even, trapped inside that awful grey world, the Breach had deposited him here. A Portal existed at the tip of one of the Breach's fractures in reality and it lay under Castle Clinton, what the people of this time called Castle Garden.

Liszt walked on until the trees parted and then he stopped. The reeling storm of his mind understood now what Cochran meant when he'd said that getting inside wasn't an option. Liszt hardly recognized the Castle Clinton towering in the gloom before him. A parameter wall stood around its boundary, beyond which the tops of narrow buildings rose up. Beyond them, the immigration depot known in this time as Castle Garden stood with its rounded walls and a central cupola atop the gentle dome. Signs for *Labor Exchange*, *Emigration* and other services adorned the exterior. It was as if they'd built on top and around the monument he knew. In his time, the high-walled structure was low in profile, a single storey, at least to the general public.

"It's not the same," Liszt whispered to himself, "but it's in there, waiting to be found again."

* * *

The official at the gate grunted his displeasure at Liszt's request to enter Castle Garden, on the pretence of looking inside for a cousin due to arrive that day, but waved him through with the assertion not to expect any preferential treatment. Liszt passed the exterior quarters and offices and paused only a moment to regard the original gate, one of the few things he recognized through the additions.

"How you changed over the years, old friend," Liszt said as he touched the masonry. More than ever now he wanted to find the Portal and get home. He didn't belong in this era, that fact was clear from the moment he awoke in the park.

Inside, the smell assaulted his nose with the acridity of the hundreds of souls inhabiting the space, all waiting to be processed. Once again, Liszt paused to take in the sight. The candles and lanterns cast a murky haze in the great space, packed with immigrants, emigrants, officials and clerks. A circle of central columns towered above everyone, supporting the domed ceiling and cupola. Stairs like wings flanked them on either side, leading to the balcony wrapping around the space above them where more wayfaring strangers awaited their due processing in those elevated cloisters.

Liszt imagined the Castle Clinton he knew from his old life in a dim, distant future. The layout in his time was simpler, the space open to the sky, with only a low, angled awning descending inward around the monument's walls. He tried to mentally place the two small hut-like buildings which in his time stood in the middle of the open grounds. In this time, with the interior covered by the full, lofty second storey and crammed with people, it felt like an entirely different place. His head swam and thought became difficult. The din of the place seemed to become a steady roar burrowing through his mind. Liszt leaned against a wall until it passed. He made his best guess at where the two huts would sit however many years in the future and so moved to the edge of the hall. He passed doors to offices and examination rooms, hoping to find something familiar to guide him. He weaved past the mothers nursing babies, children curled on the floor playing games with whatever detritus they found, men with pipes humming quiet melodies. They watched Liszt as he walked by, some hopeful, some tired. A man bumped into him and muttered an apology in a thick accent.

Liszt found a clear patch of floor by a door and stopped. When he felt the tug in the pit of his stomach, a curious pulling sensation, he knew he was in the right place.

Liszt regarded the door, which sported no label or sign. The grimy paint flaked and peeled. He expected it to be locked when he reached out and turned the knob, but it wasn't. He went inside.

* * *

164

The room afforded little space to move. Liszt reached into the coat that had once belonged to Cochran and took out the man's small box of matches. He shut the door and struck one alight. Dust and cobwebs covered the walls of the claustrophobic empty room. Liszt touched the stone, feeling the gritty texture under his finger tips. After a half dozen paces, he reached the other end of the room

··more of a storage closet, he mused··

and had to shake the match out as it reached his fingers. He lit another one and looked around, certain this was where he was supposed to be.

That's when he saw the other door, sunk into the wall standing not even two feet square from the floor. Liszt knelt and moved the match closer. It caught a draft of air and winked out. Liszt lit another match, careful to keep it away from the moving air, and scrutinized the door. This one was unpainted, but thick and solid, with ornate iron hinges and door handle. Liszt wrapped him fingers around the cold metal handle and pressed the release. There came a clunk as a bolt fell open and Liszt pulled at the door, holding the match high and away from the gust of air he expected. It hit him like a strong breeze, stale, but oddly more fresh than the air inside the depot.

The match danced and threatened to go out as Liszt illuminated the passage inside the door. The shaft dropped straight down and as the match grew hot near his fingertips, he let it fall and craned his head to watch it descend. It didn't get more than five feet down before going out, but Liszt saw iron rungs jutting out from the wall of the shaft and knew he was going to climb down.

* * *

Slipping out of the small room, Liszt crept toward a sleeping family in the shadows. He peered over their belongings, didn't see what he needed and moved on. Near them slept a man wrapped in a dirty blanket, next to two sacks tied with a drawstring. Liszt moved to the next group, a larger family, laying about their luggage and crates. There he found what he was looking for. The small mass of wax could hardly qualify as a candle inside the unlit lantern, but it would have to do. Liszt sauntered over, careful that his boots made little noise on the stone floor. He glanced about to see if anyone was watching and eased the lantern off the crate. With it, he walked back to the door just as he saw a group of policemen and depot officials crowd in through the main entrance. Liszt looked down at his own uniform and knew why they were here. Cochran's body had been found.

Liszt ducked back into the tiny room and waited. He set the lantern down and gripped the nightstick, holding it close. He leaned in and peered through the crack between the door and the frame. He saw the police and depot officials split up. He watched the team moving in his direction as they poked through the waiting immigrants and tested each door they found. They opened them, looked inside and then headed to the next. One policeman stopped to question the onlookers and Liszt caught his breath when an old woman pointed in the direction he'd gone. The officer, bulky and muscled, thanked her, said something to his colleagues and pulled out his own nightstick. Backed up by another cop, one younger but just as well-built, the two approached his position. Liszt grabbed the lantern and scrambled to the miniature door, having to find it by touch. He pulled the door open and climbed inside, holding the lantern in his mouth by the handle.

"Let's check in here," said the older policemen outside the room. Liszt twisted onto his stomach and flailed his legs to find the rungs embedded in the wall. His foot caught one and he eased himself in. The pointed cap on his head bumped the top of the passage, knocking it crooked as he pulled himself in, stepping down the rungs.

The unmistakeable creak of the outside door opening made Liszt freeze.

"Dark as a tomb in there," said the younger policeman.

Liszt realized the small door was still ajar.

"Anyone in there?" the older policeman called out. "Now's your chance to show yourself. Don't make us drag you out."

Liszt waited.

"Sean, bring that lantern," said the older policeman. "Damned if I can see my hand in front of my face in there."

Liszt took the chance and grabbed the small door's handle. He resisted pulling it hard shut, not wanting to risk slamming it. As the miniature door slid back into its recess in the wall, the narrow room beyond grew brighter.

Again, Liszt froze and waited, listening and watching the sliver of light under the door.

"Someone's been in here," said the older policeman. "See the footprints in the dust? And the dirty, wet ground? I'd say it's a good bet our man came in here from outside. Come on, let's keep looking. He's bound to be here somewhere."

The policemen left. When the outside door clicked shut, Liszt whistled a sigh of relief through his teeth, which still clutched the lantern handle. By touch, he found the top-most rung and began to descend the shaft, heart pounding in his chest.

* * *

"Listen up, I need all eyes on me," barked Captain Villa.

The recently-promoted Sergeant Liszt stood before the unit now under his responsibility. Being a fresh assignment for both him and this squad, Captain Villa took it upon herself to orient them to the facility as a group. Having seen their barracks and the mess hall a level above, Villa now guided them to the research facility. They passed quickly through the antechamber outside the vast main laboratory and Villa brought them to a halt. They peered through the thick glass at the consoles, computers and equipment beyond. The captain dropped her voice to a speaking level as her troops quieted down at once. "Here's a little history lesson: As you know, this facility is located under Battery Park and the Underpass. It was built with the utmost secrecy, but the modern labs you see behind me are only the latest additions. When we come back here in a moment, we'll go over the protocols for the lab, but for now there's a room you need to see. Knowing about it may save your life if this facility is compromised."

Villa led the group away from the main lab to the other end of the antechamber as she spoke. She stopped at a door, swiped a card key through the reader and the door unlocked. She opened the door and continued her lecture as they walked down a cramped brick corridor, one much older than the modern part of the facility they'd just left.

"We're going to pretend we're in the Way Back Machine and jump all the way back to the 1800s," Villa said with a smile. "And I'll be damned impressed if any of you get that reference."

Liszt didn't get it and neither did the others.

"I didn't think so," said Villa, shaking her head. "Anyway, you'll be fully briefed on what's being studied in the lab back there, but suffice to say it's very old. It was first discovered in the mid-1800s and it's part of what we call the Breach."

Villa stopped at a metal door which looked like it dated from World War II.

"We're below Castle Clinton now, just so you have your bearings," Villa said, pointing upwards. "As the story goes, when it stopped being a fort and was renovated into a performance hall, a team working on either a drainage system or trying to dig a substructure came upon the Breach and were slowly driven mad by it, but not before they formed some kind of cult and worshipped it for years. There's a story that they all finally snapped during an underground ritual, the same night as a Swedish opera singer named Jenny Lind was singing at Castle Garden so many yards above them. Only one of the cultists survived and he drooled on about it for years at Ward's Island. A doctor there helpfully wrote it all down. We have that report archived and it makes for fascinating reading if you don't ever want sleep again."

The soldiers did not easily hide the nervousness in their quiet laughter. At this, a hint of a smile crossed Villa's face. She unlocked the metal door and it groaned as it opened. Darkness lay beyond.

"Follow me," the captain said, not hesitating at all as she entered the room. The troops did hesitate, just for a moment, and that's when Liszt spoke up.

"You heard the lady! Move!" Liszt ordered them.

The troops filed into the black chamber, Liszt bringing up the rear. The shaft of light from the hallway illuminated a sliver of stone floor and wall, but little else. Villa's voice spoke from the darkness.

"Sergeant, please close the door," she said.

"Yes, sir," Liszt replied and shut the heavy door behind him. Not even a thin line of light penetrated the seal. Liszt looked around, hearing the murmurs of the soldiers, his eyes struggling in the complete blackness to see something.

"Am I the only one seeing this?" asked one of the soldiers. Liszt thought it was Ramirez.

There was a shuffle of feet and another soldier balked out a "Watch it, man!" as someone no doubt bumped into him.

"Hey, I see it, too!" said Private Hamlin.

Liszt moved to his right, hand out to catch anything he might bump into.

And then he saw it.

A faint glow grew in the room as his eyes adjusted. It towered over them, gradually becoming clearer. Liszt squinted at it in the dim light. It rippled, the way light bounces off water in the dark. Curious as it was, the light seemed to house no colour, yet all the colours at once. As Liszt squinted more he caught bits of blue, then red, then green, but almost as soon as he saw them, they disappeared into cold white and he wasn't sure he'd seen anything different.

The awe in the troops' voices as they each saw what Liszt saw made him turn and he could make each of them out. He straightened up as Villa stepped forward, standing between them and the glowing whatever-it-was.

"Ladies and gentleman, what you're looking at is a visible part of the Breach," Villa said. "That light you're seeing is actually coming from the main lab back the way we came, where Dr Stevenson and his team are studying the Portal. Again, we'll explain that in more detail later, but in layman's terms, the light from the lab is travelling through the Portal along the Breach and we can see it here. Yes, you with your hand up. Private Decker."

"Sir, is it safe to, you know, touch it?" Decker asked, pointing her finger at the glow.

"Excellent question, Private," Villa said. "If we were to turn the lights off in the lab, you would not be able to see this glow and you very likely would have no idea this was even here. If you walked through it to the other side of the chamber, you'd feel nothing. We run tests regularly. You all had to fill out a shit ton of forms when you came on this assignment and spent a day getting samples taken from every part of your body, all to give the medical staff a baseline to work from. We've run tests on everyone who's been working in the facility since it was built, past and present, and no one seems to have suffered any physical ailments we can conclusively attribute to this phenomenon. There are sensors in every room monitoring radiation levels, which are still well within acceptable parameters."

Villa tapped an app on her watch, then selected an option which brought up a display noting the background radiation around them.

"See? We're pretty safe in here, it seems," Villa said. "The lab is an entirely different story. Radiation is not the issue there, but the protocols for being around the Portal to the Breach are strict and there for very good reasons, all of which we will cover before any of you set foot inside."

Villa tapped off her watch's display and looked to Liszt.

"Sergeant, please go to the door and there you'll find a dimmer switch," the captain said. "You should be able to see it now that your eyes have adjusted. Please turn it on, gradually if you would."

"Yes, Captain."

Liszt did indeed see the switch on the wall by the door, connected to cables running up to the ceiling. He turned the dimmer switch and eased light into the room from fixtures hanging above. As he did, the glow from the Breach, already faint in the dark room, disappeared against the brighter work lights.

"You can't see it anymore, but obviously it's still there," Villa said. "Notice we marked the floor and walls to indicate where it is."

The troops looked down and saw the yellow and black tape running across the room, marking the boundary. The tape ran up both solid stone walls and even across the ceiling.

"Sir, this Breach travels through the walls?" Decker asked.

"Through walls, through rock, through the bay... Yes, Private," Villa said, nodding toward the wall opposite the door they'd entered. The soldiers looked at each other, murmuring again, the full extent of the nature of the research here beginning to sink in.

"Sir?" Decker said, putting her hand up again, only for Villa to wave it down, "is this the room where the cultists killed each other?"

Villa smiled, making no attempted to hide it.

"Yes, Private, it is," she replied, giving the group a moment to let that sink in. She went on, "Remember when I said this part of the tour might very well save your life? Above us is Castle Clinton. Tourists are buying tickets up there to go to Liberty Island. They obviously don't know we're down here, but there is a tightly guarded back door located up there, part of the mid-19th Century renovations: A shaft leading down to this room. Both it and this chamber were built by our poor friends the cultists. Notice the rungs up that corner of the wall? If there's a problem exiting the facility through the main entrance, that shaft will take you to a guarded station in Castle Clinton."

Villa crossed the room, mindful of the caution tape on the floor, and headed to the door.

"Sergeant, please turn off the lights as we leave, thank you," she said and opened the metal door.

"Yes, sir," Liszt replied.

The soldiers filed out and Liszt turned the dimmer down until all that remained in the room was the soft, almost imperceptible glow of the Breach.

* * *

171

Liszt awoke in the same spot where he fell asleep, propped up in the corner of the chamber, with Cochran's uniform jacket folded into a pillow. He didn't notice the dryness of his mouth and throat as he turned his gaze to the beautiful glow of the Portal before him. Unlike in his time, where the Breach Captain Villa showed had the group extended though the chamber and into an area that would become the main laboratory, here and now in the past, the Breach did not yet reach that far. In his when, the Portal at the tip of the Breach was in the lab, which had been built around it. In this when, the Portal still remained in the chamber the cultists built to worship it, the chamber Liszt now occupied. Then and as now, the Portal made its presence known in dramatic fashion. It rose up from floor to ceiling, a column like shifting water, bending and distorting light, an aberration of reality. It emitted no light itself, but when light came close, as it did now with the stolen lantern sitting before it, he saw the gentle ripple extend a few feet along the path of the Breach beyond the Portal.

Startled, Liszt scrambled to his feet, letting the coat fall to the floor. He intended only to rest his eyes, but it seemed he fell right to sleep. The candle burned low now and Liszt wasted no more time blowing it out. He didn't mind the dark. It soothed him and allowed for no distractions. He felt for the small computer on the floor and picked it up, carrying both items back to the corner of the room. He ignored the pain in his hand from when he'd pounded the chamber wall in frustration two sleeps before. Time had no meaning down here without a clock or daylight, its passage marked only by the times he slept and the time he was awake. Often, Liszt spent the wakeful periods shrouded in blackness, not lighting the lantern at all. He expected this to be one of those times.

The control computer's power cell no longer held a charge. After escaping down the shaft days earlier and discovering the Portal in the chamber, Liszt tried at once to activate the device. When he pulled it from his cargo pocket and turned it on, horror replaced his excitement. The blinking orange rectangle indicated the power cell's imminent demise. Still, he tried to calibrate the device. According to Cochran, the date was

October 28, 1886 and he was under Castle Garden in Battery Park. The small control computer accepted the data, not prompting him much as it calculated the relative position of the Portal during this time period and the frequencies needed to open it. The computer worked away, taking minutes, then an hour. Liszt went from holding his breath in anticipation to pacing back and forth, trying not to watch the screen. When the orange rectangle reappeared, replacing the creeping progress bar, Liszt stopped and watched as his fears were realized. The computer flashed a message in red text below the power cell warning which read:

Power: 0.02%
Please replace cell
Shutting down

And the screen went black. No amount of taping or button pressing could bring it back to life, Liszt knelt on the chamber floor, holding the computer, trying to will it to give him a little more run time, just enough to open the portal so he could return home. He prayed. When that didn't work, he cursed. When that failed, he set the computer down, rose to his feet and let out an agonized wail. He pounded the walls with his fists, leaving them bloody and aching. He tried to enter the Portal anyway, stepping into the column of distorted reality, but apart from a headache and nausea brought on from a dizzying sensation, nothing happened.

The Portal here was closed to him.

Two sleep periods later, having woken up from a dream about his former captain and his first visit to this room—·

Years in the future, yet part of my past, Liszt thought. He giggled at this.

—Liszt lay defeated in the blackness. He no longer wanted to think. He no longer wanted to do anything. He lay in the hollow chamber, yet the hollow chamber was also his soul. He had nothing else, just memories of his old life.

"Why did I volunteer?" he asked. "If Stevenson wanted this damn thing probed, he should've done it himself, or gotten one of his egghead lackeys to do it. But no, stupid me, I had to say 'Sure, I'll go out with your team to this other Portal in Buttfuck, Nowhere, push the button when you tell me and see what happens.'"

Of course, neither he nor Stevenson carried the blame. The mission was to open a second Portal along the Breach, which the scientists had never tried before.

"Oh, but they were fucking confident, weren't they? Bunch of fucking Know-It-Alls," Liszt spat. He wondered when his voice had become so hoarse, his mouth so dry.

Despite it being him alone stuck in the past, no one could take the blame. He'd agreed to the mission. Once on site, he'd agreed to stand before this newly discovered Portal in the mountains –location classified, of course. Welcome to the Army, situation normal, all fucked up. And Liszt had agreed to do so without his sidearm or even his watch. When he asked the ranking scientist on site why he couldn't wear his watch, but he was holding this small control computer, the scientist shrugged and said Stevenson wanted to eliminate as many variables as possible.

Brilliant man, that Stevenson, truly he was, but goddamn if he lacked some basic common sense sometimes.

So, when at last the cameras and sensors were set up, tested and everything was ready, the good Dr Stevenson relayed the go-ahead to the team on site. Liszt did his duty and tapped the screen as instructed.

At first there was nothing and then there was something. The column of broken reality in the mountains twisted even more, there came a great wrenching sound, high-pitched and piercing, and before Liszt could react, the Portal grabbed him. He didn't see it, but he felt it, in the pit of his stomach, holding him still. The distortion advanced on him like the maw of a great monster and Liszt closed his eyes, hoping the end wouldn't hurt.

However, the end didn't come for Liszt that evening, only the start of a long nightmare being lost in the Breach, a horrible grey, smoke-like world.

Liszt pushed the memory away, wanting again to be empty, soulless in the black chamber deep underground, but the knot in his gut wouldn't go away, no matter how much he tried to will it to stop pulling.

I'm trapped here, he thought. *Leave me alone!*

He leapt to his feet, fist clenched in rage.

"FUCK YOU!" Liszt cried, advancing to the Portal even as he couldn't see it. "I'll rip you open with my bare hands!"

He knew he was in the midst of the Portal, that column of broken reality, when the wave of dizziness hit him, but it only fuelled his rage. He clawed at the air in the blackness, seeing nothing, but not letting that stop him.

"You hear me?! I will open you if it's the last thing I do! I don't need a fucking computer, I'll break you with my mind! If not here, than somewhere else! You think you're the only fucking Portal on this planet?" Liszt's voice gave out on the last word and he stumbled, overcome with nausea. He fell against a wall, gasping, but as his equilibrium stabilized, the solution came clear. He started giggling again, running his hand through his hair, tucking again at his sleeves. When he spoke to himself, his broken voice a whisper, he didn't notice his chapped lips were bleeding. "I'll find another Portal. That's the solution. There are others. It'll be my quest!"

Liszt gathered his belongings, found his way to the shaft in the dark and made the long climb up to the small door. Once inside the narrow room, he peered through the crack between the door and the frame and saw the immigration depot much as he'd left it days before. The temporary residents huddled in the dark and most slept. Liszt straightened his stolen policeman's uniform and slipped out of the vast holding area. He passed a group of officials, but did not stop until he made it outside the building. The fresh air hit him and he breathed it in with deep gasps. The fog and rain had cleared out and Liszt could see the stars. When he reached the guard at the gate, the man didn't even look at him, so distracted was he with the crowd beyond. Hundreds of people filled the Battery, standing in awe watching over the harbour and the bay. Fireworks riddled the sky and the onlookers chattered in wonder. Liszt joined them to watch this spectacle, making his way through the crowd. The people stepped aside for him. He reached the railing at the water's edge and took in the enthralling sight of the bay filled with ships. Fireworks rained overhead and the statue he recognized stood alight across the water.

"Worth the wait, wouldn't you say, Officer?" a scruffy looking man asked him.

"How's that?" Liszt asked.

"Bartholdi's statue out yonder there," the man said. "They finally lit it. I came out here three days ago to see this, but all the rain and muck forced a delay."

"Ah, yes," Liszt nodded, feigning understanding. "It's quite something."

"Most certainly is, Officer," the scruffy man said. He gestured to the statue of the lady holding her torch high out at Bedloe's Island. "Symbol of freedom, that is. You feel it, Officer, the freedom?"

Liszt nodded.

"Why, yes," he agreed. "I do feel free."

Liszt left the man at the shoreline and pushed back through the crowd. Beyond the park, Liszt saw the buildings which overlooked it, the rooftops lined with even more onlookers watching the festivities. His stomach growled and he decided to find something to eat, then he'd start his quest.

"Oh, but which way will I travel?" he wondered aloud.

The answer lay in the tugging sensation in his gut.

West.

Liszt didn't question it because the answer lit as bright as the fireworks behind him.

West.

176

18

November 1, 1886
Orchard Bend

Rose's fingers slipped between Emery's, their warmth comforting both women as they watched the lit candle float away down the river, a tiny speck of light in the darkness. Above them, to the south east, the waxing crescent moon hung as a pendant in the sky. Emery spotted the reddish pin-point of Mars right above the river.

"It's almost midnight," Rose said.

Emery nodded, watching the candle drift further and further away. When it disappeared from view, Emery and Rose left the landing by the river and walked through the starlit streets of Orchard Bend, saying nothing. At Rose's cottage, they made passionate love and fell asleep soon after.

* * *

November 2, 1886
Orchard Bend

Bit by bit, the town came to life that cold Tuesday morning. Emery accompanied Rose on her walk to the church that was her schoolhouse, leading her horse behind them. Both ladies bundled up against the chill. White flakes drifted down from the overcast sky, beginning to dust the ground.

"The snow falls early this year," Rose said, tightening her long cape around her, "and it brings with it an awful chill."

"Do you have wood for the stove?" Emery asked. "You'll want to light it first thing today."

"Yes, but I'll ask the Statlers for more," Rose said, looking down the street. "If I start using it this early, I'll run out before spring."

"Good morning, Miss Adelaide," Rebecca Clarke called out from the boardwalk as she and Billy Howard approached. "And you, Ms Dale."

"Good morning, Rebecca. Good morning, Billy," Rose smiled. "How would you two like to set the stove alight for me? I'll be inside in a few minutes."

The teenagers exchanged a look and a smile and then agreed. Rose gave them the key with instructions to leave it on her desk. "And be careful with the matches."

The two hurried inside and Rose turned to see Emery smiling as she checked her saddle.

"Think you can trust those two alone?" Emery asked.

"I won't give them time to get up to anything the Holy Spirit wouldn't approve of," Rose said, grinning. She looked up and down the street then leaned in and whispered, "Thank you for last night."

Emery blushed and she too cast about to confirm no one was within earshot.

"You're welcome, my dear Rose," she said, keeping her voice quiet. She put her boot in the stirrup and climbed atop her horse.

"Give my best to Gertrude for me," Rose said, stepping away toward the schoolhouse.

"I will," Emery replied.

Rose climbed the steps to the schoolhouse and Emery rode off, heading east. She passed groups of schoolchildren wrapped in scarves, mittens and layers in the late fall morning. She counted more adults accompanying their children, as it had been in the days following the murder of Laura O'Malley. The men tipped their hats to her as she passed and the women gave her but cursory glances. While pleasantries offered to her were rare, Dale sensed this gloom ran deeper.

The farms she passed lay quiet, the wheat harvest and replanting done, with few fruits and vegetables remaining. Dale passed the McCabe Orchards and ascended the hill where their grand house overlooked the town. Dale trotted around the back of the house and found Henry cleaning out a stall. He stopped, leaning against his shovel and waited for her to arrive.

"That one at the end is freshly cleaned, Ms Dale," Henry said, using his sleeve to wipe some sweat from his brow despite the cold.

Dale tipped her hat to him and guided her horse into the stall.

"I'll make sure he has some water," Henry said, coming over to her.

"Thank you, Henry, I appreciate that," Dale said.

Henry shrugged and avoided eye contact. Dale watched him as she rooted through her saddlebags and retrieved her satchel. His eyes went from her sword to her guns. She looked at his cheek and saw the thin white scar left there years before by the bullet of a man named Saunders. She draped the satchel's strap over her shoulder and smiled at the young man.

"How are you, Henry?" Dale asked.

This made him look up and Dale wasn't certain what she saw there; surprise, perhaps that she was asking after him, but also confusion. Or maybe fear. His gaze went to the sword on her back again and Dale thought she understood, the dramatic scene still fresh in her mind so many years later.

Saunders' gun shone silvery in the moonlight as the hammer clicked back, seeming to echo in the vast space of the barn. Then her blade cut the moonlight, cutting Saunders' head from its neck as his finger squeezed the trigger, firing the round that missed killing Henry but left the graze on his cheek.

Henry had lived through that, only to see Sheriff Wilson take his own life after moaning about failing to solve Laura O'Malley's murder.

"I'm fine, I guess, Ms Dale," Henry said, stuffing his hands in his pockets. The heavy work gloves did not let them go too deep.

"Talk to your mother or father if you think you need to," Dale said, hoping this shred of advice would help. "Or come talk to me."

179

Henry blinked and simply stared at her. Dale passed him as she left the stall, giving him a warm smile, wondering if he'd take her up on the offer.

Dale walked around to the front of the house and found Burke smoking a pipe at the far end of the front porch. He nodded and she nodded back, reaching up to knock on the door.

"He's in his study, you can go right in," Burke said. "Mrs McCabe is in the parlour with the young Owen. She disapproves of me indulging this around her now, saying she no longer appreciates the aroma."

As if to highlight his displeasure, he took a few puffs from the pipe. Dale nodded and reached for the door handle to let herself in.

"He's not in the most agreeable of states this morning, either," Burke said. "This business with Wilson has him in a foul mood."

Dale nodded. Burked turned away to look back out at the view of Orchard Bend.

"And expect questions about Ashleyville," he added.

* * *

"Beech dropped the ball!" Dale said, her arms crossed.

McCabe gave her a hard look across his desk. He held in his hand a communiqué from Beech on CUC letterhead. Sent the morning after the incident at the Police Station, Beech couriered it to Orchard Bend via rail while Dale traveled home by horse, thus it reached McCabe a full two days before Dale arrived.

"You think that matters?" McCabe sighed. "I have business ties with the CUC. Land. Shipping. The optics of the situation are these: one of my employees is at the forefront of a *bloodbath* with the railroad police. It does not reflect well on said ties. Not to mention what Beech calls a '...flagrant disrespect for his authority and the interests of the railroad.'"

"I've worked for you for *years*, Mr McCabe," Dale said. "You know if I was at fault I would own up to it. Beech failed to anticipate the betrayal of one of his own and lives were lost as a result."

"The problem, Ms Dale, is that this goes far beyond what I think or even what Beech thinks," McCabe said, leaning back in his chair. "He's sent this to the CUC Head Office, who no doubt will decide to review their relationship with me. Beech is a bureaucrat with a nose more brown than the rug you're standing on, its how he got to where he is now. He has allies in the CUC. You're nobody to them."

Dale sighed and her gaze fell to the ornate brown rug under her boots. The designs weaved intricate patterns, fooling the eye with misdirection.

"So I'm fired then?" Dale asked.

"Ms Dale, if I intended to have you fired out, I would have started this conversation with that fact," McCabe said, his tone wary. "I intended to travel east to meet with some allies of my own in the CUC. I expect the damage is not irreversible. The timing of all this could not be more inconvenient, however, what with the matter of Wilson taking his own life."

"I'm sorry your son had to see that," Dale said.

"Such a thing will linger with him for a time, but I expect Henry will put the memory in its proper place," McCabe said. "I should have seen that Wilson could not carry the burden of responsibility demanded by the job. Then again, that harpy Mrs O'Malley only made the entire matter worse, grief or no."

"Who are you going to offer the job to now?" Dale asked.

"We put advertisements in the county newspapers calling for experienced lawmen to apply," McCabe said. "We'll see who shows up next week."

* * *

Just as Burke said, Dale found Gertrude McCabe in the parlour, going over arithmetic lessons with Owen on the sofa. Dale paused at the door, watching them, thinking of the night Saunders came to kill them all. Another lawman, broken with grief, but unlike Wilson who took his own life, Saunders sought revenge on Maxwell McCabe by killing his wife and sons. He almost succeeded.

Gertrude saw Dale at the door and beckoned her in, rousing Emery from her thoughts.

"Owen, take your work over to your desk, will you, honey? That's a good little man," Gertrude told her son, directing him away from the sofa as Dale joined her. Gertrude offered her to sit and Dale did.

"I hear you had an eventful trip," Gertrude said. "I'm glad you came back safe."

"Two good men were not so lucky," Dale sighed. "One of whom I knew well."

"Yes, I was privy to that," Gertrude said. "Such a dangerous job you have in my husband's employ. We should be thankful your skills allow you to come through unscathed."

"Unscathed indeed," Dale said, taking in the view from the window, gauzy and pale grey through the thin curtain.

"I've taken to drawing again, did you know?" Gertrude said as she poured two cups of tea.

"I did not," Dale said, picking up her china tea cup and taking a sip.

"With Henry older and doing much of his studies with his father now, I find I have more time to indulge," Gertrude said, her excitement coming through. She took the black leather ledger from the end table and opened it up. Dale recognized the sketches on the first number of pages, including two of Emery herself. She should've expected the sudden headache when she saw them, but they hit with such intensity this time, more so than when it happened seven years previous. She set her tea cup down with a clatter and pressed the bridge of her nose between her finger and thumb.

"Are you not well?" Gertrude asked, touching Dale's arm.

"It'll pass," Dale said, even as the pain intensified. She couldn't shake the sense of familiarity in the pictures, as if she was looking in a mirror but seeing someone else. Then from the depths of her mind another memory swept in.

The blonde girl, swinging a wooden sword at me, Dale's mind struggled to make sense of it. *Is it her I see in Gertrude's sketch?*

Dale realized it was.

The pain broke almost as fast as it came and she opened her eyes.

Who was that girl? Someone from my old life, but who?

"Emery, you're pale," Gertrude said with concern.

"I get these headaches from time to time," Dale said. "They tend to come on unexpectedly."

"Yes, I have to admit I've seen them," Gertrude said. "Have you spoken to Dr Shaw about them?"

"He knows, but there's little he can do. They appear unrelated to any physical ailment he can detect," Dale sipped her tea, trying to hide the mix of confusion and excitement brimming under the surface. This wasn't the first memory to surface from her old life, but in some ways it was the most important, a connection between two disparate fragments. A reason for elation, without a doubt, but it raised more questions than it answered.

"Forgive my directness," Gertrude said. "And I hope in our friendship you understand I ask this from a place of concern, not base curiosity, but might it be related to your past?"

Dale tensed and Gertrude saw it.

"I'm not asking you to confide your life's story to me," Gertrude hastened to add. "I merely suggest it may be wise to look there for answers, to examine what you carry with you."

Dale smiled.

"You are observant and insightful, Gertrude," Emery said. "And before I forget, Rose sends her greetings. I believe she started the list you asked for, of the school's financial needs. After recent events it provides her a welcome distraction."

"Recent events," Gertrude shook her head. "I lament if this town will once more experience normalcy. Things have not been right this last year. There was such optimism a year ago, do you remember? Then after our Hallowe'en soirée..."

She looked at Dale, her eyes glassy and distant.

"...Everything changed that night," Gertrude said, not attempting to hide the sadness in her voice. Across the room, oblivious, Owen hummed to himself as he worked on his arithmetic and drew simple pictures of rabbits.

* * *

The sun peaked through the clouds over the autumn landscape. Dale slowed her horse to a stop at the crest of a hill, taking in the near desolate beauty of the scene. Fewer gold and orange leaves covered the trees edging the farms, the distant memory of the heat of summer.

A chilled gust made Dale adjust her hat and she continued on her way west. She did not expect to see the lone figure of a woman wandering on the road up ahead, dress rippling in the breeze, hair sailing about unkempt. She wore no jacket or coat, nor a shawl or cape or bonnet, nothing but her dress and boots to protect her from the elements. Dale approached her from behind and the woman did not turn or even seem to hear her. When Dale passed her and came about to face the woman, she finally stopped. She didn't look at Dale at all, her eyes focused on nothing, not even blinking as her hair danced about her face in strands. Dale leaned forward to ask whether she needed help and her question caught in her throat when she saw who this woman was.

"Irene?" Dale asked.

No reaction came, just the same vacant stare to some far off point. Dale dismounted and went to her, stopping only when Irene put up her right hand.

"No, don't," Irene said, gaze still distant.

"What are you doing out here, Irene?" Dale asked. "It's freezing. You're not dressed for this weather."

Irene twitched and shook her head, but the gesture took effort. Dale could only watch as anger burned in the pit of her stomach. She cursed Wilson for his selfishness. No matter what the sheriff felt about Laura O'Malley's murder, his suicide brought Irene to this state.

"How about we go home, back to town, where you can warm up by the fire. And we can talk," Dale suggested.

With another furious shake of her head, Irene took a step back. She wagged her finger at Dale, which would have been comical if it wasn't so heartbreaking.

"No," Irene said. "No, I have to do this."

"Do what?" Dale asked.

Irene answered with more head shaking.

"Irene, I'm your friend," Dale said. "Remember when we first met? Do you remember that? I do, clear as day. You warned me to be wary of Mr McCabe. You didn't *have* to tell me that, I was a stranger, but you did, because I saved Miss Adelaide's life. Do you remember that? I was grateful for what you said. I was new here and you were kind to me."

Irene only stood there.

"I want to help you, Irene," Dale said. "You're not alone."

"You don't understand, Miss Dale," Irene said. "It's all her fault."

"Whose fault?" Dale asked.

Irene threw up her hand and tossed her head back, letting out a groan of frustration.

"People told me what she said, that I'd feel great pain before I die," Irene said. "She made this happen. She made Clem do it, with her foulness and evil!"

"You mean Mrs O'Malley?" Dale said. Rose had told her about the grieving mother's outburst at the opening of the Town Hall.

"DON'T SAY HER NAME!" Irene screamed, pointing to Dale with the knife she held in her other hand, the one she'd been hiding at her side behind her billowing dress. The move came with such quickness, Dale ducked and drew her gun without thinking. Just as fast, Dale lowered the six-shooter and holstered it. The hand holding the knife trembled and Irene wept, "Please, Miss Dale, I have to do this. She's evil."

"It won't bring Clem back, Irene," Dale said. "I know it hurts, but if you kill her, you'll surely hang. You're my friend and I don't want to lose you. And Miss Adelaide... *Rose*... she's your friend, too, and it would break her heart if you did this."

Irene wavered, the knife shaking in her hand. Her lips quivered and tears rolled down her cheeks.

"Clem wouldn't want this," Dale said. "He was a kind, good man."

"And he's GONE!" Irene bawled.

"Not in your heart," Dale said. "He's still there and you still love him. The pain will ease. It's impossible to see it right now, but you have to trust me. Killing *her* won't take the pain away."

"She deserves it," Irene cried in a whisper.

Dale watched Irene's face, the agonizing battle as revenge lost out to grief. At last, the young woman could not hold on to what little composure she had left and she dropped the knife and bent over, letting out a bloodcurdling wail. Dale stepped forward, kicking the knife aside with her boot as she put her arms around her friend. Irene collapsed and Dale eased her to the ground, where they knelt in the cool sunshine. Irene sobbed, her hand clasping onto Dale as each fit of pain came. She blubbered incoherencies and Emery consoled her until the bout of sorrow ran its course.

Dale fetched a blanket she kept in her saddle bag, taking the opportunity to retrieve the knife from the ground and pack it away safe. She wrapped Irene in the blanket, offered her some water from her canteen and helped her onto the horse, where she sat slouched over in exhaustion.

* * *

"The poor girl," Rose said after Emery told her what happened on the road. Upon returning to town, Emery left Irene with Dr Shaw and then fetched her mother from their tavern. With nothing more she could do, Dale indulged in some whiskey at Sully's, had a meal as she watched the late afternoon sunset, had one more shot and walked with her horse under the darkening sky to Rose's cottage. She now sat before the wood stove, soaking in its heat, feeling drained. Rose made her some cocoa and sat next to her. Rose took Emery's hand, warming it in hers as she went on, "It's a miracle you found her when you did. I believe that."

"So I'm an agent of the Lord, then?" Emery said with a wry grin.

"Don't mock," Rose said. "I know we don't share the same views on these matters, but you are not wicked. You have a bright soul and a unique strength. God does not control your actions, you have free will, but at least consider that he acted *through* you to save Irene Sullivan."

"He works in mysterious ways, is that it?" Emery asked, closing her eyes and rubbing them with her free hand.

"Sometimes not so mysterious," Rose said.

Emery stared at the glowing window of the stove and after some time of companionable silence she spoke without looking at Rose.

"I can't continue working for Maxwell McCabe," Emery said.

Rose sat up.

"He didn't terminate your employment?" she asked, incredulous.

"No, nothing like that," Emery said, still watching the flames inside the stove as they flickered and danced. "He doesn't even know. I didn't even know until just now."

"Are you sure you wish to leave this job?" Rose asked.

"I think I am," Emery said. "The man who died in Ashleyville, Quick Harry, he wasn't a close friend, but we'd known each other for five years. He was a shady character, always looking over his shoulder, hustling, mixed up in that life. Watching him die that way, gunned down because he was in so deep, I began to wonder if his life had any other possible outcome. And I don't think it did. If it hadn't been the deal he made with the railroad to be their mole, it would've been in a dirty slum bar in a back alley, or at a poker table. He was doing something good, sure, but he wasn't doing it to get out of that life, you see? It was just another deal, a good payday and a favour to be owed to him by the railroad."

When Emery looked at Rose she saw the schoolteacher understood, her expression full of sadness and love and relief.

Emery's throat tightened against the rise of feeling within her. Tears formed in her eyes, stinging them, and she looked away.

"There are other reasons, too," Emery said. "When I first took this job, I had to evict a family of homesteaders from a McCabe property after a run of poor crops. The Nobles. I told myself it was a job, to not let it get personal, that I was only the messenger. But it stuck with me, the looks on their faces, the feeling that I was sentencing them to exile or death or whatever fate had in store for them."

Emery felt the tears running down her cheek and wanted to wipe them away, embarrassed by this display, but she could make no effort to do so. Her head felt light, almost dizzy, and her muscles spent.

"It was the part of the job I hated most," Emery sighed, almost whispering. When Rose did not reply, Emery looked to her. The teacher's eyes were wide, her lip trembled.

"It takes great strength to walk away from such poison in your life before it corrupts your soul," Rose said. "I know some things about that, lessons learned with pain, but I know my life is better for leaving that all behind. It led me here... And then to you, after all."

Rose leaned in and kissed her, the schoolteacher's hand cupping Emery's breast. Emery pulled Rose to her, pressing her body close, wanting nothing more right now than to be with her.

19

November 11, 1886
Orchard Bend

On the stage in the cavernous Town Hall, Henry McCabe sat next to his father at the table. Maxwell McCabe insisted that this would be a valuable part of the boy's education in the matters of local politics. Flanking the McCabes were Mr Allman, the town's young undertaker, and Mr McManus, Orchard Bend's aging blacksmith. The three adults all sat on the Council of Alderman for the town, the Council representing the extent of the local government. Their duty today consisted of interviewing prospects for the position of Sheriff. Henry had to admit it was rather funny having him here considering the circumstances of Sheriff Wilson's death.

The last man to be interviewed that day sat at his own smaller table on the floor, looking up at the aldermen as the light coming through the windows began to fade. Henry hoped his father would bring the interview to an end very soon. His stomach tightened and growled with hunger. The sooner they finished, the sooner they could eat. Maxwell had promised his son a dinner at The Harvest Moon hotel after the interviews. They just had to get through with this man, Turnbull. Henry wondered how Turnbull came by the ugly but somehow impressive scar on his cheek.

"Mr Turnbull," McManus said, going over the man's résumé, "you spoke about your duties with the railroad police, your skills and so forth, but can you tell us why you left?"

"Yes, sir," Turnbull said. "I recently came to realize that I needed a change. I'm not sure if you heard, but there was an investigation into the railroad police by the company. While I hate to bring it up, because I assure you I was not involved in any wrong doing, those who were corrupted by greed and power were brought to justice. I did my part in their apprehension—"

"And some of those corrupt men were killed rather than apprehended, isn't that true?" Maxwell McCabe chimed in.

"Yes, sir, it is," Turnbull said.

"I'm familiar with the events that transpired, Mr Turnbull," McCabe said. "Rather unfortunate how it all played out."

"Yes, sir," Turnbull agreed, with his jaw set, trying not to let it show that this line of questioning bothered him. "I feel now I need a fresh start. I've already resigned from the railroad police. If you agree to hire me, I hope we can work together to keep Orchard Bend safe."

McManus nodded and scribbled some notes. The elder McCabe looked to Mr Allman.

"Do you have any additional questions, Edgar?" McCabe asked.

"No, I don't, Mr McCabe," the undertaker said, consulting his notes. McCabe turned to McManus.

"Earl?"

"No, that's it for me," McManus said, still scribbling and not looking up.

"Very well," McCabe said, addressing the candidate. "On behalf of my fellow aldermen, thank you for travelling all this way, Mr Turnbull. We will make our decision known tomorrow at 5 o'clock. Do you have accommodations arranged?"

"I had a mind to stay at Sully's, unless you could suggest another place to stay, sir," Turnbull said as he stood and collected his things.

"Sully's is a fine establishment," McCabe said. "We will send word to you in either instance, whether we offer you the position or not."

"Thank you, sir, that's much appreciated," Turnbull said, donning his coat. "5 o'clock tomorrow, then."

"Have a good evening, Mr Turnbull," McCabe said. "Henry will show you out."

Henry jumped to his feet, relieved the interview was over. He descended the stairs from the stage, picked up Mr Turnbull's bag and escorted him out to the foyer, trying not to look at the man's scarred cheek.

Turnbull put on his hat and took his bag from the boy.

"It's an exciting story," Turnbull said.

Henry blinked, not understanding.

"The scar," Turnbull said, smiling. "I saw you looking at it. Everyone does. If I get this job, maybe I'll have the chance to tell you about it."

Henry thought he'd been inconspicuous in his glances at Turnbull's face, but clearly he'd failed. Turnbull pushed the large door open and left the Town Hall. Henry shivered in the draft of cool air and went back to the assembly hall. Halfway across the floor, as he admired the craftsmanship of the columns, Henry heard the front door open behind him. Thinking Turnbull must have forgotten something, Henry turned as the door to the great hall opened.

It wasn't Turnbull who entered, but someone in a cloak, hooded. Their boots clicked on the hardwood floor. Henry's jaw fell open when the stranger pulled back the hood.

Emery Dale gave him only a glance as she strode by, her attention fixed on the men on the stage.

* * *

She came to a halt at the small table and looked up at the aldermen. By now, the three council members ceased packing up and regarded her with interest.

"Evening, Ms Dale," Earl McManus said, coat in hand, weathered satchel open on the table. "What brings you here?"

"If the sheriff's position is still open, I'm interested," she said.

"The job is not available, Ms Dale," McCabe said at once.

"The last interview just left, you can't have decided yet," Dale replied.

"You're correct," McCabe said, "that *was* the last interview."

"I'm not even to be considered?" Dale asked.

"A *woman* sheriff?" McCabe balked, amused and incredulous.

"You more than anyone know the extent of my skills, Mr McCabe," Dale said. "I was in your employ for seven years. I

191

have fought and bled for this town. I have saved lives and nearly lost my own while acting to protect the citizens of Orchard Bend."

McCabe's glare pressed down on her, but Dale remained undaunted. Allman and McManus exchanged a look.

"I think she's serious, Maxwell," McManus said. Dale walked to one of the large columns, took off a glove and put her hand on a crater chipped in the wood the size of a quarter, about head high. Dale traced the scarred wood, now varnished over but still visible.

"This is where Daniel Underwood and I fought," Dale told the men without looking at them, letting her voice echo in the fine acoustics of the hall. "He came to Orchard Bend bringing death, like his father before him."

She turned to face the men on the stage and McCabe spoke up.

"If I recall correctly, it was young Sam O'Toole who gunned down Daniel Underwood in that spot, saving you from almost certain death," McCabe replied.

"Yes, it was Sam O'Toole who stepped up when needed," Dale agreed. "And had I not saved him seven years before, he'd not have been there to return the favour."

"I can't say I'm convinced of your argument," McCabe said, putting on his coat.

"I am," McManus said, his dry voice quiet and hard.

McCabe turned on him.

"Earl, do you hear yourself?" McCabe asked, ice in his tone.

"I do, Maxwell," McManus said, looking at him. "I hear myself very well. Do you know where I was when Daniel Underwood shot Sheriff Anderson dead in the street? I was hiding next to my forge. I told myself it was because the town was ordered off the street, but I could've taken up a gun and searched with the rest of them. To my shame I hid and this woman did not. She didn't hide that day and she didn't hide when she saved Sammy O'Toole and the schoolteacher."

"That's right," Allman said.

McCabe spun around and saw the young undertaker shrink away. McCabe crossed his arms, head tilted back in defiance.

"Mr Allman, do you have something to add?" McCabe asked in a voice that could freeze the water in the pitcher on the table. Allman looked from McCabe to McManus to Dale, then back to McCabe.

"Mr McManus is right," Allman said. "If he votes for her to be sheriff, I do too."

"I do so vote. Write that down, Mr Allman. On the record," McManus said, looking at her. "I think she'll do fine."

"I agree, Mr McManus," Allman said, furiously jotting this unexpected development into the minutes of the interview.

"Listen to the two of you!" McCabe threw up his hands. "A *woman* as sheriff? Orchard Bend will be laughed off the map! We'd be practically inviting ruffians and criminals to test our mettle."

"Ms Dale," McManus said, not looking at McCabe, "how would you feel about a probationary period of one year?"

"How would that work, Mr McManus?" Dale asked.

"Yes, Mr McManus, do enlighten us," McCabe said.

"One year," McManus went on. "If during that year the Council of Aldermen decides your performance is not satisfactory, we all go about our separate ways and pretend this didn't happen. If at the end of the year we feel you did the job well, we will make the position permanent. Mr Allman, how does that sound to you?"

"Perfectly acceptable, Mr McManus," Allman said. "I support the notion."

McManus turned to McCabe, his confident expression almost challenging McCabe to disagree.

"Mr McCabe, what say you?" McManus asked.

"With a two-to-one vote in favour of this ludicrous idea, what *can* I say?" McCabe blustered at his fellow aldermen. He turned his attention to the undertaker. "As council secretary, Mr Allman, it falls to *you* to draw up the agreement and have it ready for all parties to sign tomorrow at 5 o'clock. Several copies will be needed."

Allman deflated somewhat, realizing the extent of the paperwork for which he was now responsible.

193

"Ms Dale, let me be the first to welcome you as Orchard Bend's new sheriff," McManus said, coming down to the floor, hand extended.

"Thank you, Mr McManus," Dale said, shaking his hand. She nodded toward the stage —more to Allman than McCabe, Henry noted— and added, "And thank you both, gentleman. I will see you tomorrow. Good evening, then."

And with that, she turned and walked back across the hall to the foyer. She passed by Henry and gave the boy a nod, something noncommittal, and for a moment Henry set his contempt for her aside long enough to wonder if the gesture was related to her offer, the one made last week to talk to her if he needed to. Or perhaps she thought there was a bond between them, forged when the man Saunders tried to kill him. If she thought that, Emery Dale was a fool. Not that it mattered anymore, Henry mused, because he knew he'd have to kill this woman for humiliating his father, just as he'd killed Edmond Reed last Halloween for sleeping with his mother. The Master of Life and Death would exact vengeance.

20

June 12, 1953
Blue Creek

Four days after the fire, what remained of *The Yellow Canary* was at last torn down. Like with the blaze, a crowd gathered to bear witness to the sad event. Not much remained by the time Todd King, Katy Falconer and Freddie 'The Fish' Beauchamp came by.

"It ain't right," the Fish said.

"No, Fish, it ain't," Todd replied. And neither of them said anything else for a long time. When from an apartment window overlooking the street someone started playing "The Clock" by Johnny Ace, it got to be too much and Todd led the group away. They wandered to the park across from the clock tower and Todd and Katy sat down on the bench. Freddie the Fish kicked a stone that bounced off the memorial plaque of the mine accident.

"It ain't right," the Fish said again.

Katy wiped a tear from her cheek and Todd clenched his jaw.

"It's like everything's turned upside down, you know?" the Fish continued. "Cal, Debbie... Now the *Canary*'s gone. Mr Dooley..."

"We know, Fish," Katy said.

"I know you know, it's just..." Freddie trailed off, putting his hands behind his head and looking at the ground. There were no stones to kick, so he targeted an old candy wrapper and gave it a swipe with his foot. Then he turned back to his friends. "We need to *do* something."

"Like what?" Katy asked.

"Anything!" Freddie said, arms wide.

Silence descended on them again until Todd spoke up.

195

"I know what we can do," Todd said. "We've put it off long enough."

Katy and the Fish looked at him, then each other. The Fish grinned and nodded. Katy understood, too, and looked back at her boyfriend.

"Can we?" she asked.

"We have to," Todd said. Freddie pointed to him, nodding.

"Exactly!" Freddie said. "Oh, the kid's gonna flip when he sees us."

"Orchard Bend is a long drive," Katy said.

"Shush with all that! You're coming, too, doll," Freddie said.

"Well of course I am!" Katy said with a glare.

"Sorry, I'm just glad to be *doing* something," Freddie grinned.

"Do we need to stop at anyone's house for anything?" Todd asked. "If not, I say we hit the road right now."

"I'm ready," the Fish said.

"Me too," Katy smiled.

They left the park, Freddie the Fish rubbing his hands together with mischievous glee.

"Cal's going to be so surprised!" Freddie said with a grin.

* * *

June 12, 1953
Orchard Bend

Stirred from her dreamless doze, Mara awoke at her camp by the river to the sound of angry voices in the underbrush. Snapping into action, she drew the knife from the sheath on her hip and tensed as she peered over the mossy rocks that concealed her position.

"There he is!" cried an angry male voice.

Weaving between the trees, three teenage pursuers zeroed in on their prey, another teenage boy. Mara could see the boy would not stand much of a chance outnumbered as he was and outweighed by each of them. They passed through the trees more than a dozen yards from her camp and into the grove of aspens. Mara followed after them, knife at the ready. The fleeing boy lost ground foot by foot and Mara knew it wouldn't be long before they caught him.

With less cover in the grove, Mara proceeded with caution, but soon the pursuing trio slowed and she saw the boy up ahead standing amongst the aspens.

He must be exhausted, came the voice of the captain.

"He must be," Mara agreed just as she heard the boy utter "Help me!" to the otherwise empty grove. The larger boys slowed and spread out, flanking their target, but Mara stayed on the middle one with the crew cut and horn-rimmed glasses. He was the ringleader.

She took a position behind one of the aspens and watched the hunted teen look to his feet and then grab a stone the size of a hardball in his bloody right hand. On the tree behind him was the carving of the rose.

"Done running, rabbit?" taunted the boy with the horn-rimmed glasses.

Mara watched and waited for her moment to strike, inching forward as the three predators closed in on the boy with the bleeding hand. She had to give him credit, the boy was defiant facing the impossible odds before him. He was prepared to go down fighting.

"What? Got nothin' to say, tough guy?" the gang's leader asked, light winking off his glasses.

"Thinks he's gonna scare us off with a rock," his red haired friend chuckled.

The boy with the glasses wasn't laughing, though. Mara knew his body language, his tone, even if she couldn't see his face. He meant business. When he gave the order to his buddies to "Grab him," Mara put her knife at his throat.

"Stop," she commanded, her tone dead serious.

Everyone stopped.

It brought a smile to her face.

The teen with the horn-rimmed glasses trembled under her knife, afraid to move, and that was good, Mara liked it that way.

"What were you going to do to this boy?" Mara asked. "Beat him to within an inch of his life? Kill him? Hope no one would find his body out here?"

Mr Glasses didn't answer.

"Cat got your tongue, big guy?" she asked.

"We, uh, we don't want any trouble," said the brown-haired friend. "We were just messing around with this guy."

"Is that so?" Mara replied, then she asked the boy with the knife at his throat, "That true? You were just messing with this kid? Giving him a scare?"

Mr Glasses grunted, nudging his head only as much as he dared.

Mara nodded to the would-be victim and said to Mr Glasses, "Well, he's a friend of mine, see, and I don't appreciate my friends getting beaten on. I think you can understand that. Do you? You understand what it is I'm telling you?"

Mr Glasses nodded again and forced out a gasp of, "Yes. Yes, I understand."

Mara withdrew the blade from his throat and shoved him forward. Their potential victim still stood ready with his stone, but Mara knew the fight had gone out of the three assailants.

"Go," Mara ordered them.

Mr Glasses looked at her, then his buddies, and backed away. He cast a look at the victim that Mara read as a warning, that this wasn't over, and then the three boys sulked off back through the grove. Mara watched them until they were out of sight, then watched some more just to make sure they weren't coming back.

"Thank you," the wounded teen said as he lowered the stone and let it drop to the ground.

"You're welcome," Mara replied. The boy looked at the bleeding gash on his hand and Mara knew it was going to leave a scar. "You'll want a doctor to look at that, but I can field dress it until you get back to town."

* * *

198

"Thank you," the wounded boy told her again as she worked on his hand at her campsite.

"You already thanked me. Once was enough," Mara replied.

"I saw you yesterday," the boy said, "at the park next to the Town Hall. And before that, by the train tracks."

Mara nodded, but said nothing, focusing instead on the boy's hand. She cleaned the wound of the dirt and much of the dried blood.

"I walked here along the tracks," she said at last, but wanted to change the subject. "Why were those boys chasing you?"

"A misunderstanding. I met his ex-girlfriend last night and he's not happy about that," the boy explained. He winced as she wrapped the dressing around the gash. Mara tried to work fast, sensing nervousness in the boy as he fidgeted. She chalked it up to his encounter with his attackers, which would be enough to get anyone amped up.

When he suddenly jerked away, she wondered if it was more. His gaze past her made her turn, but she saw nothing there.

Or did she?

Just for the moment, there might have been something, a shape over her shoulder, gone in an instant.

"What is it? What do you see?" Mara asked.

The boy looked at her, his expression odd, his eyes flicking about her face. She saw uncertainty and confusion and thought she understood.

"Is it a ghost?" Mara asked.

"Yes," the boy stammered. "She's right behind you. She's looking at you."

Mara thought of her dream and of the spectral figures that moved about the grove. She supposed she shouldn't be surprised by any of it.

"It's this place. Lost souls gather here," she said. "I think there might be two of them. I've caught glimpses, quickly and out of the corner of my eye."

"I can see them," the boy said. "I know that sounds utterly nuts, but—!"

"I believe you," Mara said.

"You do?"

199

"Yes. I've seen some odd things in my life, so yes, I believe you can see them," Mara said as she bound the dressing.

"But I couldn't see them before yesterday, before I saw you," the boy said. "Did you do something to me? To my sight?"

Now that *was* odd, she thought, this boy ascribing such strangeness to her.

"No," Mara said. "I don't have any magical powers. *You* might if you can see ghosts, but I don't."

The boy said nothing, pondering what she said. Disappointment lined his face.

Mara finished dressing his wound.

"Don't try to make a fist and avoid using the hand if you can. And go see a doctor. You don't want an infection," she ordered as she stood up. The boy rose and stuck out his good hand.

"Thanks," he said. "My name is Cal. Cal Watson."

Mara took his hand and gave it a firm shake.

"Good to meet you, Cal," she said. "I'm Mara Dale."

21

June 12, 1953
Blue Creek

Tyler Brand only came prepared the night before to break into Owen McCabe's house and steal his ledger; he did not come prepared to flee Orchard Bend in such a hurry afterwards. He didn't regret the decision, since the magnitude of what he'd done demanded immediate flight from town. Ty only wished he'd brought more with him than just the clothes on his back. When the day began to warm up as he walked along the road, he tied his dark brown cardigan around his waist. Brand's white undershirt already felt clammy with sweat under his arms and down his back. After hours of walking, the blisters that formed on his aching feet burst and he dreaded taking off his shoes when the time came. It wouldn't be pretty.

Most of all, Ty Brand regretted not taking his car in for routine maintenance more often. When it broke down in the moonless night, he'd opened the hood and stared with his flashlight at the vehicle's inner workings with little comprehension as to the problem. He poked and prodded and tried to glean some understanding, but the mess of wires, tubes and metal offered no insight. At first, Brand waited, sitting with the car door open watching for someone to drive by, hoping they'd give him a lift. Or better yet they might know how to fix what was wrong with his car and could send him on his way. So Ty waited. And waited. He thought of Gabby, how proud she'd be that he'd avenged her by stealing Owen's ledger, a book full of the old man's madness and a record of his murderous deeds. Ty imagined Sheriff Thorn leaving for work in a few hours and finding the ledger on his porch where Brand

201

left it. Ty would like to have handed it to the man in person, but it was just too dangerous. Owen "The Barber" McCabe had people everywhere and one of them would find him. Fleeing when he did was the right move. For all he knew, Owen McCabe had even now discovered his ledger was missing and was already making calls.

Brand had got out of the car and looked back the way he came, then ahead down the road. With Ashleyville behind him and Blue Creek still an hour's drive southeast, he had a long way to go to get out of reach of The Barber. This being farm country, Brand knew he'd have to come across *someone* out here, someone like a helpful farmer. So he set off in the direction of Blue Creek. It didn't take long to begin to understand the difference in perception between when a man drove these roads and when he had to walk them. The acres of farmland stretched out all around him under the stars. He passed unmarked side roads, but fear of getting lost out here became a real concern and Ty stayed on the road he knew. He found a long driveway that appeared to go nowhere, so continued down the road as the sky began to lighten. The next driveway he came across ended with a house and a barn and Ty's hopes began to rise. He made the long walk to the two-storey brick farmhouse and knocked on the door, but no one answered. He yelled up at the windows, expecting the bedroom light to come on, but the house remained dark. Ty waited, parking himself on the comfortable porch swing, intent on staying put until someone who lived here found him. Didn't farmers get up at the break of day? Wasn't that how it worked? Ty thought it was, so he waited, watching the sky continue to grow brighter. His body welcomed the rest. He took off his cardigan and propped it up behind his head.

When he snapped awake, the morning sun shone bright in his face. A glance at his watch told him he'd been out for over ninety minutes. He looked for any sign that the occupants of the farm were up, but saw none. He pounded on the door again and once more walked around the house calling out, asking if anyone was home.

No one was.

At the back of the house, Ty spotted a solitary gravestone under an ancient-looking tree which read:

Margaret Noble
Wife, Mother, Grandmother, Sister, Aunt.
R.I.P.
1879

Brand considered the grave for a moment, wondering if it was real, guessing it probably was.

"Better get moving or The Barber will put me in one of these himself," Ty said without humour. Slumped forward, he started back down the driveway, his aching legs protesting.

* * *

The service station at the side of the road glittered white against the green and gold scenery in the distance, picked out by the afternoon sun pouring through the clouds.

When he reached the I & G Friendly gas station, a middle-aged man with a round face and rotund form came out of the station holding a cup of coffee and sporting a work cap and oil-stained white coveralls. He watched Ty, sipping his drink, and gave a nod as Ty waved.

"Afternoon," Ty said.

"Right back at you, young feller," the attendant said. Ty saw the monogrammed name on his coveralls was 'Irwin.'

"My car broke down," Ty said, pointing back down the road. "I don't know how far, a good many miles that way, at least, I've been walking all day and there's been hardly anyone out on the roads. No one stopped to give me a lift if you can believe that. Can I get a tow? And I assume you do repairs here?"

"We do," Irwin said between sips of his coffee. "And we can get you towed. How about you come inside for a cup of coffee? You look like you could use it."

"Thanks, but I'm in a bit of a rush," Ty said, looking up the road.

"We can't go anywhere until my partner shows up," Irwin said. "Someone has to mind this place. He'll be here in, oh, say, fifteen minutes. Time enough for you have that coffee."

Ty wanted to press the matter but got the sense it would be useless. Still, he couldn't shake the feeling that McCabe was closing in with every passing second. He looked back in the direction of his car and resigned himself to waiting.

"Okay, coffee sounds good," Brand said. "It's been a long morning."

"Come on in, I'll fix you up a mug. On the house for a weary traveller," Irwin smiled.

Inside the station's office, Irwin poured Ty some coffee as the reporter stood next to the fan on the desk, letting it cool him down.

"Hope you like it black, son," Irwin said, handing Ty the mug. "Gill's supposed to bring some cream and sugar today, seeing as we're all out."

"Black is perfect, thanks," Ty said.

"What brings you out this way this early, if you don't mind me asking?" Irwin said, sitting behind the desk.

"Heading to the city," Ty said. "Long overdue vacation. Figured I'd leave early and get to the city before noon. That doesn't look likely now."

Irwin nodded, finished his cup and poured himself another.

"The city, huh?" Irwin said with disgust. "I don't have a lick of time to spare going to a place like that. Full of degenerates and liars, you know? If I were you, I'd stay out of the city."

"I'm only going there to catch a flight," Ty said, hoping Irwin's partner Gill would show up soon so they could get on with fixing his car.

Irwin didn't respond as he leaned back in his chair and sipped his black coffee. Ty looked out the window out toward the road just in time to see a police car pull up to the gas pumps. He froze, heart pounding, fresh sweat forming on his brow.

"That'd be Deputy Berger," Irwin said, his cheerful tone returning. "He comes out here instead of filling up in town because our gas is cheaper. He pockets the difference. The deputies are supposed to fill up each morning at Cole's, but not Berger, no-siree."

Deputy Berger's doughy form climbed out the squad car and the policeman began the ritual of filling up. Irwin got up from behind his desk and went to the door.

"Help yourself to another cup, if you need," he said to Ty as he went outside.

Brand recognized Berger from the cemetery meeting a few days earlier and now wanted very much to flee. From the office, a second door led to the garage and he wanted to slip out of sight and find a back door. But running would only make things worse. Ty wouldn't get very far, for starters. And if Berger wasn't looking for him right now on Owen McCabe's orders, running would draw attention to him anyway. Ty's only hope was for the deputy to finish his business and leave. With any luck, he wouldn't find Brand's car on the side of the road either and this would all blow over.

Irwin and Berger chatted as the deputy filled up the tank. When another car pulled into the service station, both men waved to the driver. Instead of stopping at the pumps, the car parked off to the side of the station's lot and a scrawny, middle-aged man in a similar set of coveralls got out. Brand guessed him to be Gill, Irwin's business partner.

"Don't tell him I'm in here. Don't tell him I'm in here," Ty muttered over and over as Gill walked with his lunch box past Berger and Irwin and they exchanged words. Gill didn't slow down, but continued toward the office. Berger and Irwin resumed their conversation and Ty stepped out of their view as Gill came in. He looked startled for a moment to see Brand standing there.

"Oh, hello," Gill said. Ty was correct, it was Gill, according to the monogram on his coveralls. "Didn't know anyone was in here."

"Irwin didn't tell you?" Ty asked, trying to sound casual.

"Naw, he was jawing away with the deputy out there," Gill said, putting his lunch box in the fridge and heading to the coffeemaker. "What brings you here?"

"Car broke down," Ty said. "Irwin's gonna bring the tow truck to pick it up."

"Well, we'll take good care of you," Gill said with a smile as he went into the garage. Ty faked a smile in return long enough for Gill to leave, then it fell away as he returned to watching Irwin and Berger.

"Hurry up and finish, Deputy," Ty muttered. "I gotta get out of here."

At last, Berger finished pumping gas and paid Irwin. The attendant started back to the office as Berger climbed into his car. The deputy started it up and gave a honk as he pulled out onto the road, heading in the opposite direction of Brand's car.

Ty felt faint as he dropped himself to sit on the edge of the desk. Irwin came in and put his empty coffee cup down on the desk next to Brand.

"I'll let Gill know where we're going and then we'll go get your car, how's that sound?" Irwin said as he took a set of keys from the hook next to the fridge.

"Sounds great, thanks," Ty said.

Irwin opened the door to the garage and stuck his head in.

"Gill, I'm gonna go with this young feller to get his car and bring it back here," Irwin called out.

"Okey-doke," Gill called back.

Irwin shut the door and turned to Brand.

"Okay, friend, feel better after that coffee? Hit the spot, didn't it?" Irwin smiled as he walked to the front door.

"You could say that," Ty said, his joints cracking as he stood up.

* * *

"Son, you picked the worst road to break down on," Irwin said, shaking his head. "I'm surprised you saw anyone out this way at all. Half of these farms are for sale, but you wouldn't know it just by looking. Is that you car up ahead?".

"That's it," Ty said.

It didn't take nearly as long to get back to the car as it did to walk all day to the service station. Ty tried not to think how far he'd have gotten if it hadn't broken down. I he hadn't, he'd be out of the country by now.

They pulled in behind the car, which still had the hood propped up. Ty hopped out of the passenger side and the blisters shot darts of pain into his feet. Irwin came around the tow truck with a toolkit in his hand.

"Let's take a look-see, huh?" he said as he passed Brand. "You jump on in the front seat and when I say, you give her a crank, got it?"

"Sure," Ty said and he climbed into the car.

"Start her up," Irwin called out.

Ty turned the key in the ignition and the motor revved but didn't turn over. He gave it another crank, to no avail.

"Alright, alright, that's enough," Irwin called out. "Let see what we've got."

Ty heard him open his toolbox, muttering about the inner workings of the engine, what to Brand's ears might as well have been a foreign language. He tuned it out and closed his eyes, his head thrumming from a combination of stress, lack of sleep and caffeine. He felt something digging into his lower back and remembered the flashlight. He adjusted his position and reached for it.

"Try it again, there," Irwin called out.

Ty turned the key and the engine revved once more. Still the car wouldn't start. When he stopped trying to turn the engine over, Ty leaned out the open driver's side door.

"Why don't we take the car to the garage and look at it there, Mr Irwin?" he asked.

"Heh, Mr Irwin," the service attendant chuckled. "That's funny. Give her another crank, would you?"

Ty did and a flick of light caught his eye in the rear view mirror. A car rounded the corner down the road behind him. He stopped revving the engine and watched the car, noting the telltale black and white. Ty stopped breathing. His tired mind began to spin.

What if it's not a police car? he thought. It was a ways off yet, so maybe his overtaxed brain was playing tricks on him.

"Mr Brand, give it another crank," Irwin called out. "I think I have an idea."

Ty got out of the car.

"Hey, let's load the car... onto..." Brand trailed off as he looked back at the advancing car. It would be on them in a few minutes, but that wasn't the problem.

Ty hadn't told Irwin his last name.

"Shit," Ty whispered.

This is where it ends, is it? he thought.

Irwin came into view around the driver's side of the car and Ty was not surprised to see him holding a gun, a .22 he guessed from the size.

"Oh look, here comes my brother," Irwin said.

"Are you going kill me?" Ty asked.

"No, sir, not unless you make me" Irwin said, gesturing with the gun toward the approaching car. "That might be *his* job, but it's not mine. How about you come away from the door, up here to the front of the car with me? Nice and slow, young feller."

Irwin backed up and motioned for Ty to follow. Ty did, feeling deflated and very, very tired now. Part of him felt relief the chase was over. He also felt something heavy bouncing in his back pocket.

His flashlight.

Ty angled his body so Irwin wouldn't see it as he moved forward. An idea half formed in Ty's mind and he knew he had to act right then. He stepped forward quickly, feigning a sway as he did, trying to look beaten.

"Whoa there," Irwin said, but Ty stopped as suddenly as he had started forward and looked past Irwin with horror.

"What the *fuck* is THAT!" Ty cried.

Out of reflex, Irwin glanced over his shoulder. In a single desperate motion, Ty grabbed the flashlight and swung it at Irwin's gun. It connected as Irwin turned back to the reporter. The blow didn't knock the gun loose as Ty had hoped it would, but it deflected the gun's aim. Acting on pure survival instinct, Ty backhanded the flashlight at Irwin's head, connecting with the man's temple. The gun dropped to the ground and Irwin brought his hands up to defend himself as he staggered back. Ty swung again, bludgeoning Irwin on the head. The man fell backwards to the ground and lay there moaning, but Ty continued his advance, almost lost in a defensive rage. He kicked Irwin as hard as he could in the gut, letting out a primal scream as he did. He stood heaving over the prone, whimpering man and remembered the gun, then remembered the approaching car.

Ty found the gun lying almost at his feet. He scooped it up and turned around. The hood was still stood open, blocking the approaching car's view of what just happened. Ty could hear the car now, it was very close. He stepped out into the middle of the road, gun in both hands, trained on the police car as it pulled up. At the sight of him, it screeched to a halt. Ty aimed the gun at the driver, Deputy Berger.

"HANDS UP!" Brand hollered.

The deputy sat there, eyes wide, his mouth dropping open in surprise.

"I SAID HANDS UP!" Brand screamed at him.

Berger did as ordered, bringing his hands into view, palms up.

"GET OUT OF THE CAR!" Brand thought about putting a warning shot through the windshield. "DON'T TRY ANYTHING OR I'LL FUCKING KILL YOU!"

Berger eased himself out of the car, which was still running, and kept his hands up.

"Put your gun on the hood," Brand ordered him. "If you draw, I'll kill you. Use your left hand!"

Berger did as he was told, reaching across his body in an awkward motion to pull his gun out of his holster.

"What did you do to my brother?" Berger asked in a shaky voice.

"Shut your mouth!" Brand was in no mood to talk. "Pull out your cuffs."

Berger paused a moment, confused, then pulled out his cuffs and started to put them on the police car's hood next to his gun.

"No, not on the hood! Hold onto them," Brand said, the gun still levelled at the deputy. "Let's see the key."

Berger dug into his pockets and produced the key.

"Toss it, out in the field," Brand said.

Berger let out a sigh and tossed the key away.

"Okay, get over here," Brand ordered, backing up.

Irwin was still on the ground, moaning, clutching his bloodied head. When Berger saw him, anger rose in his face.

"You piece of shit, Brand, what did you do?!" Berger snapped.

"I told you to shut the hell up, that's what I did!" Brand snapped back.

"Irwin, I'm here. You'll be okay," Berger said.

"Help him up," Brand said. "And keep those cuffs handy, you're going to need them."

* * *

With the brothers cuffed to the grill of Brand's car, Ty picked up Irwin's tool box from the ground and brought it back to the tow truck. He picked the flashlight up off the ground, slipped it into his back pocket and walked over to the still-running police car. Berger's .38 police special lay on the hood. Ty switched the .22 revolver to his left hand and held the .38 in his right. The weight felt good and something primitive inside him swelled with power as he held both weapons in his hands, looking from one to the other. The panic and fear of the day had left him. He took in the horizon, the farmlands and distant hills. Insects buzzed in the otherwise quiet air. He looked west to the lowering sun, where Blue Creek lay, with Sutter Grove beyond and eventually the city. He turned to face east, toward Ashleyville and Orchard Bend, toward Owen McCabe.

Yeah, Ty thought, gripping the pistols tighter. The guns felt very good in his hands.

22

June 12, 1953
Orchard Bend

Davis ascended the steps to the front entrance of the Town Hall, his shadow cast broad on the sturdy old wooden doors. He passed through the foyer as his cigarette reached the end of its life. He crushed it out on the wall above the waste bin, next to a photo of the Town Hall as it looked the year it was built. The old Town Hall in the photo didn't feature the additions built onto it later, like the Sheriff's Office and Post Office. Next to this photo hung another image, this one of the 1887 Council of Aldermen standing shoulder to shoulder on a stage. Looking at the photo, Davis took out his pack of smokes and drew another, placing it in his mouth and pulling out his lighter. He read the names under each and saw listed as absent one Maxwell McCabe. Davis brought the lighter up, flicked the cap open, placed his thumb on the spark wheel and then stopped. He closed the lighter, put it away, took the cigarette from his mouth and replaced it in the pack, leaving the foyer and heading into the hall. He passed the thick columns and made his way to the interior door of the Sheriff's Office.

"Oh, hello!" said the girl behind the front desk. She looked to Davis like she should still be in high school. He guessed her short haircut was pretty, if you liked that sort of style. "How can I help you?"

Davis looked at the nameplate on the desk.

"Would you be Miss Dickson, darling?" Davis asked, taking off his fedora.

The girl laughed.

"No, no, I'm her assistant, Grace," the girl said. "Mrs Dickson will be back in a moment."

Davis nodded.

"I'm here to see Lieutenant Pine, Grace," he said. "Would he be around?"

"Yes, he is," Grace said. "Let me page him for you."

"No need, Grace," called Lieutenant Pine from behind her. He stood at the door of the sheriff's private office and waved Davis in.

Davis rounded the desk and followed Pine into the office.

"You get promoted to sheriff?" Davis asked.

"Of course not," Pine said, throwing himself down in the sheriff's chair behind the desk. "Thorn's wife died last night, so he's on leave and I'm in charge. It's easier to run things from in here, as opposed to the closet they call my office."

Davis nodded.

Pine leaned forward.

"Why are you here?" Pine asked.

Davis pulled out a slip of paper and handed it to Pine. The figure on the check made Pine let out a long sigh. He looked up at Davis.

"Mr McCabe appreciates your efforts in making that old case disappear," Davis said, looking around the sheriff's office.

"The Emery Dale case," Pine said, shaking his head.

"The Barber is a generous man," Davis said. "He wants your girl out there to go to a nice college."

Pine looked through the glass at his daughter Grace and then to Davis.

"I can see the resemblance, Lieutenant," Davis said. "Pretty girl, though I'm not a fan of the hair-do."

"Enough about my daughter, if you don't mind," Pine said, dropping the cheque on the desk. "Maybe I should give this back, because Mr McCabe is *not* going to be happy when I call him. I'm sure he's waiting by the phone right now."

Davis watched as Pine let out a miserable groan and stretched back in the sheriff's chair. Davis rolled his eyes and wished he'd lit that cigarette after all.

"What seems to be the problem?" Davis asked when it became clear Pine wasn't going to just tell him like a normal human being.

"Ty Brand broke into McCabe's house last night and stole something from him, something valuable," Pine said. "McCabe put it on me to find him, as if I don't have enough crap going on. But Brand is gone, took off with what he stole and that could seriously fuck with everything."

"What did he steal?" Davis asked.

Pine looked away, thought about it a moment, wrestled with it and finally gave up, "The ledger. McCabe's black leather ledger, the one he carries around everywhere. God only knows what's in it, but I tell you, he's scared. He tried to hide it, but I've never heard The Barber scared like that, he's—"

Davis was in Pine's face in a flash, he hands slapping the sheriff's desk as he bent over Pine.

"You keep that little fact to yourself, Lieutenant!" Davis said low. "It doesn't leave this room, understand?"

Pine nodded, inching back in his seat.

"When did all this happen?" Davis asked, standing back up.

"Last night," Pine said. "McCabe called me this morning. I've been all over town looking for Brand. There's an A.P.B. out for him in the county, but who knows where he is now?"

"Hiding," Davis said, "or running."

Pine let out another groan of frustration.

"Then there's this other matter," Pine said. Davis very much wanted that cigarette, but didn't want to chance it. It his experience, people remembered the little things, especially witnesses. The smell of his cigarettes would linger in their mind and that could be the difference between remembering something and remembering nothing about a man. Sometimes Davis wanted a person to remember him, sometimes he didn't. Grace Pine out at the desk might remember her father talking to a man who smoked, but probably wouldn't remember much about a man who didn't.

"What 'other matter'?" Davis asked.

213

"McCabe instructed me to find this other person, some woman who he says just arrived in town," Pine said. "How is that for vague, huh?"

"He must have given more than that to go on," sometimes Davis felt like a schoolteacher leading children to the answer. And this man Pine was a police lieutenant, to boot. So much for keen deductive acumen. He looked out through the blinds toward the main office, empty now near the end of the day. He saw a woman come in and join Grace at the front desk. Davis picked her out as Mrs Dickson.

Behind him, Pine flipped through his notebook and found the right page.

"Blonde, about five-foot-six," Davis said. "Early thirties. Light green eyes, McCabe said. Very light, almost white."

"'Almost white,' you say?" Davis asked, turning back to Pine.

"Yeah," Pine said, "that mean something to you?"

"Met a girl in Blue Creek who fit that description," Davis said. "She looked good in a uniform."

"A uniform?" Pine asked.

"Waitress," Davis said. "Worked at the now-closed *Yellow Canary* diner. You say she's in town?"

"If it's the same person, yes she is, at least according to McCabe," Pine said, his interest piqued. "You've seen her. You think you can find her?"

"That's not my job right now," Davis said.

"Oh, is that so?" Pine said, reaching for the phone. "How about I call Mr McCabe and see if he thinks it's you job to find the girl he wants found, the girl *you* say you met once. I'm sure he'll agree that it's best you don't help look for her."

Pine started to dial and Davis's iron grip seized his wrist just as fast as he got into Pine's face a moment ago.

"You don't want to make that call, Lieutenant," Davis said, his eyes fixed on Pine. "And you don't want to test me."

The two locked glares and Davis had to admit that Pine did have some guts somewhere in his belly.

"Alright, Lieutenant," Davis said. "If you need my help that much, I'll poke around for this waitress. When I find her, McCabe will be informed in great detail as to your inability to follow through on his request. I doubt he'll be pleased, unless you find Brand and get back what he stole."

Davis let Pine's wrist go and he left the office, noting Grace and Mrs Dickson didn't even glance up at him as he departed, so involved were they in reviewing the girl's performance.

Outside, Davis lit his long awaited cigarette and took a deep drag from it, watching the sun drop lower in the sky.

23

June 12, 1953
Orchard Bend

Detective Tom Reed pulled his car up to the curb under the shade of a bigleaf maple standing tall on the Thorns' front lawn. Reed sat in the car with the radio playing, tapping the wheel and staring at the house from across the passenger seat. Varetta Dillard's "Easy, Easy Baby" finished and went right into the B-side, "Letter In Blue." Reed made up his mind and turned off the engine, cutting the radio just as the song started. He climbed out and rounded the car, passing the mailbox. He paused a moment when he saw the names stencilled on the side.

Brian & Maryanne Thorn

The flag was up, so Reed opened the box and took out the contents. He didn't look at them, only made his way up the path to the front porch. He watched the windows and listened, hoping he'd hear something from the grieving man inside and at the same time hoping he wouldn't. Reed didn't know what to expect, but something told him anything was better than silence. Well, just about anything.

Reed climbed the stairs and saw the covered casserole dish at the door. He picked that up, too. It still radiated warmth, so whichever thoughtful neighbour delivered it had done so recently. Tom listened at the door, craning his head. Hearing nothing from inside, he knocked. The sheriff might ignore a doorbell, because people being polite always rang the doorbell and today he'd probably received his share of polite visitors. Police, however, knocked and Reed hoped doing so would illicit a response. He waited and listened, but heard nothing. He knocked again, hard, tempted to call out to the sheriff, but thought Thorn might ignore him. Reed waited again, then heard a soft creak, followed by another. The footsteps approached the door and the detective braced himself.

The door opened a crack and one bloodshot eye peered out. Reed didn't know if he should speak first, but when the sheriff said nothing, the detective decided he'd better.

"Sheriff, I'm sorry about your wife, I really am," Reed said with an awkward mix of hesitation and rambling. "I wanted to see how you were doing and... um... One of your neighbours left you a casserole. And I have your mail."

The bloodshot eye blinked and the door closed. Reed let out a long breath and wanted to kick himself. It had been a mistake to come here, he should've left well enough alone.

There came a click and the door opened again, wider this time. The sheriff looked pale, both eyes bright red and his expression one of great fatigue, but Reed saw alertness in the man's eyes, the kind you don't see when a man's had too much to drink. He wore a sweat-stained white undershirt beneath the suspenders of his pants.

"What do you really want, Tom?" Thorn asked.

"Can I come in, Sheriff?" Reed asked.

Thorn looked at him so long Reed thought the sheriff would say no, but he stepped back and waved the detective in with a motion that seemed to take a lot of strength.

"Thank you, Sheriff," Reed said, stepping inside. "I know it's a difficult time right now and I wouldn't have come if—"

"Stop talking, Detective," Thorn said, taking the casserole from him and walking through the living room to the kitchen. Reed followed a few steps behind, keeping a close eye on him. He waited in the living room, but through the open kitchen door he saw a cardboard box on the kitchen table. The glass necks of a half dozen bottles stuck out of the top of the box. Thorn put the casserole down next to the box, bumping it and making the bottles clink. He came back out to the living room and eased himself onto the sofa, leaning forward with his elbows on his knees. He began rubbing his temples. Reed waited and when the sheriff finally stopped, he looked up at the detective and gave a curt nod to the chair next to Tom. Reed sat and put the mail down on the coffee table. The sheriff stared at him, then gave a gesture that said, *Well, what do you want?*

"The Barber is looking for Tyler Brand," Reed said. "Lieutenant Pine put out an all-points bulletin on him, for burglary of all things. I don't know what Brand is supposed to have stolen, but Pine's worked up over this. It's a serious matter for McCabe."

"Pine, huh?" Thorn said, looking out the window.

"Yes," Reed said, "I have a feeling he's responsible for making the Emery Dale case disappear; all that evidence we collected at the Hansen property."

"Do you really want to go down that road?" Thorn asked, still looking out the window. With the late afternoon light pouring in on Thorn's face, Reed thought the sheriff looked ten years older and in dire need of three days of straight sleep.

"I want to find Brand," Reed said. "I want to find out what he knows. If we get him to a district attorney, it could end McCabe."

"Big 'if,'" Thorn said.

"We know Brand is in McCabe's pocket, or he *was* until this morning," Reed said. "The county-wide A.P.B. means he's either skipped town or is hiding. Can you think of any place he might be?"

Thorn brought his gaze from the window to the picture on the end table. In it, he and his wife Maryanne, both ten years younger, stood arm in arm healthy and happy on the old boat landing downriver from the McCabe Mill. Their carefree smiles radiated from the black and white photo.

"Ty Brand is a reporter," Thorn said, looking at the photo. "Reporters are like police detectives. They have contacts and sources. They know people. *He* knows people, not all of them are loyal to McCabe."

Reed waited for more, but Thorn put the picture back and got up with a world weary groan.

"Thank you for coming by, Tom," Thorn said. "Tell Shelly Dickson I'm okay. I'm sure she's worried sick, though she'd never show it."

Reed wanted to ask him for more to go on, but didn't. He rose from the chair and started for the front hall. Thorn followed him out. Reed glanced toward the study and saw a medium-sized package lying discarded on the floor.

"Getting a lot of deliveries today, I suppose, huh?" Reed asked.

Thorn looked at the package, shrugged and opened the door for him.

"Sheriff, some sleep might do you good," Reed said. "And call someone, maybe. You shouldn't be alone right now."

"My sister is on her way," Thorn said. "I won't be alone. She'll be here in a few hours, enough time to have a nap, I think."

"Do you need anything?" Reed asked, stepping out onto the porch.

"No, Tom. Thank you," Thorn said, his voice still heavy with emotion, but the gratitude sounded genuine.

"Call me anytime, day or night if you need," Reed said.

Thorn gave him a nod, but said nothing as he left.

Reed made his way to his car, got in and looked back at the house.

"Contacts and sources," Reed said. It wasn't much, but it was something. He started the car and the radio came on to the DJ announcing the next song as "K.C. Loving" by Little Willie LittleField. Reed pulled away from the house and cruised along the street, his detective's mind gearing up.

"It's a case, just like any other," he thought aloud, tapping on the steering wheel to the rhythm of the song. "A missing reporter. The obvious leads are dry, his job, his home. So move onto the less obvious ones, lesser known associates..."

Reed had an idea about that and headed downtown. This idea required coffee.

* * *

219

Thorn watched Reed from the study as the detective pulled away. When the car disappeared from view, Thorn bent over the desk, trying to contain the trembling and the sobs threatening to overwhelm him.

"It's too much," he gasped, his words almost unintelligible. "It's too much, Maryanne. I *need* you back!"

Shaking, Brian Thorn sat in the hard wooden chair at his desk, clutching his arms and rocking back and forth.

"Nothing makes sense, Maryanne," he whispered. "Nothing makes sense without you here."

He shouldn't have looked at the photo, he thought. With Reed here, for a few minutes, things were okay. Not good, not by any measure, but his distracted mind was okay. But of course there was the picture. If it hadn't been the picture, he'd have spotted some other memento of his life with Maryanne. The house was full of them, so there was no escape.

"I can't do it anymore, Maryanne," Thorn whimpered. "It's too hard. I just want to be with you, somewhere better than this."

Brian opened the desk drawer and pulled out his service revolver and cleaning kit. He set the kit on the desk and opened it. The shaking eased, as if his body knew the suffering would end soon. Thorn checked the cylinder of his .38, confirmed it to be fully loaded and closed it again.

"I'll see you soon, honey," Thorn said.

He put the gun to his head and thought of happier times, like the day his sister took the photo now sitting on the end table. Of course he'd lied to Reed. Brian Thorn had not called his sister to come over, nor had he called anyone else today, except the undertaker.

He felt the hard metal against his temple and pulled it away an inch, not wanting that to be the last thing he felt. Tears streamed down his cheeks, blurring his vision. He blinked the moisture from his eyes, looking out the window, wanting the last thing he saw to be the pleasant view of the bigleaf maple on his lawn. He leaned back in the chair, stretching his tired legs and back.

Might as well be comfortable, he thought and gave a teary little chuckle.

The wheel of his chair caught something and he looked down at the floor. The package left on his porch that morning sat wrapped in newspaper and looking plain. Whoever left the package had written 'Sheriff Thorn. Important" on it.

"What could be so damn important?" he muttered. The pounding in his head would not let up and he'd welcome the relief that would come from pulling the trigger. With her dying words, Maryanne had asked him to stop drinking and in his grief he'd agreed. So try as his might, Brian had gathered up the bottles lying about the house, each in various stages of full. He wondered for a moment what Tom Reed thought when he saw them in the kitchen. Did he see Thorn was dry today? Thorn thought Reed did spot that.

"Fine," Thorn said to himself and put the gun down, figuring it could wait a few minutes. He picked up the package and unwrapped It. Inside he found a black, leather bound ledger. The first pages looked more like some talented artist had used the pages as a sketchbook. Detailed and rather beautiful pencil work depicted scenes of life in Orchard Bend. He found a curious looking map and a sketch of a tree with a carving on it, then sketches of people, including some nice drawings of a blonde haired woman.

As pretty as the pictures were, Thorn didn't see what was so important about the book until the sketches stopped and entries like in a diary appeared, some with newspaper clippings dating back around 70 or more years.

Orchard Herald
May 5, 1879
UNDERWOOD GANG TERROR COMES TO ORCHARD BEND

...proclaimed the first clipping. It told of Emery Dale's heroics saving a boy and a schoolteacher on a road outside of town a few days before. Below that, from the same date, another clipping's headline read...

MCCABES WELCOME SECOND SON 'OWEN FREDRICK'

221

Thorn scratched his chin and flipped ahead, curious about the rest of this make-shift scrapbook diary. He found another set of clippings...

Orchard Herald
November 3, 1885
LOCAL MERCHANT DEAD IN STOREHOUSE FIRE

...one read. Below that, the diary's author had written "Reed Storehouse – Henry's doing."

Thorn started from the beginning of the diary portion and began to read, getting up from the desk and leaving the study. He walked through the front hall, the living room and into the kitchen. He didn't want to put the ledger down, even to make coffee, but his stomach growled from not having eaten anything all day. The smell as it brewed triggered a need to eat, so Thorn popped some bread in the toaster and read another few diary entries before pausing again to gather up his meal and return to the living room. Next to the photo of him and Maryanne, Brian Thorn resumed reading, fascinated as the dark, twisted history of the diary's author unfolded page by gripping page. He stopped at one point and stared at an old notice glued in sideways, appearing to date from November of 1886.

THE ORCHARD BEND COUNCIL OF ALDERMEN
HEREBY ANNOUNCES THE HIRING OF
MS. EMERY DALE
TO THE POSITION OF TOWN SHERIFF
WITH ALL ACCOMPANYING
JURISDICTION AND AUTHORITY

In the middle of the notice, a simple but expressive drawing of Emery Dale looked back at Sheriff Thorn from across the decades.

"The lost sheriff," Thorn said. He sipped his coffee and read on.

24

The aldermen's notice on the door of the jailhouse fluttered in the cold morning breeze. Emery Dale stood looking at it, debating whether to remove it. She'd hoped to take the job with little fuss made, at least in public, but the announcements posted all over town made that impossible. As she'd ridden into town moments earlier, Dale did see one of the notices come down, removed from the General Store & Feed window by the owner, the widow Mary Reed. Mrs Reed took the paper off her door, folded it and saw Dale passing by on horseback. Without a word, Mrs Reed went back inside and Dale continued on her way.

She decided to leave the notice up at least for the rest of the day, unlocked the door and went inside. Memories came of her first days in Orchard Bend; being locked up by Sheriff Anderson, mocked by US Marshall Saunders, both in this very jailhouse, and at Sully's only seven months ago when Deputy Wilson asked for *her* help when Daniel Underwood kidnapped Sheriff Anderson.

"All those men are dead," Dale said under her breath, which wisped frosted from her mouth. She went to the potbelly wood stove, noting it as the same make and model Rose had in the schoolhouse. With some newspaper as kindling, Dale lit the stove and stood up. She took off her sword and cloak, hanging both on the hook in the office across from the jail cells.

On the desk sat Wilson's sheriff's badge and a locket. She reached for the badge, hesitated, then touched it with two fingers, but left it where it was.

223

Behind her, the door opened and Deputy Allen Green entered, bundled against the chilling breeze. He saw Dale and stopped inside the door, pulling his scarf from his face.

"Oh, you're here already," Green said. "I was hoping to get here first and have the stove lit, but it looks like you took care of that."

"I did," Dale said. She didn't know Green very well at all. He'd been hired by Wilson at the beginning of the summer. "And good morning, Deputy Green."

"Yeah, good morning, Sheriff," Green said, coming in and hanging his overcoat on the hook next to her cloak and sword. Seeing the latter, he stood with his hands on his hips and gave it a good long look. "Well, wouldn't you know? There it is."

"I presume word of the sword precedes me?" Dale asked, searching now for the coffee supplies.

"Yes, ma'am," Green said. "I reckon most everyone knows you have it, though they haven't seen it on your person in a long time."

"Well, there it is," Dale said, pulling the bag of coffee grounds and a coffee pot from the cabinet by the desk. "And no, you may not touch it."

Green lowered his hand and looked sheepish. She saw him glance at the pair of cherrywood handled knives under her jacket and the pair of Colt Peacemakers on her hips.

"Deputy, how old are you?" Dale asked.

"I'm twenty-one, ma'am," Green said.

"You're of the family who owns the farm east of here, aren't you?" Dale said, measuring out coffee grounds.

"Yes, ma'am," Green said.

She stopped what she was doing.

"Okay, right off the bat, don't call me 'ma'am' and I won't call you 'kid' or anything like that, deal?" Dale said with amusement.

"What should I call you? Just 'Sheriff'?" Green asked.

"That would be fine," Dale said. "Tell me, how do you feel working for me?"

In didn't surprise Dale to see the deputy uncomfortable with the question.

"This is your first day, so I can't really say this way or that," Green shrugged.

Dale resumed preparing the coffee.

"How do you feel about working for a woman?" she asked.

Green stood up straight.

"I can rightly say I've never done it, until today," he said, head high.

"It's a day of firsts for both of us, then," Dale said and handed him the coffee pot. "Would you mind fetching us some water, Deputy Green?"

He took the coffee pot and retrieved a bucket from under the table by the door without a word. He left to get the water and Dale took off her jacket as the stove warmed up the room. She fed another thin log to the fire, returned to the desk and looked out the window as the people she'd sworn to protect went about their business on Anderson Street.

* * *

"EVIL WALKS *FREELY* ABOUT THIS TOWN!" Mrs O'Malley cried out. Parents on the boardwalk gathered up their children and hurried indoors while other townsfolk stopped what they were doing and watched the grieving mother. Unlike her last visit to town, this day she clad herself in a heavy black dress and shawl. Scattered snowflakes descended from the afternoon sky. She walked slow and steady through the middle of the street. Everyone kept their distance.

"A monster lurks in the dark corners of Orchard Bend," Mrs O'Malley continued, casting her malicious eye from person to person. "It took my daughter's head from her body and it is evil, but just as foul are all of *you!*"

The woman in black gripped the gold cross hanging from her neck.

"You pass the days fretting about your insignificant lives, blind to how someone pure and full of light was taken from this world!" Mrs O'Malley proclaimed. "But not Sheriff Wilson! His eyes were opened and he was made to see. The guilt of his failure drove him to take his own life! He rightly burns in hell!"

225

"You," said the quiet voice from the shadows of the boardwalk. Irene Sullivan stepped onto the hard dirt of the street. "You don't get to speak his name."

"Hush, harlot!" Mrs O'Malley held the cross up high, straining its chain around her neck. "I promised you pain and you deserved it, distracting our sheriff WHEN HE OUGHT TO HAVE BEEN HUNTING DOWN LAURA'S KILLER!"

The murmurs from the townsfolk ceased at the awful sound of Mrs O'Malley's rage given voice. Her words seemed to smother the onlookers and their attention went to young Miss Sullivan, standing alone now on the snow dusted street.

"I forgive you," Irene said.

Mrs O'Malley gasped as if slapped across the face.

Irene wasn't finished.

"I felt the pain you wrought, but it no longer poisons my soul," Irene said, her voice never rising above a clear but quiet timbre. "I wish you peace. We all wish you peace, but your putrid ravings have no more power. That's why you shall not invoke Clem Wilson's name ever again in such a fashion."

"You know *nothing!*" Mrs O'Malley seethed.

"Leave here," Irene said with pity. "Come back only when you find peace."

Mrs O'Malley opened her mouth to say something, but the words left her. A heartbeat later she turned and walked away back down the street, head low. Irene and the townsfolk watched her as she rounded the corner and was gone. One by one, people returned to their affairs. Irene started back to Sully's and only then saw Emery Dale on the boardwalk looking at her.

"Miss Dale --I mean, *Sheriff* Dale— I didn't see you there," Irene stammered. "I'm sorry to cause a fuss, but she had to be stopped."

"Yes, she did," Dale said, giving her a hug. "It's a relief to see you in better spirits, Irene, a relief beyond description."

"I was not myself when you found me," Irene said, her gaze following after Mrs O'Malley, "but you helped me, Sheriff."

"It warms my heart to know that," Dale said. "And please, call me Emery."

"Come visit me at the tavern later," Irene said, starting to shiver in the cold. "We run a tab for the local constabulary, you know?"

"I will," Dale said as Irene walked back to the tavern.

* * *

The early darkness made it seem later than it was in the jailhouse. Dale read Doc Shaw's autopsy report on Laura O'Malley and Green brought her up to date on Sheriff Wilson's investigation.

"To be frank, Sheriff, Wilson had just about come to his wits end," Green said as they sat drinking coffee. "He talked to just about the entire town, everyone who knew Laura and all the farmers in the area where she was found. He even asked Sully and Mr Trask about anyone new in town. It was a burden on him, I could tell. Even the night he... well, you know, *that* night, the night of the Town Hall opening. When I arrived at the jailhouse, he had so much on his mind. He left the locket and Doc Shaw's report on the desk, but what I found really odd was that he left his badge. I should've seen right then and there that he was breaking, but as curious as it was, I didn't think he'd go so far as to... do what he did."

"It's not always easy to see when someone is that close to the edge," Dale said, picking up the badge and turning it over in her hand. "There's no shame in saying you didn't see it coming."

"Maybe if he'd stayed a few moments longer instead of going off on his own that night, I might have seen it," Green sighed. "Instead, young Mr McCabe finds him distraught and has to see such a horrible act."

Dale nodded, pondering how one act of violence in Orchard Bend, the murder of Laura O'Malley, could destroy so many lives, its effects rippling out further and further.

"On Monday, we start the investigation over," Dale said, putting the badge back on the desk next to the locket. "I want to see where the body was found. I trust you can take me to the spot."

"Yes, I can," Green said, "though the memory of her body there is about as unpleasant a thought as I can muster."

"I understand, Deputy," Dale said. "Do it for Sheriff Wilson, and for Laura."

Green smiled a sad little smile.

"Not to worry, Sheriff, I've made my peace with it," Green said. "I just don't like picking at old wounds."

Not long after, Green went to Sully's for dinner and Dale sat by the lantern light alone. Rose expected her to visit the cottage tonight, so she planned to retire soon. A knock came at the door. Earl McManus entered.

"Ah, good thing I caught you, Sheriff Dale," he said, taking off his gloves. "That title still has a funny ring to it, doesn't it?"

"Mr McManus, I haven't had a chance to thank you for supporting my application for this job," Dale said.

McManus waved her off.

"All I did was see to it you get a fair shake," the blacksmith said. "There are grumbles from the other aldermen, those loyal to Maxwell McCabe and those who think it ain't a woman's place, so don't go thanking me just yet."

"I expected the opposition when I decided to walk into Town Hall two days ago, but it was something I had to do," Dale said.

A gust of wind buffeted the walls of the jailhouse and the wood creaked and groaned. Dale glanced out the window. Snow whipped about the street leaving a thin sheet on the ground.

"I have something for you, Sheriff," McManus said, taking a small bundle of cloth from his pocket. He handed it to her and she unwrapped it.

"It's lovely, Mr Manus," she smiled.

She held the badge up to the lantern light and read the letters stamped into the brass.

ORCHARD BEND
SHERIFF

DALE

"Worked on that the last day and a half," McManus said. He looked past her at the desk and pointed. "I made Sheriff Anderson's badge, too. That was a good many years ago and I thought it was time for a new one. I tried to add some flourishes to the design. I've learned a thing or two over the years."

Dale picked up the old badge from the desk and held one in each hand side by side. Anderson's badge, weathered and patinated, was a simple star with rounded points. Dale's freshly polished brass featured ornate, if uneven detailing.

"Thank you, Mr McManus," Dale said. She held out the old badge to him. "You should take Sheriff Anderson's badge and place it in memoriam in the Town Hall. He was a good man, as was Sheriff Wilson."

"May they rest in peace," McManus agreed, taking the badge from her and admiring his long ago handy work. "I'll see to it that gets on the docket for the next council meeting."

"They deserve to be remembered," Dale said.

"Too right you are, Sheriff Dale," McManus said. "I should be on my way. The little lady at home won't wait much longer for my return before she feeds my dinner to the mutt."

He gave the badge in her hand a tap.

"Don't go losing that, mind, I'm not making you another," McManus said with a wink.

Dale lifted her cloak and fumbled to pin it on her coat. McManus reached over.

"Allow me," he said and Dale let him secure it to her coat. He took a step back and gave it an appraising look. "Fine bit of craftsmanship there, I dare say."

"You best get on home to your missus," Dale shooed him to the door. He tipped his hat and left the jailhouse. Dale went to the window and looked at her reflection, admiring the metal.

The headache came swift, a splitting migraine. Her hands went to her temples and massaged them, then she pressed the bridge of her nose between her thumb and forefinger.

"Congratulations, Major," said a man in uniform with many medals on his chest. She recognized the voice, one of strength and sternness, a hard voice she knew to follow. *"Your service to*

your country on a difficult assignment should stand as an inspiration to the officers and soldiers under your command."

"Thank you, sir," Dale heard herself reply.

Her C.O. leaned in and said in a quiet, but still gruff voice, "You made the right call out there. You saved lives. Don't let anyone tell you different."

"Thank you, sir," she said again, "I have no doubts..."

The scene of the medal ceremony changed in a heartbeat. The air became hazy. Low, indistinct huts and shacks surrounded her and her soldiers.

"Fire," she ordered, but not with the bludgeoning force of other commanding officers she knew, but with a sharp, precise voice that cut through the dusty brown wind.

The rapid crack of automatic weapons sounded almost like fireworks, but her attention stayed fixed on the row of people in shrouds and loose-fitting clothes. One moment they pled and argued with her and the next they dropped dead in a bloody hail of bullets.

When the shooting stopped, Dale stood over the bodies and waited, her own service weapon ready in case any of them weren't quite dead. But they were dead, the entire group—

A family. Clearly a family, she thought as she stood in the jailhouse reliving the moment.

—and when she was certain of it, she faced the unit under her command.

"Sergeant Rateliff, let's get back on the road," she said. "We have a mission to complete."

"Yes, Major!" Rateliff replied.

Dale staggered back, almost knocking the lantern to the floor, overcome by nausea. She hit the bars of the cell back first and slid to a crouch against them. When the nausea passed, Dale stayed seated on the floor, replaying the fragments of memories again and again.

"What did I do?" she whispered. "Who was I?"

25

November 15, 1886
Orchard Bend

"Cheat found her there," said Deputy Green, pointing up ahead.

The brittle waist-high grass crunched beneath their boots in the field northwest of town. Their horses stood tied to a tree near the road.

"Who owns this land?" Dale asked, her breath visible in the cold air. It drifted out from under the hood of her cloak as she looked across the horizon.

"The town owns these acres from the road to the gully west, just over yonder," Green said, pointing to a cluster of barren trees. "That's where the watering hole is, where Laura and her friends went swimming before she disappeared. On the other side, north, are the railroad tracks. That's CUC railroad land. Looking east, the field goes on until it hits..."

"Freddy Wood's land and a few others, including the old Campbell farm," Dale finished his sentence. She'd spent Sunday in her cabin in the ravine reading Sheriff Wilson's notes from his investigation. He had checked alibis and tried to establish leads. Dale had hoped to spot something Wilson had missed, but the man had been thorough, alibis established for those close to the victim and those living in the area where the body was found. Dale found herself rooting for Wilson as she read his notes and lamented his inability to crack this murder. She could understand his frustration. She smiled at the mention of Rose, from when Wilson had spoken to the schoolteacher about Laura.

They walked on for a few more minutes, then Green stopped and pointed to the ground.

"Here," he said.

It looked like just about any other section of the field, but Green's expression told Dale he knew this was the spot.

"How was the body positioned?" Dale asked.

Green didn't reply, only stared at the ground where Laura's headless body once lay.

"Deputy," Dale said, gentle but firm.

Green roused himself and apologized.

"Um, she was on her back," Green said.

"Which way were her feet pointing?" Dale asked.

"Well, um, one leg was pointing to the road, the other was kind of lying bent at the knee under the straight one, if that makes sense," Green said.

Dale wished Wilson had thought to bring a camera out here. The best she could do was try to picture the scene in her mind. Doc Shaw's report said she was strangled from behind, that's what killed her. Based on Green's description, as she went down, it wasn't a clean fall, but she ended up on her back.

Dale stood where she guessed the killer had been behind Laura, trying to picture the victim dropping down as the killer strangled her.

"He would've knelt as she collapsed, as he squeezed the life from her throat," Dale said, turning the scenario over in her mind. "Deputy, stop me if you think I get a detail wrong."

"Alright," Green said.

"When he let go, Laura dropped onto her back," Dale continued. "He then would've stood up with his ax or hatchet and taken her head off."

"Sheriff, is this necessary?" Green asked, wincing.

Dale ignored the question.

"But then what?" she asked herself. "What would the killer do next? Deputy, what do you think?"

"I couldn't rightly say," Green said.

"Take a guess," Dale prompted him.

"Sheriff, I've never thought about murdering another person," Green protested.

"To solve this, we have to try to think the way the killer did," Dale explained. "You've just killed a girl you know and cut off her head. Tell me, Deputy, was there a lot of blood?"

"Sheriff there was more blood here than I ever cared to see in my lifetime," Green said, shaking his head in horrified awe at the memory.

"So the killer was probably covered with it himself, does that follow?" Dale asked.

"It sure does," Green said, turning a little pale. "So if he was covered in blood, how come no one saw him?"

Dale watched him as he considered the problem. She had her own ideas and wanted to see if Green arrived at a similar conclusion.

Green looked up from the spot where Laura O'Malley's body had been and took in his surroundings.

"He'd be seen on the road," Green said.

"My thought exactly," Dale agreed.

Green looked west.

"He wouldn't go back toward the swimming hole either," Green deduced.

"If he goes east, he risks being seen crossing the farms," Dale said.

"North," Green said, turning to face the railroad tracks. "He went north after he killed her."

* * *

The two moved slowly northward from the murder scene, walking their horses through the tall grass under a sky growing more leaden by the hour.

"We searched all over the field to find her head, Sheriff," Green said after ten minutes of walking, "and to find the murder weapon. We had twenty or more men out here."

"We're following his route to the tracks," Dale said. "I don't think either Laura's head or the weapon is out here, not in this field, anyway."

"So why...?" Green asked.

"To see what he saw as he fled," Dale said.

"I must say, Sheriff, I find this more than a little peculiar," Green confessed.

Dale said nothing, her eyes casting back and forth from the grass before her to the approaching line of trees and the rail bed. When they arrived at the edge of the field, Dale brought them to a halt a dozen paces from the fence between the field and the tracks.

"What is it, Sheriff, do you see something?" Green asked.

"Over there," Dale point, east along the fence line.

Green saw it at once.

"Where the fence is broken, I see it," Green said. "You think he crossed there?"

"I would, but let's not assumed anything," Dale said, adding silently, *well not any more than we're assuming already, that is.* "We start here and move along the fence in either direction, just to be sure. If he climbed over, maybe he left a clue."

They tied the horses off again and split up, each walking a ways along the fence, but found nothing. They rendezvoused at the broken section where the top crossbar had rotted from the posts long ago. The rest of the fence was not in much better shape.

Dale turned and looked back in the direction of the murder scene, wondering if the killer had done the same as he carried Laura's head. With Green following, she passed through the break in the fence, through the tree line and climbed up the steep bank to the tracks.

"I hope there's not a train due anytime soon," Green sighed, looking in both directions.

Dale took in the farmland on the other side of the tracks.

"That's Ellie and David Langford's place," Dale said, pointing north. She knew the property from before the young couple bought it from Maxwell McCabe. It was a small plot, which was why McCabe had been willing to part with it. The land would afford them a modest living if they put the work in and the weather cooperated.

"Yes, it is," Green said. "The Pictons and the Langford in-laws were both visiting their children there the evening of the murder. They didn't see anything out this way, but it's not surprising since in the summer all these trees are covered in leaves." Green gestured to the row of trees between the Langfords' farm and the tracks.

"So," Dale said, "east or west?"

Green weighed his options, once more looking in either direction.

"I'm sorry, Sheriff, the path we're on is less clear now," he said.

"Three of Laura's friends, the ones she went swimming with --including Rebecca Clarke-- live in that direction," Dale said, pointing west. "Two others, the Morley girls, live south of here. It's possible the killer went that way, but your search parties were also scouring the land west and south-west in the days after Laura disappeared, so I think perhaps east is a good choice."

Snow began to fall, but not the thin flakes of the last two weeks. This snow was heavier, wet, sticking in clumps to the ground.

"There's a road that meets the tracks near the trestle bridge over the east river," Dale said. "Take the horses and meet me there. I'm going to walk the tracks and see what I see."

Green did as ordered and Dale watched him untie the pair, climb on his horse and guide both back across the field, then she started east along the railroad tracks.

* * *

The truth was Dale wanted some time alone to think. She moved along the tracks, scanning either side, hoping something would stand out, but mostly she wondered how she could possibly continue this investigation any better than Wilson had done. After all, he'd covered a lot of ground and come up empty.

She walked for close to an hour while the snowfall became thicker. She began to worry that a train might catch her on the track before she had a chance to get out of the way. She stopped every few minutes and gripped the metal rail, hoping to feel a vibration. No train came by the time she reached the intersection near the trestle bridge. A few yards away down the

235

road, the horses were tied to a thin old stump, but Green was not there. Dale noticed the snow was letting up.

"Green?!" Dale called out, approaching the trestle bridge.

"Sheriff! I'm down here," Green answered from somewhere up ahead.

Dale went to the bridge as the skies lit up and the snowfall ceased.

"Green? she called out again.

"Here, Sheriff," he replied again and Dale found him climbing about the large rocks and stones in the middle of the river, balancing himself with a long stick.

"What are you doing?" she called down.

"Come down and I'll show you," Green said. Dale noted the excitement in his voice.

She descended the bank and he manoeuvred his way to her.

"Sheriff, sorry I didn't wait for you," Green said, "but on my way over here, as it was snowing, I got thinking how I hope it snows a lot this winter because it was really dry this past summer. I got thinking about the swimming hole the kids used, how low it was this year along with the rivers. That got me thinking, if you were right about the killer heading east, maybe he tried to throw the murder weapon into the river from the bridge, thinking no one would find it, because normally this is much deeper."

"Deputy, did you find something?" Dale asked.

Green reached into the deep pocket of his duster and pulled out a hatchet.

Dale stared at it in amazement.

"You pulled this from the river just now?" Dale asked, still hardly able to believe her eyes.

"About ten minutes ago," Green said. He pointed to a rock jutting up from the running water. "It was there, next to that big rock. I saw the wood of the handle and pulled it out. Our man must have thrown it from the bridge."

There came a blast of a train's horn above them. Heading east, a locomotive rocketed across the bridge with a deafening clatter. They watched from the shore until it was gone and the world quieted down around them.

"Well, there's your train, Sheriff," Green said.

"Yes, indeed," Dale said.

She took the hatchet and looked it over. A brown stain covered parts of the wood handle, but aside from the maker's mark, there was nothing to distinguish this tool, no engraved initials, nothing unique. But Dale had to guess this might be the murder weapon.

The snow returned a moment later, thicker now, and Dale decided they should return to town. The snow would make further investigation of the area extremely difficult. Finding the hatchet, though, Dale could only shake her head in near disbelief.

When they reached their horses, Dale stopped Green before he could mount up.

"Deputy Green... *Allen*, you did exceptional work today," Dale said.

"Thank you, Sheriff," he replied.

"This find stays between you and me, understand?" Dale said. "The killer doesn't know we have it and that might be valuable, make them keep on thinking they got away with it, you follow?"

"Yes, I do, Sheriff," Green said. "I'll say no word but mum."

Dale smiled.

"Shakespeare," she said.

"Is that where it came from?" Green asked. "My mother says it all the time."

With that, they mounted up and rode back into town.

* * *

With a healthy layer of snow gathering on the ground by the time they reached Orchard Bend, Dale and Green brought their horses to the Statler Livery and walked down Anderson Street's covered boardwalk to the jailhouse. As they neared, Dale saw a man sitting on the wooden bench by the jailhouse door. He wore his hat low and the collar of his wool coat high, blocking his face. Dale threw back her cloak to reveal the badge on her jacket and to expose her guns should she need them.

As they got closer, the man turned, his collar still covering his face. He saw Dale and stood up.

Dale stopped and Green followed suit.

"Afternoon, *Sheriff* Dale," the man said, "Congratulations are in order."

He turned to face her and she relaxed when she saw the ugly scar on his cheek.

"Good afternoon, Officer," she said. "How are things in Ashleyville?"

"In shambles when I left," he replied. "My name is Turnbull, by the by, and I don't work for the railroad police anymore."

"Is that so?" Dale asked.

"I gave my notice last week," Turnbull said. He gave her cloak a once over. "I like the new attire, I must say."

Dale turned to Green.

"Deputy, please lock the item in the cabinet, would you?" Dale said.

"Absolutely, Sheriff," Green said. He hurried past Turnbull and went inside.

"What brings you to Orchard Bend, Mr Turnbull?" Dale asked.

"Looking for a job, frankly," Turnbull shrugged and smiled. "I applied for the position of sheriff, but it went to someone more qualified, it seems."

"Yes, well," Dale said, "best of luck with that. Perhaps the CUC will hire you back."

"Oh, I'm not returning to Ashleyville," Turnbull said. "There's nothing for me there, but I thought maybe you'd need another deputy."

Dale gave him an appraising look and nodded.

"Well, I suppose I can look into it," Dale said with a hint of a smile. "It's the least I can do after you refused to arrest me."

"Mr Beech was none too happy with that," Turnbull said. "It made my decision to leave that much easier."

"Where are you staying in town?" Dale asked.

"Sully's, down the way there," Turnbull pointed. "I can afford a couple of nights at least. If you can find out before then, I'd appreciate it. Otherwise, I have family in Blue Creek and I'll head there."

"I'll let you know as soon as I know," Dale said.

"Thank you, Sheriff," Turnbull tipped his hat and ventured down the boardwalk to Sully's. Dale watched him go and then went inside the jailhouse.

* * *

Closer scrutiny revealed what Emery Dale already suspected, that the hatchet found in the river bore no distinct markings to set it apart. The handle bore obvious wear from use and damage from being submerged for three months, so Dale didn't expect it had any secrets left to share apart from its very existence.

Leaving Green to mind the jailhouse, Dale crossed the now snowy street to Reed's General Store & Feed. She stomped the snow from her boots and shook more from her cloak before entering. The bell above the door rang and Mary Reed's eldest son Quinton stepped out from the back room.

"Oh, good day, Ms Dale," the boy smiled. Dale was struck by the resemblance to his father, the late Edmond Reed. In his teens now, the boy was almost as tall.

"Good afternoon, Quinton," Dale said. "Might I take a look at your catalogue?"

"Absolutely, Ms Dale," Quinton said, reaching under the counter. "I'm sorry, I meant *Sheriff* Dale."

"It takes some getting used to, I know," she smiled.

"Are you planning to make an order?" Quinton asked, laying the catalogue on the counter.

"Perhaps closer to Christmas," Dale said, opening the book. "Just browsing today."

"Lots of snow out there. Good thing we got that shipment of shovels, picks and augers last week," the boy went on. "Dad's habit was always to get the essentials before people knew they needed them."

Dale looked up from the catalogue.

239

"Your father was a good man," Dale said. "You honour his memory doing such a fine job in his store."

Quinton beamed.

"Thank you, Ms –*Sheriff* Dale," he said and left her to browse as he straightened up some shelves.

Dale returned to the catalogue and searched through the tools. She found the model of hatchet that matched the one Green had found and she jotted the details down in her little notebook, a gift from Rose when Dale got the job.

"Tell me, Quinton," Dale asked, "have you sold any hatchets in the last few months. Do you have that information recorded?"

"Yes, we do," Quinton said, returning to the counter. "We keep the inventory up to date, especially things like tools."

He retrieved a thick ledger from below the counter and put it down with a soft thud.

"The last five months, give or take," Dale said.

"That far back, huh?" Quinton asked. "What's this about? If I can ask, that is."

"Can you keep a secret?" Dale asked, leaning in.

Quinton looked around and leaned in, as well.

"I sure can, Sheriff," he whispered.

"Two farmers, I can't name names, one says the other stole his hatchet," Dale lied. "The second farmer says he *bought* the hatchet fair and square."

"Ooh," Quinton nodded.

He flipped through the pages, eyes scanning the columns.

"We sold one in June, two in July," he pointed to the separate notations, "here and right here, see? Then... Oh, and another in early August... And that's it, as far as I can see. Axes and saws, those have been popular, too."

"Nothing after August, you say?" Dale confirmed.

"No, ma'am," Quinton said, looking again through the pages. "What does that mean? Is it important?"

She gave the boy a wink.

"It means someone's lying to me," Dale said. She thumbed back through the catalogue, having spied something in the jewellery section. She flipped the pages and found the locket's listing, the same as Laura O'Malley's.

She started copying the information into her notebook, then stopped as she read a particular sentence.

Our charming LOCKET allows you to display TWO photographs inside, and features a HIDDEN, SECRET compartment so your tiny KEEPSAKES are always close to your heart!

A secret compartment.

Dale jotted that down along with the rest of the details, thanked Quinton and went back to the jailhouse.

* * *

"The catalogue didn't show how to open it?" Green asked, standing over Dale's shoulder as she sat at the desk examining the locket.

"No," Dale said. "It was probably in with the packaging, but I have no desire to visit Mrs O'Malley if I can avoid it."

She turned the locket over, examining the hinge which opened the regular compartment that housed the photos of Mr and Mrs O'Malley. She traced her finger along the edge of the base and the lid, hoping to trigger a release, but nothing happened.

"We can try prying it open," Green suggested.

"If we must, but I'd like to avoid damaging evidence if we can help it. After all, there might be something delicate inside," Dale said.

"Maybe there's something under the photos," Green said. "Try taking those out."

"Good idea," Dale said and gingerly she worked the photo of Laura's father out of the locket. Finding nothing underneath, she did the same with the photo of her mother. Again, there was nothing significant hidden behind it. Dale examined the surfaces behind the photos with a keen eye, but at last put the locket down.

"I need a break," Dale said. "Do you want to give it a try? I'm going to make some coffee."

They switched spots at the desk and Dale went to the stove to brew up a new pot. As she prepared the coffee, Green started tapping the locket on the desk.

"Don't break that," she reminded him.

"I'm being careful," he replied, giving the locket another round of taps on the desk.

Dale stepped outside to get some air while the coffee brewed. It had stopped snowing again and the sun peaked out from behind the clouds, lighting up the snow now blanketing the town. Students rounded the corner from Wood St to Anderson, laughing and kicking at the snow. She spotted two older ones walking hand in hand and recognized them as the Clarke girl and the Howard boy. According to Wilson's notes, Rebecca Clarke was Laura's best friend and was with her at the swimming hole that day in August.

Dale stuck her head in the jailhouse door.

"Check on the coffee, would you?" she asked the deputy. "I'll be right back."

"Okay, Sheriff," Green answered.

Dale walked across the street and intercepted Billy and Rebecca. They saw her approach, saw the badge on her jacket and stopped.

"Rebecca Clarke and Billy Howard, am I correct?" Dale asked.

"That's right,' Billy answered.

"Ms Dale, when I heard you were going to be the new sheriff, I couldn't believe it!" Rebecca said, grinning. "A *woman* sheriff. Who would've thought it possible. I wonder if you're the first!"

"I wanted to talk to you a bit about Laura, if that's alright?" Dale asked.

Rebecca's smile faltered.

"Anything we can do," Billy said. "Sheriff Wilson asked us a lot of questions and I'm afraid we weren't that helpful."

"Laura had a locket, a birthday gift from her parents," Dale said.

"Oh, she absolutely adored that locket!" Rebecca said. "It was one of her favourite things! It was really pretty and before she died I wanted one, too. I even teased young Mister Howard here about buying me one."

"If I made enough at the mill, I would have," Billy said playfully. "This Mister Howard takes care of his sweetheart."

Rebecca blushed.

"I've heard some of those kinds of lockets have a little secret compartment hidden in them," Dale said. "Did you know if Laura's had such a thing?"

"A secret compartment?" Billy asked.

"If hers had one, I didn't know about it," Rebecca said, looking a touch hurt. "We were very close, but maybe she kept it a secret."

Billy put his arm around her and gave her a squeeze.

"That's all I wanted to know, thank you," Dale said. "It's cold out here, you two should run along."

"Sheriff?" Rebecca said, "I'm glad you're looking into Laura's death. I mean, I'm glad you haven't forgotten about her."

"I'll do my best to solve this, Miss Clarke," Dale said.

Rebecca blinked tears from her damp eyes and left with Billy, hand in hand once more.

26

December 24, 1886
Orchard Bend

From across the street, Emery Dale saw Reed's General Store & Feed bustling with activity. As she approached, the first stars of Christmas Eve shone over the town in the clear blue-grey dusk. She pulled back her hood and took in the cold peaceful air, then opened the door and slipped inside the busy store, letting the warmth envelope her.

Quinton Reed hurried up the aisle, key in hand, and saw Dale standing in the doorway.

"You're lucky, Sheriff," Quinton said, wagging the key. "My mother just gave the order to lock the door. No more customers are being let in."

"Quinton, did my package arrive?" Dale asked.

"We actually did get a shipment," Quinton said. "I think it was the one that was supposed to arrive last week, so your order may be with it. I'll take a look after I finish letting the customers out."

"Is this normal for Christmas Eve?" Dale asked, watching the men and women pick through the shelves.

"Every year," Quinton smiled. "My dad used to say 'You can give people 365 days to do their Christmas shopping and they'll still leave it to the last minute.'"

"Ain't it the truth?" Dale sighed.

"Sheriff Dale, Merry Christmas!" said Ellie Langford as she headed for the door with her purchases.

"Merry Christmas, Mrs Langford," Dale said, taking off her gloves. "I saw your husband at Sully's just now. Heading home, are you?"

"Yes. And I hope all he was drinking was coffee," Ellie laughed.

"Near as I saw," Dale said.

A rush of cold air came in as Quinton opened the door to let a customer out. No sooner had he done so than a gloved hand grabbed the door from outside and held it open.

"I need to come in, sonny!" barked the man stopping the door from shutting.

"Mr Adams, we're closing. I can't let anyone else in," Quinton said, blocking his path.

"What about all these people?" Adams pointed to the customers milling about the store.

"We're serving them and then we're closing up. It's already 5 o'clock," Quinton said.

"I can see what I want right there on the shelf," Adams said, pushing forward. Behind him, two other men started inching forward, crowding the door.

"I'm sorry, Mr Adams," Quinton said, giving the group his best sympathetic smile.

"I'll just grab it fast and be out of your hair, sonny boy," Adams said, charging forward. Quinton tried to close the door, but Adams wasn't having it. The man barrelled into the boy and the boy went down on the slippery floor.

Adams didn't make it more than two steps into the store before Dale had his arm wrenched behind his back, doubling him over in pain. She shot a look at the two men trying to come in behind him, one that told them to be on their merry way. They backed up, deciding they'd come back after Christmas.

"Apologize to young Mr Reed," Dale told Adams, applying more pressure to his arm. The man cried out between gasps.

"You're breaking my arm!" he said.

"No, but if I wanted to, I could," Dale said. "Now apologize."

"I'm sorry, sonny!" Adams cried.

"Be thankful it's Christmas and I'm in a charitable mood," Dale said. "Be on your way once I let you go, understand?"

Adams nodded emphatically and Dale released him. He massaged his shoulder and glared at her, spreading his broad shoulders. Tall as Dale was, Adams had a few inches and sixty pounds easy on her.

Dale rolled her eyes.

"Changed your mind, did you?" she asked, incredulity not masked in the slightest.

"I don't take orders from a woman," Adams said, "badge or no."

"Look, I have plans this evening and they don't involve throwing you in jail," Dale said, then pointed to the customers watching the exchange. "No one here is impressed with your little display. The store is closed to you. Get out."

In her time in Orchard Bend, Dale faced opponents both quick and nimble, but Adams turned out not to be either. With little effort, Dale dodged his ham-fisted lunge and drove a fist into his kidneys. He swung with a backhand and she caught it, rolled with it, and used his momentum against him, bringing him to the floor. She pinned him with her knee and could have broken his wrist and elbow, and had half a mind to do just that, but Doc Shaw deserved a Christmas Eve free of treating patients, so Dale restrained herself.

"Like I said, I have *plans*," Dale told Adams through gritted teeth. "You are *not* going to win this fight."

She looked up at Quinton.

"Open the door," she said. "I'm going to escort this man from the premises."

Quinton opened the door and Dale hauled Adams to his feet, his arm still locked behind him. Guiding him out the door, they crossed the snowy boardwalk and onto the street. With a shove, Dale released Adams and he staggered forward in the snow. When he regained his balance the glare returned and Dale was done talking. She dropped to a ready position for hand-to-hand combat and hoped he wouldn't pull a weapon. With just her bare hands, she could deal with him acting a fool, but things would get deadly if he pulled a knife.

All Adams did, however, was let out a chuckle, then a mocking laugh. He gave a dismissive wave, turned and walked away down the street through the snow. Dale watched him go and heard him laughing the entire way until he turned down Wood St.

Dale found her gloves in her jacket pocket and slipped them on, making her way back to the store.

"Merry Christmas, Sheriff," a familiar voice called out. Deputy Turnbull approached, the collar of his wool coat pulled up against the cold, his hat tucked low on his head.

"And to you, Deputy," Dale said. "If you're hoping to get in some last minute shopping, Reed's is closed."

"No, Sheriff, I finished that business weeks ago," Turnbull said. "I'm out enjoying an evening constitutional after a satisfying meal at Sully's, then I plan to return home and retire, very likely write a letter to my family. My mother gifted me with a copy of Dicken's 'Christmas Carol,' so I expect I'll read that tonight with some brandy."

"Don't indulge too heavily, Deputy," Dale said, walking back to Reed's store, "you're on duty tomorrow, remember?"

Turnbull waved and began whistling as he strode down the street.

Dale slipped back inside the store as a customer was let out. She waited until the last one left and Quinton went to look at the shipment. His mother opened the till and began her evening count.

"Sheriff Dale," Mary Reed said after a moment, "thank you for keeping the violence to a minimum with Mr Adams."

"A large part of my job is to keep peace in Orchard Bend," Dale replied. "I tried to keep the situation from escalating."

"You take an unusual approach to your job, Sheriff, there's no denying that," Mrs Reed said. "And thank you for coming to my son's aid."

"You're welcome, Mrs Reed," Dale replied.

Silence fell between them and Mrs Reed returned to counting the till.

Quinton came from the storeroom shaking his head.

"It wasn't there, Sheriff, sorry," he said.

"Shipments get backed up this time of year," Mrs Reed said without looking up from her count. "We're much lower priority out here, not to mention delays caused by heavy snow.

Sometimes I think we're lucky we get any stock for inventory at all."

"I'll check back in on Monday, I suppose," Dale said. "Merry Christmas to you."

"Merry Christmas, Sheriff!" Quinton replied.

She pulled her hood over her head and walked down the aisle to the door, with the boy following to lock it behind her.

"Wish Miss Adelaide a Merry Christmas from us, too, Sheriff," Mary Reed called out from her counting, not looking up.

Dale looked back.

"I will, Mrs Reed," Dale said.

* * *

"Emery, I love it!" Rose exclaimed as she unwrapped the ornate silver frame. "I know just what I'll do with it, too! How thoughtful of you!"

Emery beamed.

"I found it in a shop in Ashleyville and knew right away I had to buy it for you," Emery said, sipping her cocoa next to the schoolteacher.

Rose held the frame to her breast and squeezed Emery's hand, then stood it up on the coffee table next to the candle burning there.

"Such detail in the carving, see how the light reflects?" Rose said, admiring the craftsmanship until she sat up with a start. "Oh, I have *your* gift, Emery Ann Dale. I likewise thought you would take great pleasure from this and I admit I had my eye on it for myself, too."

Rose took the present out from the modest cabinet in the dining area and brought it back to the sofa. Giggling, she handed it to Emery.

"I hope you don't mind that I wrapped it in newspaper," Rose said. "Some frugal habits are hard to break."

"You spend wisely," Emery said. "No one could accuse you otherwise."

She tore open the wrapping and beheld a novella with no dust jacket and a green cover. Emery read the text on the spine.

STRANGE
CASE

She opened the book and upon seeing the title page sat moved by a wealth of emotion.

"'*Strange Case*," She read aloud, "*of Dr. Jekyll and Mr. Hyde*, by Robert Louis Stevenson."

"Jee-kill," Rose said. "It's Scottish."

Dale looked at her, eyes wide. Rose smiled.

"You mispronounced it with a soft 'e' instead of a hard 'e'," Rose explained.

"Ever the schoolteacher," Dale said, trying to sort through the feelings welling up. She looked back down at the book, one she'd never read, yet one so familiar. "I've... I've heard of this book."

"It became something of a rage after the *Times* gave it a glowing review," Rose said. "I had to be discreet in obtaining it. Such a book in the hands of a schoolteacher might cause a scandal. I had a cousin send it to me rather than place an order through Reed's."

Emery traced her fingers over the book, finding it hard to grasp why she felt the way she did. She knew this story. Much as she remembered little of her own old life, this story was one she knew, or some version of it. She opened the book to the title page once more and read the year of publication, *1886*, and realized in part the source of those feelings. After almost eight years in the past, a woman out of her time, here was a tangible connection to the future, to something of her old life. Not a memory, but something familiar.

"I love it, Rose," Emery said as she leaned back on the sofa, putting the book down on her lap. It rested on something hard in her pocket and Dale reached down to pull out Laura O'Malley's locket. She held it up by the chain, letting it hang silhouetted by the candle.

"It's sad how she won't see this Christmas," Rose said, looking at the locket. "How her family has come apart so."

"I wrote to the company that makes this locket, in my official capacity as sheriff," Emery said, "and I asked them for a complete set of instructions so I might open the secret compartment. I received no reply, so I ordered a locket just like this one, which naturally will have the instructions."

"A secret compartment, you say?" Rose said, fascinated. "And you're unable to open it?"

"I've tried," Dale said. "My deputies have tried. The only solution might be to break it open with force, but that seems the wrong way to go about it. I don't want to break or damage what it might be hiding. I'm also starting to consider the possibility that what it holds likely has no bearing on the case."

"May I try?" Rose asked.

Dale handed the locket over and sat up. Rose turned the locket over between her fingers.

"My students occasionally come to class with puzzle games," Rose said, intent on the locket. She opened the cover to expose the photos of Laura's parents and examined the inside. "I sometimes have to confiscate them and some are truly quite clever."

"We looked under the photographs and found no clue there," Emery said.

"That would be too easy," Rose said, her tone wry. "The trick is to keep the curious and sneaky from finding their way in."

She closed the cover and it clicked shut.

"Well, isn't that something?" Rose said under her breath.

"What, do you see something?" Emery came forward, leaning in close.

"Let me try..." Rose said, her voice trailing off as she pressed down on the little hook that held the chain in place. Both of them heard another click, very soft, but nothing happened.

Emery waited, not breathing as Rose moved her fingers along the edge. Still nothing happened. She pressed the hook again as she squeezed the release that normally opened the lid and there came a *pop* that made the ladies start. As Rose opened the secret compartment behind the photo of Mrs O'Malley,

Emery squeezed the schoolteacher's arm between her own, then reached out to take the locket from her.

Inside the compartment was a tiny folded piece of paper.

* * *

"Bring the lantern," Dale said, trying to hide her excitement and failing. Rose retrieved the lantern from the dining area and brought it to the coffee table, turning it up as bright as she could. Dale unfolded the paper and held it up, squinting to read the cursive penmanship, made small to fit on the paper.

My heart yearns, but I have to wait. His heart yearns also, I know it. I long to be with my Mr H.
Someday.
Someday M and F will understand.

Dale read the note again, considering what it meant, weighing options, her mind trying to fit this piece into the larger puzzle.

"What does it say?" Rose asked. "Can you tell me?"

"Read it," Dale said, handing it to her. "You can confirm that's Laura's handwriting?"

Rose took the note and read it, hand over her mouth. Emery got up and stretched and walked to the window. She parted the curtains and took in the darkness outside.

"Poor Laura," Rose said at last.

"It's her handwriting?" Dale asked.

"Yes," Rose said. "I'm quite certain."

"Right now, you and I are the only two who know that paper was in her locket," Dale said. "If her killer knew, he'd have taken it. I doubt her parents knew about the secret compartment and I asked her friends Billy and Rebecca if they knew about it and they didn't."

"Billy..." Rose said, looking at the note.

It came to Dale at the same time.

Billy Howard.

Mr H.

She turned and looked at Rose, who looked up at her, the schoolteacher's expression sad in the understanding of what it could mean.

Dale went to her.

"Rose, you can't speak of this note to anyone," Dale said.

"I had no such intention, Emery," Rose said.

"I know," Dale said. "I trust you."

Rose nodded, her gaze dropping back to the note.

"I pray it's not true," Rose said, handing the note back to Dale. "I cannot even fathom such a thing."

"Rose, we don't yet know what this means," Dale said, "but we will get to the truth."

27

December 25, 1886
Orchard Bend

If not for the seriousness of their duty that day, Emery Dale would have enjoyed the splendour of the winter scene to the fullest. A thick blanket of snow coated the farmland in the bright morning light. Riding out of town Dale and Deputy Turnbull made their way to the Howard farm.

"I will say, Sheriff, this is not how I expected to spend my Christmas morn," Turnbull said wistfully. "I volunteered for duty today because I have no family here and few acquaintances, all of whom I expect are warm beside a fire, making merry with their loved ones. For a bachelor in Ashleyville, Christmas Day duty at the station was something of a much sought after post. Often there were three of us and with very light duties ·-and practically no emergencies. We'd pass the day with stories and laughter and hot drinks. Coffee was the most common, but some years we'd have cocoa. One man, Aaron Lock, a good officer, he'd bring in tea. Never cared much for coffee, he always drank tea. Michael Pitt's wife, Jane, she would come by in the afternoon with freshly baked cookies. Even on the coldest Christmas Days, her cookies arrived still hot. In the evening, the railroad would send over a prepared goose or ham. We always promised to leave some for the shift after ours, but we'd end up stuffing our bellies and laughing that the food was just too good."

Turnbull let out a longing sigh.

"I'm trying to recall now exactly why I left that job," Turnbull said.

Dale looked at him from under the hood of her cloak and he smiled back.

"You know I jest, Sheriff?" Turnbull said with a wink.

"I had harboured no doubt, Deputy," Dale said. "I, too, wish this trip was unnecessary, but alas, we must follow this lead."

"I'll say it again, it's quite impressive you were able to open the locket at last," Turnbull said. "Its makers should be proud of their design. It had us at our wits end, to say the least. And now you think we can break his alibi, that of being at the mill?"

"The proximity of the swimming hole, the murder scene, the railroad tracks, the trestle bridge, the river and the mill is such that I consider it possible the timeline may allow for a discrepancy, a window of opportunity," Dale said.

"A rather narrow one, it seems," Turnbull said.

"I admit, it may prove too narrow," Dale said. "Or just narrow enough for our killer to slip through."

* * *

"How did you feel about Laura?" Dale asked.

Billy Howard sat across from her at the table in the kitchen of the little farmhouse. Behind him stood his father, arms crossed, a scowl twisting his features in stark contrast to the home's cheerful holiday decorations.

"She was my friend," Billy said.

"They've been friends since they were little," Mr Howard added.

"That's right," Billy said.

"Mr Howard, please let your son answer," Dale said.

From outside came the sound of laughter as Billy's younger sisters played in the snow. Mrs Howard was with them and called out for them to be careful throwing snow at each other.

"Did you have any other feelings?" Turnbull asked, standing by the front door. "Maybe more than friendship?"

"No, it was never like that," Billy said, surprised.

"Were you aware she had feelings for you?" Dale asked.

"She... what? Feelings for *me?* No," Billy replied, looking from the sheriff to the deputy. "Where did you get that idea?"

"New information's come up and we're re-examining everything," Dale said, "including where everyone says they were the day of the murder."

"Billy was at the mill, working," Mr Howard said.

"How long does it take you to walk home, Billy?" Turnbull asked.

"Three quarters of an hour," Billy said.

"You spoke to Sheriff Wilson twice," Dale said, consulting Wilson's notes. "The first time, the night of the disappearance, you said you didn't see her that day and didn't know where she might have gone."

"That's right!" Billy said.

Dale put Wilson's notes down and fixed him a hard stare.

"The second time, after her body was found, you said you left and came straight home," Dale said. "You would have passed the field where Laura was killed and you didn't see anything? Not a soul?"

"No!" Billy said. "I wish to Heaven I *had* seen something!"

"You didn't see the Morley twins coming back down that same road after they left the watering hole at five o'clock?" Dale asked.

"That would've been the same time you got off work," Turnbull said. "You didn't cross paths coming home?"

"No, we must have just missed each other," Billy said.

"No doubt," Dale said. "And you didn't see anything out of the ordinary while walking that road?"

"I keep telling you, NO," Billy said, his fist clenched. "I didn't see anything or anyone?"

Dale reached into her pocket and took out a length of bright pink ribbon.

"Ever see *this* before?" Dale asked.

Billy looked confused.

"I don't know," he said. "It's a piece of ribbon."

"A piece of ribbon that belongs to Esther Morley," Dale said. "You know Esther?"

"Yes, I suppose," Billy said, uncertain. "I know the Morley girls from school. Esther sometimes wears a pink ribbon in her hair."

"That's right," Dale said. "And her twin sister Willa often wears a blue ribbon."

"We stopped by the Morleys' on the way here and asked if we could borrow Esther's ribbon," Turnbull said.

"You see, Sheriff Wilson found this ribbon after Ester lost it," Dale said.

"She lost it on her way home from the swimming hole the day Laura was murdered," Turnbull added.

"And Sheriff Wilson came upon it tangled in the grass on the side of the road," Dale said. "The road you take coming home from the mill."

Billy went pale looking at the ribbon. Dale scrutinized his face, watched his eyes dart about as he processed this information and grappled with how to respond. Then he relaxed and wagged a finger at the ribbon.

"I don't know how I could've let it slip my mind," Billy said. "I think I remember it, like you said, all caught up in the grass. I guess I didn't give it much thought, being it was just a piece of ribbon."

"So you did see it?" Turnbull said.

"Yes, I'm pretty sure, now that you got me thinking about it," Billy said and smiled, "Funny how memory works, huh?"

"Yeah, it's very interesting," Dale said. "The only problem is that Esther Morley didn't lose this ribbon on the road that day, or any other day."

"Wait, wait," Mr Howard said, coming forward and putting his hands on his son's shoulders. "You *lied?*"

"Yes," Dale said. "And so did your son."

Mr Howard look flabbergasted at Dale.

"You...." Mr Howard stammered.

"Billy, you didn't come straight home from the mill, did you?" Dale asked.

"I did, I swear!" Billy cried out.

His father swatted the back of his head.

"William Howard!" Mr Howard barked. "You best tell the truth to the sheriff NOW! They think you killed Laura."

"I didn't!" Billy said, afraid and panicking.

"Where were you?" Dale said.

"I..." Billy couldn't find the words.

"Speak up, boy!" Mr Howard said. Dale glanced at her deputy and he nodded, ready to step in and take the father aside. Mr Howard was afraid, too, afraid they were right about his son. There was no telling what he might do.

"I was..." Billy's lips quivered. "She and I..."

"Dear Lord, no!" Mr Howard backed up. Turnbull moved to put himself between the father and his son.

"You and Laura?" Dale asked.

"NO! Me and Rebecca!" Billy pounded the tabled. "I snuck off... I snuck off work early. No one noticed. I do it sometimes. Mr Van Owen doesn't always check, he... he drinks a lot on the job, there in his office. You can tell when it's a good day to knock off early, so I did. I knew Rebecca and the girls were swimming, she told me, so I snuck out to try to catch Rebecca alone."

"Son, if you shamed that girl, God help me..." Mr Howard said, regaining his composure, fear replaced with anger and disappointment.

"We kissed! That's all," Billy said. "We talked and we kissed."

"Did you see Laura?" Dale asked, her own relief setting in that she didn't have to arrest this boy for murder.

"I did," Billy nodded, tears swelling in his eyes. "I watched all the girls get out of the water and get dressed. The Morleys went off across the field like you said. Rebecca and Laura would've walked west along the tracks because it's faster for them to go that way, but I met them at the swimming hole. Rebecca and I took the tracks to be alone. Laura wasn't very happy about it and left across the field. That's the last I saw of her."

Dale consulted Wilson's notes, but already knew what they said, that Rebecca claimed she and Laura left the swimming hole together and split up between their farms. It was why the search parties started looking for Laura west of the swimming hole, while her body lay in the field to the east.

"You didn't see anything unusual out there?" Dale pressed. "Anyone else hanging around?"

257

"No, I swear it," Billy said, miserable and deflated. "I'd tell you. I've thought about it, over and over. I'm sorry. I'm sorry I lied!"

"You damn well better be, boy!" Mr Howard said, coming forward to hug his son, his own eyes wet with relief.

Turnbull looked to Dale and she nodded. It was time go.

Outside, they said a quick goodbye to Mrs Howard, who wasted no time gathering her girls up and hurrying them inside.

As they rode back to town, they said nothing until they were a good distance from the Howard farm.

"We should check his alibi with Rebecca," Turnbull said. "His *real* alibi."

"I will," Dale said. "You head on back to town at the crossroads up ahead. I'll make my way to the Clarke farm and speak with her, then I'll catch up with you at the jailhouse. Have pot of coffee waiting, will you?"

"It'll be nice and hot, Sheriff," Turnbull said.

"Thank you, Deputy," Dale said. "And good work back there. I'm glad we were able to eliminate Billy as a suspect."

"Where does that leave us?" Turnbull asked. "He didn't harbour affection for Laura O'Malley. Whatever she felt for him, Billy didn't kill her."

"No," Dale agreed, "but someone did."

28

December 31, 1886
Orchard Bend

"Sheriff Dale," Gertrude beamed as Emery stepped inside the McCabe house, "it has been far too long since you graced our home with your presence."

The pleasant aroma of apple cider and freshly cooked turkey filled the home. The soft, warm glow from the sconces bedecking the walls reminded the sheriff of the many hours she'd spent here over the years and part of her had to acknowledge that, while she did not regret her decision to quit working for Maxwell McCabe, she missed the familiarity of this place.

"Until your invitation arrived, I had no reason to visit," Dale said.

"Such nonsense," Gertrude chided her friend. "You are always welcome in this home."

"I wonder if your husband shares your sentiment," Dale said. "He was resistant to my leaving his employ and more-so to my taking this post. I also heard from Mr McManus that his was the solitary vote against my request to hire a second deputy. I inferred then that he feels ill will towards me. I didn't feel it prudent to put you in an awkward position with my presence."

"You are here as my guest tonight and any other time you wish to visit, Emery," Gertrude said, taking her arm and walking with her to the parlour. A table full of trays covered with food and bowls of cider and punch lined one end of the room. The bread, cheese, fruit and meats made Emery's stomach growl. From the study, Dale heard the laughter of men and the booming voice of Maxwell McCabe telling a story with his usual flair.

Doc Shaw sat at the upright piano in the corner of the parlour, playing and singing to a cluster of guests. Next to him, Rose sipped a glass of punch, singing along. She gave Emery a wave as Gertrude guided her friend to the buffet.

"Where are the boys tonight," Dale asked.

"Owen went to bed early," Gertrude explained. "A nasty cold hit them a few days ago. Henry is about somewhere here, he's feeling much more himself."

Gertrude turned suddenly from the food on the table and let loose a heavy bout of coughing.

"You sound like you may have come down with something yourself," Dale said.

"I'm feeling infinitely better than I did some days ago. I may retire early, however, but for now I am in wonderful spirits," Gertrude said and left to visit with her other guests.

Dale helped herself to some food and punch as Doc Shaw finished a rousing version of "Camp Town Races" and announced, "Here's a song I learned in the war," and went on into an uptempo rendition of "Young Hunting."

Rose joined Emery and whispered, "You're late, Sheriff."

"I was enrapt by an excellent book I received as a Christmas present," Emery smiled. "I could hardly put it down."

"I look forward to reading this book of which you speak," Rose said, sipping her punch. "Soon, if at all convenient, now that you've finally started it."

"I expect to complete the task any day now," Emery said. "The ending may prove unexpected for the reader."

"Hush," Rose said. "You need not spoil it."

Emery put a finger on her lips.

Gertrude returned and took Rose by the arm.

"I have wonderful news, Rose," Gertrude said. "I've been waiting for the right moment and now that Emery has arrived, I wanted to tell you that Maxwell and the aldermen have voted in favour of an increase in funding for the school."

Rose was taken aback.

"Oh my!" she gaped. "An increase of how much, may I ask?"

"The entire amount you requested," Gertrude smiled. "On your behalf, they placed an order for the books you listed and the supplies you outlined."

"Surely you jest!" Rose breathed.

"Not at all," Gertrude said, taking her hand. "And starting next week, you can expect a raise in your salary."

Rose stood speechless, looking from Emery to Gertrude.

"I took a liberty and I expect you'll not mind too much," Gertrude went on, "but with the modest increase you requested I felt I had to step in."

"Oh," Rose said, "I'm sorry it was too much..."

"My dear, sweet, Rose" Gertrude said, "I took it upon myself to present a case to my husband that the amount you put forth was insufficient, so I doubled it. Truly, Rose, your modesty is a virtue, but your salary should reflect your value to this community."

"I think I need to sit down," Rose said, easing into a chair nearby and Emery and Gertrude laughed.

Dale sipped her punch and balanced the plate of food as she felt a hand touch her arm.

"Sheriff Dale?"

She turned to find Henry McCabe at her side, looking quite the gentlemen in a suit and tie.

"Good evening, Henry," Dale said. "Don't you look ever the refined gentleman this evening?"

"Thank you, Sheriff," he replied, turning his attention to Gertrude. "Mother, I checked in on Owen and read him a story. He's sound asleep now."

"Thank you, Henry," Gertrude smiled.

Henry turned back to Dale and leaned in.

"Sheriff, can we talk?" he asked, at once looking anxious. "You said if I ever needed... that you..."

"Yes, Henry, I remember," Dale said low. "I'll find you at the stalls. Will that be okay?"

"Yes," Henry said and stepped away, mingling his way through the guests.

Major, it's me!

Dale spun around at the voice, her head throbbing.

Gertrude and Rose didn't notice, engrossed as they were in their discussion of the school's new budget. Dale shook her head and chalked it up to her imagination.

Major!

The pain in her head exploded in a sudden sharp burst, joined by a stinging pain in her bicep and above her knee, pain she thought long behind her.

Major, come with me, said the man's voice, one she knew but couldn't place. She sat down and closed her eyes, rubbing the bridge of her nose as the pain in her head seemed to drill into her mind.

And just as suddenly it let go.

Dale opened her eyes and beheld a smoke-like grey world, identical to her own, but somehow translucent.

"Major, you have to come with me," said a shadowy figure before her. The features were hard to make out, except for the face, the gaping holes for eyes and the deep pit of a mouth. It looked wretched, yet she recognized him. She started to speak, but the shadow raised a black, indistinct hand. "Don't speak, Major. I'm a prisoner here, no one else can see me and I can't hold you here much longer. But you need to see. You need to come with me so you can end this!"

The voice assaulted her aching mind, a flooding combination of words, images and ideas. They were scattered, but she thought if she had the time she might be able to make sense of some of them. This thing spoke so fast it was difficult to keep it all straight.

Dale didn't know why, but she trusted this apparition. She'd seen him before and had seen this world before, glimpsed as she knelt over the dead body of Daniel Underwood months earlier as she had struggled to remain conscious. This wraith had been there, too, and...

There was more, she knew, much more, but it wouldn't come to her.

Dale got up and followed the being to the front door. It passed right through, and she opened the door to follow, grabbing her cloak as she went outside.

In the grey world, the cold seemed diminished. Still, she put up the hood of her cloak and passed some guests smoking cigars on the porch. They tipped their hats with a polite acknowledgement of "Sheriff."

The grey world started to slip back to normal as she rounded the side of the house.

"We must hurry," the Prisoner said. "You must trust me."

"I do," Dale said and the Prisoner stopped. Despite his need for haste, he turned. The gaping holes where eyes ought to be regarded her and that feeling of deep familiarity hit her again.

"Good," the Prisoner said, but there came more images and ideas than that single word conveyed and this time Dale caught more.

A soldier.

The desert.

A place of metal and computers.

Laughter.

The crying of a boy.

The Prisoner led her to the barn and the grey world was nearly gone by then, his form a mere black wisp, one she knew she'd seen before.

And as Dale reached the door, the Prisoner faded away and the world returned to normal, the ache in her mind and in her wounds gone with it. She no longer saw the grey world and now took in the deep blue dusk of the sky. The half moon made the winter landscape glow under its light. The lonesome whistle of a freight train carried across the orchard in the distance.

The Prisoner wanted her to see something in the barn, so she went inside. Tools and harvesting gear lay unused for the winter amid stacks of apple crates and baskets, sorted with tidy precision. To her left, the pale light pouring in from outside lit the wall of smaller tools above a work table. Everything had a place, even the tool that wasn't there.

A hatchet.

Three of them hung on the wall, but the empty space between the second and third told Dale there ought to be a fourth one. And the unmistakable outline, made from years of dirty, sweaty hands taking the missing hatchet from the wall and putting it back over and over was clear as day.

At once, Dale suspected that the hatchet recovered from the river belonged in the empty space next to the others on the wall, the hatchet found in the river below the railroad track, the track which ran from the field where Laura O'Malley was murdered to the edge of the McCabe property.

Dale stood cold in the barn, but not because of the winter air. Like when the Prisoner had spoken in its mix of words and images, Dale's mind flooded with details.

Laura's secret note...

> My <u>heart</u> yearns, but I have to wait. His heart yearns also, I
> know it. I long to be with my Mr H.
> Someday.
> Someday M and F will understand.

Mr H.

Someone Wilson didn't question, according to his notes. And why should the sheriff have thought of this person? He didn't attend school with Laura O'Malley. Sheriff Wilson wouldn't think to ask him.

Mr H.

Henry McCabe.

Maybe Wilson *did* question Henry. The thought made her sick, that Wilson might have figured it out, or at least thought to ask Henry the night of the Town Hall opening. Maybe Mrs O'Malley said something that made him consider Henry. So Wilson went to talk and somehow Henry got the best of him.

Henry, the only witness to the self-inflicted shooting of a man no one thought suicidal.

Laura O'Malley, strangled and then beheaded.

Henry McCabe, who as a child witnessed a man named Saunders beheaded in this very barn as he tried to kill the boy himself.

"Now you have to die like the others," said Henry behind her.

264

She drew both guns and spun around to see Henry charging. Henry raised Dale's own sword in his hands. In her haste to follow the Prisoner, Dale had left the sword in the house. She ducked and fell to her right, feeling the rush of cold air as the blade swept past her. The sword hit the frozen dirt floor, bouncing off with a ringing sound. Dale pivoted on her knee, trying to get a clean shot as she twisted her body, but Henry was on her again. His swing lacked momentum but slashed with enough force to make her roll out of the way. One gun slipped from her cold hand as she hit the solid ground shoulder first. Henry's swing brought the sword back up over his head. He grinned wide and mad as he saw his opportunity. He brought the sword swinging back down. Dale fell onto her back and fired from the hip. Henry staggered back, looking at the sword's grip where Dale's bullet had ricocheted off the pommel. The bullet left it dented and deformed. She took aim again, but Henry dodged to his left, slashing at her. She rolled and came up on one knee, bringing her gun to bear on Henry as she saw her sword coming back around. Her free hand went to one of the knives under her jacket as the blade curved through the air in the direction of her neck. Her angle was bad for a shot with the gun, so her hand brought the knife up to parry the sword's blade. In the next motion, Dale fired, emptying her six-shooter into Henry's body. The sword dropped from his hand and hit the dirt as Henry fell backwards.

Dale grabbed her fallen gun from the dirt and kept it trained on Henry as he writhed on the ground, gasping and coughing up blood.

"Why?" Dale whispered, her voice struggling to form the words. "Why, Henry...?"

Henry convulsed, his body so damaged and beyond repair, yet his eyes focused on her, burning with hate. His words came out in a blubbery mess of blood and gasps.

"I'm the Master of Life and Death..." Henry choked.

Dale didn't see the wisps of black as the Prisoner approached until he stood over Henry. The Prisoner knelt down. Henry shook his head as if hearing the Prisoner speak and Dale watched in fascination. Henry snapped his gaze away from the

Prisoner and looked Dale in the eye, the hate and madness gone; urgency and fear radiated beneath the blood on his face.

"You can't let him!" Henry said to Dale. "Key... list..."

And Henry McCabe died.

Dale looked for the Prisoner, but saw only darkening shadows in the hollow of the barn.

She holstered her guns and stood alone over the cooling body of Laura O'Malley's murderer.

About The Author

Patrick Lemieux is a Canadian artist and writer based in Toronto. He has exhibited his work internationally and it has featured in magazines and album sleeves.

He is currently working on the third *Orchard Bend* book. He's also toying with the idea of another *Chronology* book. The second collection of his artwork and the collection of his photography are both still forthcoming. The second volume of his comic series *Horizon Line* might take a little longer than originally planned.

You can find him on Facebook and Instagram at *Patrick Lemieux Artist* and on Twitter @MadTheDJ